Not Working

Not Working

A Novel

LISA OWENS

THE DIAL PRESS
NEW YORK

Published in the United States by The Dial Press, an imprint of Random House, a division of Penguin Random House LLC, New York.

THE DIAL PRESS and the HOUSE colophon are registered trademarks of Penguin Random House LLC.

LIBRARY OF CONGRESS CATALOGING-IN-PUBLICATION DATA
Names: Owens, Lisa.
Title: Not working : a novel / Lisa Owens.
Description: First edition. | New York : The Dial Press, 2016.
Identifiers: LCCN 2015042040 | ISBN 9780812988819 (hardback) |
ISBN 9780812988826 (ebook)
Subjects: LCSH: Unemployed women workers—Fiction. | Self-actualization (Psychology) in women—Fiction. | Self-realization in women—Fiction. | Psychological fiction. | BISAC: FICTION / Contemporary Women. | FICTION / Literary. | FICTION / Humorous. | GSAFD: Humorous fiction.
Classification: LCC PS3615.W4695 N68 2016 | DDC 813/.6—dc23 LC record available at http://lccn.loc.gov/2015042040

Printed in the United States of America on acid-free paper

randomhousebooks.com

2 4 6 8 9 7 5 3 1

FIRST EDITION

Book design by Mary A. Wirth

For my parents

Not Working

I

Wallflower

There is a man standing outside my flat wearing khaki-greens and a huge "Free Palestine" badge.

"Are you the owner?" he asks, and I turn to see if he is talking to someone else, but there is no one behind me. It buys me a second to remind myself which side of the Israel-Palestine conflict I am on.

"I think so, yes," I say, and then with more confidence, because now I'm sure, "Yes, I'm definitely the owner."

He scratches his neck, which is gray with dirt. His ears have the same ashy hue.

"You need to get the buddleia removed. It's a hazard."

"Oh right," I say, looking up to where he is pointing, to a plaster pillar on the front of the building, topped by an ornamental detail. I've never noticed it before, but now I'm embarrassed to see that the paintwork is cracked and filthy. If anyone had asked me to name it—if a million pounds had been resting on it—I would have guessed it was called a balustrade. "Does it not serve a structural purpose?" I say.

He stares at me, tugging on his beard, which tapers into a slender plait.

"It's a weed. It's not supposed to be there," he says, and now I understand: there is a plant sprouting from the top of the thing, a spray of purple flowers. It's quite pretty.

"And . . . sorry, who are you?" I ask, wondering if he is from the city council, a neighbor or an interfering passerby.

"Colin Mason, MBE," he says and offers a dusty hand.

I hesitate for a fraction of a second before good manners kick in and I take it.

"Claire," I say.

"Shall I deal with it, then?" he asks, nodding up at the buddleia. "I'll do a bit of a paint job while I'm up there too."

"Mm, just . . . I'm going to have to talk to my boyfriend about it first. Because we share ownership. How can I reach you?"

"I'll be around," he says. "You'll see me about."

I go inside to wash my hand and call Luke. A woman answers, his colleague Fiona.

"He's scrubbing up for surgery," she says. "Can I get him to call you back?"

"Would you mind just holding the phone to him so I can have a quick word? Two seconds, I promise."

There's a fumbling noise and then Luke's voice.

"What's up?"

"There's a problem with our flat. A buddleia needs removing."

"A what?"

I sigh. "It's a weed. A purple flowering weed? The guy outside said it needs to go."

"What guy?"

"Colin Mason."

"Who's that?"

"He has an MBE. He was pretty adamant."

"So what do you want to do? Do you need to call someone? Can I leave it with you? Claire," he says, "I've got to go."

"Yes, leave it with me. What do you want to do for dinner?"

"He won't be home for dinner," Fiona says. "He's going to be working late."

"Oh," I say. I think I'll sit tight on the buddleia thing for a while; see if it develops.

Tube

Three women opposite talk about the weather as if it's a friend they don't much like.

"And that's another thing," says one, leaning in. "My no-tights-till-October rule has gone straight out the window."

Her companions bob their heads, uncross and recross their nylon-clad legs.

Wallflower

My mother phones me on her lunch break. I can hear she's in a cafe.

"Where *are* you?" she asks, as though she's picking up a baffling background cacophony, instead of the silence in my kitchen.

"At home."

"I see. How's the you-know-what going?"

She means "job hunt": calling it the "you-know-what" is, incredibly, less annoying than the question itself.

"Yep. Fine. Just trying to push on."

"Listen, before you go, what do you make of this? I had an awful dream last night that I saw Diane, the . . . Diane from work. It was definitely Diane, but in the dream I thought she was someone else, a stranger."

Until now I have only heard my mother describe her as "Diane the black receptionist." I have a feeling there is more to come.

"Funnily enough"—this is said as though it's just occurred to her—"I *did* see a woman who I thought was Diane yesterday in town, and went to say hello but then realized it wasn't her." She laughs. "Claire, what do you think? Do you think she would have been offended?"

"Who," I say, because I can't resist, "Diane or the person you thought was Diane?"

"The other lady. Not Diane. Do you think she would have known that I confused her with someone else, with another—"

"Another woman of color?" I help her out.

"Oh," my mother says, "I don't think that's very PC. I don't think you can say 'colored' nowadays."

Tube

A few seats down the car, there's an old man knitting, bald and cozy in a big white woolen cardigan. I smile at him and raise my eyebrows, and when I do, I see the earrings, purple dangly ones, and realize it isn't an old man at all but a woman, not so old, my mother's age maybe, who has lost all her hair. She grins at me, the needles clicking away, and I keep my eyebrows up, smiling hard at my hands, which lie still in my lap.

Wake

After the main course is cleared away, the waiters—who are really just teenagers—bring out dessert: bowls of melting ice cream and fruit swimming in syrup. I'm sitting at the children's table with the other children. (We're all over twenty-five.) My cousin Stuart, who beneath his suit jacket is wearing a "No Fear" T-shirt, asks me what I'm doing these days.

"I'm working that out," I say. I've had a lot of wine: it keeps coming and I keep drinking it. "I quit my job two weeks ago so I could take a bit of time to try to figure out why I'm here. Not in a religious way, but I believe everyone has a purpose. Like, how you were made to be in computers. That makes total, perfect sense." I stop, worried suddenly that he's a normal engineer and not a software engineer, but he nods.

"Marketing wasn't your calling, then."

"Creative communications," I correct him.

"Won't lie: I never really knew what that meant."

"It . . ." I prepare to launch into an explanation, then realize I may never need to again, "doesn't matter anymore."

"There aren't any spoons," Stuart says, and I beckon one of the teenagers over.

"Could you bring us some spoons, please?" I am indignant that I should even have to ask, and my tone is pleasingly chilly. The boy waiter smirks. When he comes back, he's clutching a bouquet of knives, which he releases in a silver cascade in front of me.

"No spoons left," he says. "No forks either. We're really busy today."

I shake my head. "Unbelievable," I mutter to Stuart as we dole out the knives. I slice off some of the shrinking ice-cream island and carefully lift it to my mouth. I look across to the table where my poor grandmother is sitting. Her husband of sixty years is only just in the ground and she's licking a speared peach-half like a lollipop.

During coffee, Stuart's dad, my uncle Richard, gives a speech about Gum. He pokes gentle fun at the pride Gum took in his "war wounds"—the scars from his many operations.

"He really *did* love to show off his war wounds," I say to our table. My cousins nod and smile, murmuring agreement. "And more!" I continue, pointing down at my lap and laughing. "Even after the heart op."

"Whoa," says my cousin Faye. "*What*? Gum used to show you his . . . ?"

"Oh—no, no. 'Show' makes it sound . . . It wasn't . . . I don't think it was really on purpose or anything," I say. Everyone is looking at me. No one is talking. "Honestly, it definitely wasn't a big deal. *At all*. I always thought it was—Did no one else have this? How it used to just kind of slip out?"

Faye is shaking her head. Her ears, poking through her thin blond hair, have turned red. I glance around at all the other cousins' faces; most are gazing into their coffee. I dump a packet of sugar into mine and stir it with the knife I saved from dessert.

Dream

At night driving on the motorway, my lights won't turn on, but each passing car has theirs on full beam, dazzling between fretful stretches of darkness.

Context is everything

"The buddleia (or buddleja bush)," according to one website, "can either be a beautiful flowering garden bush attractive to butterflies or a vile, destructive, invasive weed."

Bus

I take the bus to the gym I can't really afford anymore. I choose a seat by the window and try to make progress with my book. (I have been reading *Ulysses* for nearly nine months.) When I've read the same paragraph five or six times, I look up, desperate for some relief from the words. An old guy in a powder-blue jacket with long, sparse hair is coming slowly down the aisle. He looks around for a seat, but they're all taken and no one gets up, so like a stoic he sets his mouth and grips the handrail next to him. I think about offering mine, but I'd have to ask the woman next to me to move. She looks important, smartly dressed as if she's going to a meeting. She's reading through some notes and I don't want to disturb her, or make her feel bad that she didn't offer up her seat. I go back to *Ulysses* and, burning with the effort of pretending I haven't noticed the old guy, I finally make it onto the next page. When the woman next to me gets off, the old man stays where he is. I watch him sway and shuffle with the movement of the bus, dancing in his orthopedic shoes.

Gym

At the gym, I try to get out of my membership contract.

"You'll need to wait until the thirtieth of the month to hand in your notice, and then your contract will end two months after that," the woman whose name badge says FRANKIE tells me. It's Halloween and she is dressed as a witch, with a hat, a cape and her nails painted black. Underneath the cape, she's in a shiny black unitard.

"But the thirtieth is a full month away," I say. "Can't we just pretend it's yesterday?"

"If only!" she says, rustling a tin of retro sweets at me sympathetically. I take a pack of butterscotches and crunch them two at a time.

She looks at her records. "I see you still haven't had your Full-body Analysis. Shall we do that now, as you're here?" I had been putting it off until I got fitter because I wanted to get a better score than Luke, but it's been two years and if I'm leaving, I might as well get it done. She comes around the reception desk and ushers me to a table, taking her plastic broom with her.

In response to the questionnaire, I tell Frankie that I don't drink any alcohol or coffee, and that I sleep for nine hours every night. My blood pressure is good and so are my resting levels, but when she tests my aerobic fitness on the treadmill, I'm so eager to impress that I nearly slide off, and my vision goes dark while I gasp for breath.

"How often did you say you come here?" Frankie asks, looking at her clipboard. "Have you thought about a personal trainer?" By the time I leave, I've signed up to three one-on-one sessions with a personal trainer named Gavin, at a specially reduced introductory rate of £99.99.

Success

I'm not sure if my mother has been storing up material for our conversations, or if it's part of the process of grieving for her father, but these days when she phones, she seems to have an awful lot of awful news to relate.

"Pippa from church, in the choir—you know her. The husband, an atheist—you wouldn't have met him. Slipped and fell in the shower: it's touch-and-go whether he'll walk again. I've sent Dad out to buy one of those rubber mats. You can't be too careful."

And: "Gordon two doors up from us, well, his son-in-law, the policeman—I told you, remember? Depressed. Several attempts, over the years, but they thought he was over all that. Anyway," she says with a sigh, "it would seem this time he did succeed."

My next move

I go to a cafe to get out of the house and bring my laptop so I can do some career research. There is a table of about eight women, all with babies, and a couple of them are breastfeeding. They're talking about how hands-on their husbands are, and while their one-upmanship makes me slightly suspicious, I can't deny that the women look great. Their skin is fantastic, and the babies are all so sweet—tiny, quiet and content.

I'm surfing websites for jobs, but don't know what I'm looking for and all my searches keep returning sales or executive positions way above my earning bracket. A woman comes in who looks about my age, balancing a toddler on her hip, a little girl. The two of them are in matching Breton-striped tops and jeans, and when she orders a coffee, she actually has a French accent. She sits at the table next to me and the child is off: behind the counter, under the table, climbing up the stairs marked NO ENTRY. She is delightful; the baristas don't mind at all.

I click on a description for a heritage job, which involves writing the blue plaques on buildings where notable figures used to live. I could definitely do that, I think, sum someone up in a couple of words. I consider how I would blue-plaque people I know: Luke = "eminent physician"; Paul = "pioneering artist"; Sarah = "educational innovator." I have a harder time with the ones who work in PR and management consultancy, and decide that's because they probably wouldn't deserve a blue plaque anyway.

The toddler is at my table, holding out her arms and waving both hands from the wrists, beaming. I do the same and she laughs, runs away, buries her face in her mother's lap saying, "*Maman, Maman!*" and the mother, who might in fact be younger than me, bends over to murmur a stream of French into her daughter's bright bobbed hair.

"Maybe I should have a baby." I'm loading the dishwasher after dinner, and Luke laughs.

"With who?"

"Right, I meant *we* should. But I'll be the one having it, won't I? I could be a stay-at-home mum."

"I thought you were finding your purpose," says Luke. "I thought that's what this was all about." He makes an expansive gesture at "this," as though the kitchen is somehow part of my plan, as though "this" is where I spend all my time now.

"Maybe my purpose is to be a mother?"

Luke nods, wide-eyed, pushing out his bottom lip, thoughtful but ultimately unconvinced. He beckons me over and I sit on his knee, loop my arms around his neck, rest my chin on his shoulder.

"I think I'm going to take French classes," I say. "Build on what I learned at school. It's a shame to let all that knowledge go to waste."

"*Mais oui,*" says Luke, shrugging my face around to his. He French-kisses me, which means we'll end up having sex.

Competition

Six p.m. on Thursday, and while I may not have applied for any jobs, I *have* made myself eligible to win a Mini Cooper, two nights in Paris and seven in Miami, £500 of vouchers for a Scandinavian clothing brand, an enormous TV (which I plan to sell), an espresso machine (which I'll definitely keep), tickets to three exhibitions, a case of Prosecco, a juicer, a designer handbag, a designer coat, a meal for two at a corporate-looking restaurant in the city including a cocktail on arrival but no wine, membership to an independent cinema franchise and a VIP package for two at a female-only spa, so no one could argue it's been a completely wasted day.

Work

Paul, my friend from university, is back from a stint abroad that took in Berlin, Tokyo, Vienna, Johannesburg. He's a conceptual artist of growing repute: I've started seeing his work mentioned in blogs (even if I always find them via links on his own). We arrange to meet at a dive bar we frequented in the old days after we'd graduated. I'd traipse into London from my parents' house in the suburbs to interview for positions whose criteria my patchy employment history—waitressing, babysitting—fell some way short of fulfilling. Afterward we'd sink bottles of wine and bemoan our lost youth (we were twenty-one) and rail about how life wasn't fair: what more could we do? Why wouldn't *someone* give us a break? But while I was spamming every arts, advertising and media organization I could think of with my resume—regardless of whether a job was on offer—Paul was secretly receiving scholarship offers from prestigious art schools all over the world. When I found out, two weeks before he left for New York, I felt deeply, righteously aggrieved.

How *dare* he harbor such dreams? Who had given him permission to aim so high? Who did he think he was?

He arrives wearing big boots, their laces agape, beard full and his newly grown-out hair pulled up into a little topknot.

"Congrats on dropping out of the rat race, little one," he says. He also pats me on the head, a paternalistic bit he always does — it's ironic, but still, he does it every single time. "After all those years of empty threats! What made you go through with it?"

I tell him about the day I was seized by a powerful impulse to start swallowing things on my desk: thumb tacks, Post-it notes, whatever would fit in my mouth.

"I got as far as putting a paper clip on my tongue before realizing there was another way. So I spat it out and went to my boss's office to quit."

"How did he take it?"

"*She* was on holiday, so I had to wait another two weeks. But as soon as I'd made the decision, it was as if . . . I'd been holding my breath for years without knowing, and finally I could let it out. And I didn't have to swallow so much as a staple."

"Suicide by bureaucracy: I like it," he says, slow-nodding in approval.

"Hey, that's a freebie. Have it for your next show."

"Mm. It's not really my kind of work. But thanks," he adds, eyes shrinking into a smile.

Ladybugs

There are ladybugs everywhere; I keep stepping on them and having to clean up their crushed bodies. They're getting in through the sash windows and startling me when they fly too close, buzzing in my face like tiny drones. Luke says he hasn't seen any and I wonder if they might be haunting me, or if it's just that I'm spending too much time in the house.

The year my dad's company relocated, we had to move, and the pavements in our new neighborhood crawled with ladybugs. I was ten, and the only friend I made that summer was a boy named Jeffrey who lived next door. One of his longer-term projects involved collecting hundreds of ladybugs in a big mason jar over several weeks. When it was full, he dropped a lit match inside. I don't remember what happened next: it's possible I walked away to the sound of them popping, but it's equally likely he put the lid back on, extinguishing the flame. Big ideas, poor execution, that was kind of Jeffrey's style.

I look up "ladybug windows" online and am gratified by the number of search results. "They are overwintering in your window frames," asserts Quizking2, who has a three-out-of-five-star user rating on the forum. I look up "overwintering." "Hibernation and migration are the best ways to overwinter," Wikipedia recommends. Both sound pretty good to me.

Wasabi

I agree to go to a party hosted by one of Luke's friends from school. This group are all finance guys except for Luke: they're in chinos or dark jeans and crisp shirts, and their girlfriends are variations on a tanned, thin theme. I feel their eyes on my hair, which is flatter than I'd like, and my dress, which in the bathroom mirror looks a bit cheap. I drained my first glass of Prosecco within five minutes of arriving, and—angling my glass to catch the eye of the pourer—accept a refill every time the bottle comes near.

"Such a shame you guys can't come to Marbella," one of the girlfriends, whose name might be Lou, is saying. "Luke works too hard. He needs a holiday." This is the first I have heard of "Marbella" as a plan, and I can't think of anything worse. I'm surprised and pleased Luke has counted us out without making me be the bad guy for once.

"Yes, a real shame," I say. "Next time, for sure."

"Definitely," says maybe-Lou, scanning the room. "I'm just going to . . ." she says and slips past, not bothering to finish making up an excuse.

I take a seat on one of the enormous leather sofas next to a long dish of wasabi peas, and toss a couple into my mouth. Luke's friend Nish joins me. He has his collar turned up and is wearing sunglasses on his head even though we're indoors and it's nighttime. Notwithstanding, he's a nice guy, good at keeping things going when the conversation starts to flag. He's definitely the best out of Luke's friends.

"Watch out, they're like crack," he says, nodding at the dish.

I look at him and reach for a fistful more, which I trickle into my mouth. My eyes stream as I grind them down.

"What's new?" I ask through the burning grit. "Any scandals?"

He fills me in on what he knows. Everyone is getting married: he points out four newly engaged couples and complains about how hard it's getting to muster the required excitement with every new announcement. Nish is single and shares my ennui at what we dub the "endless parade of the engagement brigade."

"My theory is, it's like grandparents dying," I say. "When it happens to someone else, it's sad in a vague, universal sort of way, but essentially you don't really care. When it happens to *you*, though, it's the biggest deal."

"Yes!" says Nish. "Exactly!"

"My granddad just died," I say. "Good to know you don't give a shit."

Nish laughs and shoulder-bumps me.

"So what have you been up to?" he asks. I tell him about the blue-plaque job that I'm thinking of applying for.

"Maybe I'll get my own blue plaque one day," I say. "Claire Flannery, Blue Plaque-smith lived here."

"Meta," says Nish. "That didn't take long, then, finding your *raison d'être*. Didn't you only quit your last job a few weeks ago?"

"I'm just exploring my options. I might not take it."

"*If* you get it," he says.

My glass, frosted with salty, greasy fingerprints, is empty. I wave it at Nish. "We have a situation."

While he's gone, I keep working through the wasabi peas. I can't stop palming them into my mouth. Nish returns, having hustled an entire bottle of Prosecco from the fridge. I cough in an attempt to mask the pop of the cork, but end up turning a few heads with my performance. The two of us laugh and clink glasses, brazening it out.

"I think I'll skip this round," Nish says, leaning back into the sofa. "Of marriage, I mean. Wait for the second wave once everyone's divorced, have my pick of you lovely ladies when the competition's diminished." He says "you lovely ladies" in a joke-sleazy voice.

I suspect that maybe, encouraged by the fizz, Nish has taken a shine to me. I am hyperaware of his denim thigh against mine, his eyes on my face, his hot breath.

"You can do better than a washed-up divorcée!" I say, feeling charming, irresistible. I haven't felt this way in a really long time.

"I've always liked you, Claire," he says, smiling now. His eyes are glossy, and his head lolls toward me, puppyishly.

Luke finds us a while later, me with my head on Nish's shoulder, his arm around me, the empty bottle at our feet. I feel Nish tense up.

"Our taxi's waiting. I'm going—are you coming or are you too comfortable?" He's joking—I think he's joking—and I throw my arms around Nish's pink-shirted middle.

"Nish's the best!" I say and grin up at Luke, who stands with his hands in his pockets. I get up and finish the wasabi peas, the tiny, runty gray ones I've rejected until now. I've had, perhaps, hundreds.

"You didn't ask if I was ready to go," I say as I follow him out. "You just went ahead and called a taxi. You always do that."

"You never want to leave."

"I didn't even want to be there in the first place. You should be happy that I wanted to stay," I say, tripping slightly on an uneven paving slab.

"Stay and flirt with Nish? You're right. Why wouldn't I be delighted with that?"

Back at home when I take off my bra, three wasabi peas skitter on the floorboards. I kiss Luke, but he rolls onto his side and turns off the light as though he hasn't noticed I was making a move.

Hangover

The next day, I feel dreadful: dehydrated and as though my insides are scorched. No amount of water seems to help. We play a lackluster set on the public tennis court near our flat; the balls keep flying at me like giant wasabi peas in a nightmare. Luke wins easily, 6–0, despite giving even less than I am.

"I'm never eating those things again," I say. "I'm never drinking again either. The party wasn't worth this."

We have pasta for dinner with a mountain of Parmesan. Luke pours himself a glass of wine.

"Sure I can't tempt you?" he asks.

"Go on, then," I say, and I even take a refill.

Bright-eyed and bushy-tailed

Hard to believe it, but there was once a time when I would iron my clothes on Sunday afternoon, hang them up, crisp and ready for the working week ahead.

Monday morning

Four new emails, none personal.

Cafe

Opposite me sits a youngish man reading a math book with a university library stamp: pages and pages of equations, it seems. I could be with someone like that, if things were different, if I were single, I think, admiring his slender fingers and strong, dark brow. Bookish (glasses), arty (music festival wristband), outdoorsy (tanned). Head for numbers, I can only assume, or at least showing a willingness to improve, and God knows I'm no good with them. His hair, though—a huge, springy mass, which is longer and thicker than mine—would have to go. I try to imagine him with short hair and no glasses, and realize he looks exactly like Luke.

Economics

What actually becomes of all this terrible art for sale in cafes, costing the earth?

Typical

"Did you ever do anything about the thing and that guy?" asks Luke, who is sprawled on the sofa.

"Going to need a few more details," I say with my back to the static roar of the soccer game, painting my nails at the coffee table (a time-consuming but so far effective regime to make me stop biting them).

"The weed in the wall. The OBE guy."

"MBE and, it turns out, the buddleia *isn't* a weed after all, or in any case, isn't *always* a weed," I say, hoping that's an end to it— but no.

"So what are we going to do about it, then?"

"Hm?"

"You heard me."

"I didn't!" (I did.)

"What are we doing about the buddleia thing?"

"Not sure," I say.

"Ignoring the problem, hoping it goes away?"

I poke the brush into the bottle so I can glare at him unhindered. "Thanks very much for the vote of confidence. I've been looking into it—I'm not going to get something *ripped* out of our *home* before I know what we're dealing with."

"Okay. So, what *are* we dealing with?"

I return to the varnish, reciting what I've learned: "The buddleia was first introduced to Britain from China in the, uh . . . something-th century as a decorative garden plant, but has since gone rogue owing to its highly dispersible seed. It thrives in urban, disturbed and neglected sites, such as railways, canal banks and old stonework."

"Go on!" says Luke, sitting up now, and though I could very

easily continue, the surging cheers of the crowd from the TV confirm he doesn't mean me. Instead, I blow on my manicure to set the top coat of a shade that someone—on a payroll, at a desk, in an office somewhere—saw fit to name "Sizzlin' Saucepot."

Job

I begin my application for the blue-plaque job exactly two hours before the midnight deadline. One section of the form requires me to nominate an historical figure for consideration under the scheme. All the good ones I can think of already have a plaque, so blind desperation—or inspired brilliance, only time will tell—leads me to the Reverend Adam Buddle, an eighteenth-century cleric and botanist in whose memory my new friend the buddleia was christened.

I read aloud to Luke, "'Buddle spent many years working on an English Flora guide. He completed it in 1708 but it was never published.' Isn't that sad?"

"But he discovered a plant—I reckon that's better."

"He didn't actually discover it. Someone else did, years after Buddle died, and named it in his memory. Buddle never even knew it existed. He was in fact more of a moss man," I say.

"If an unpublished book and gardening hobby is all it takes to get a plaque nowadays, what about my uncle Ian?" I can hardly hear Luke above the racket he's making: riffling through the cutlery drawer, pulling plates out from between other plates, hurling cupboard doors shut.

"I'm already not feeling great about this: please don't make it worse. There isn't enough time to start again."

"Claire, you've been talking about this job for ages. I don't understand why you've left it so late."

"If you want to be helpful, instead of incredibly unhelpful, stop crashing around and tell me this: what other words can I use to do with heritage?"

"'Old,'" says Luke, "'history,' 'historic,' 'past' . . . No, wait, 'the past'?"

"Or leave?" I suggest.

He does, with full mug and plate, the fruits of his deafening kitchen concerto, but moments later, from the living room he calls, "'Posterity'!"—and actually, that's not a bad shout.

I get the application off with three minutes to spare. Afterward I read it a few times over, pleasantly surprised by how good it is: I've transformed a handful of flimsy biographical details into quite a compelling argument. I'm particularly proud of my closing statement: "It is fitting that Buddle achieved posterity through the very medium he championed in his lifetime. He is not only a credible candidate for a plaque in his own right, but a powerful embodiment of, and argument for, the concept of heritage itself."

"That last bit," says Luke, "feels like it might be a bit of a stretch."

"I've already sent it."

"And stretching is *good*," he says, hands on hips, sinking into a wide-legged lunge.

Company

Before Luke, I was embroiled in a long non-relationship, where I'd be summoned via text message late at night to Shepherd's Bush. I'd make the fifty-minute journey across town every time just to lie next to a man who preferred to kiss a joint and caress his guitar.

Revisionism

In the morning, I reread the heritage application, expecting it to fire me up for a productive day of job-seeking; but minus the eleventh-hour adrenaline, and plus the effect of three cups of coffee, it's far from the typo-free triumph I'd hoped.

Mum

A phone call from my mother; her voice is low and quailing.

"Mum, are you okay?"

"Did you tell Faye that Gum"—she takes a breath—"exposed himself to you?"

"What? No! Oh my God. That's not—"

"I've just come off the phone with Dee," she says. Dee is her sister, my aunt, Faye's mother. "She said that at the funeral—*at your own grandfather's funeral*—you were making God knows what kind of claims about him. About my father."

I try to explain that it was probably accidental, that it usually just popped out in the bathroom. I say "popped out" a few times, to play up the atmosphere of spontaneity. I tell her I'd had too much wine at the wake, and maybe I'd made it sound worse than it was.

"The bathroom?" she says, her voice getting higher. "Why would you have been in the bathroom with Gum?"

"To look at his war wounds," I say. A terrible thought occurs to me. "You haven't told Grandma, have you? Or Dee—she wouldn't have said anything, would she?"

"Of course not."

"Good. There's really no need for her to know."

"Just the rest of the family."

"I'm sorry, Mum," I say, and I start to cry. "I'll ring Faye; I'll
ring Dee and tell them it really wasn't a big deal. He never
touched me, I promise."

"I can't talk to you right now. I need some time," she says and
hangs up the phone.

Dinner

We're in a restaurant with my oldest friend, Sarah, and her newest
boyfriend, Paddy, an outing that took many weeks to organize
given Luke's schedule. The boyfriend, whom I've only met fleet-
ingly twice before, doesn't look at Luke or me throughout the
meal and directs his few words into the space between us. He
works in "industrial interior design"—what this entails is no
clearer after ten minutes of interrogation during our meal.

"So tell me: is that like factory design?" I ask.

"Not really," he says.

"Warehouses?"

"Not really," he says, then in the same monotone concedes,
"kind of, maybe, it depends."

"What . . . materials do you work with? Wood?"

A nod.

"Metal?" Luke asks.

"Both of those, yeah. Wood, metal . . . stuff like that," Paddy
says. It's the chattiest he has been all evening.

"So you work with your hands," I say firmly, pleased to be getting somewhere.

"Not really. It's more kind of concept-driven." There's a silence
and I nod as though all is now abundantly clear.

"What's . . . your favorite thing about it?" I take a long swig of
wine. I have been drinking more than my fair share; I must be two
glasses ahead of everyone else.

"The hours aren't bad."

"And how ... did you ... end up in that area?" This from Luke. Good one, I think, and nudge him with my knee. He squeezes it in reply.

"Just fell into it, really."

Sarah is oblivious, delighted by the fact we are finally double-dating and on even more strident form than usual. She corrects Luke when he mispronounces the word "epitome" and laughs longer than the mistake deserves, while Paddy gnaws on his fingers. His nails, I notice, are worse than mine: red and stumpy and sore-looking.

"Now there's someone who gives nail-biters a bad name," I say to Luke on the way home.

"If she was really as clever as she thinks she is, she wouldn't be so desperate to prove it all the time," Luke says. Hard logic to argue with, but the criticism annoys me nonetheless. I turn silent, going slightly too fast for him to comfortably keep up on the walk from the Tube station to our flat.

Car

A parked car is shining in the road, lacy with suds. I nearly trip over the bucket beside it, brimming with dark water. A film of soap scum slow-swirls on the surface. I didn't think anyone still washed their car by hand.

When I was a child, my father's windscreen was always spattered with shit. We must have lived under a busy flight path — or maybe there were more birds around then. Every couple of months when it got too dense, Dad would pull on his odd-job jeans and head out with a bucket and the yellow sponge, a primordial-looking thing that was older than me. I'd beg him to let me help, but after a while I'd start to whine about my soaking cuffs and cold hands.

Once, my mother appeared in the driveway with a plate of chicken nuggets, fresh from the oven, and fed me one with her fingers. I had just started to call her "Mum" instead of "Mummy" and stopped holding her hand in the street. The chicken burned, and I sucked down fresh air, flapping my wet hands in front of my mouth while I fought back tears I didn't understand.

I look around; there's no one in sight and no door open to any of the nearby houses. I pick up the bucket and toss the water over the car, so the suds won't dry and leave spots.

Availability

A few rings and in comes the smug automaton: "Sorry, but the person you've called is *not* available."

"The person" is my mother and she's screening my calls.

Retrospect

"One stupid comment when I was a bit drunk and she's acting like I said he molested me!"

"You did *sort* of say that, didn't you?" Luke butters some toast, apparently confident the stir-fry I'm cooking won't satisfy his appetite.

"No!" I lift the lid and check the rice. It's still very far from done. "What I said was, when he showed me his war wounds, I often saw more than I'd bargained for."

"Can you not hear how that could sound a bit . . . off?"

I think about it. "I can see how someone could interpret it that way; but it isn't at all how I meant it."

"How did you mean it?" He takes a bite of toast—half the slice in one go—and drops another piece of bread in the toaster.

"I don't know. Funny?"

"Funny 'ha, ha' or 'peculiar'? The distinction is pretty crucial."

"Both. You met Gum—he was a funny character! My uncle's speech at the wake was all about his little foibles."

"*Little foibles.*" Luke smirks. "I hope you didn't call them that."

"Don't be gross!" I go to kick him, but he's too far away.

"Seriously, Claire, it *is* pretty odd. If my sister told me our granddad had done that, I would have said it was weird."

"Yeah, well, I didn't have a brother to point stuff out to me, and I'm still fine, aren't I? It's not some dark secret I've carried with me all these years—it was just a thing that happened. Okay, it was slightly weird maybe—but it's not like I'm *scarred*. The moral here is, I should say nothing, ever."

"Well, at least you learned something," says Luke, while I crunch still-raw rice grains between gritted teeth.

The principle of the thing

The frothed milk in my latte is—don't ask me how—so stiff and solid the spoon's standing up unaided. I know there are worse things going on in the world, but that doesn't mean I should suffer in silence and drink, or, rather, eat this.

Gym

Personal Trainer Gavin has a cheesy Friday night vibe—the sort of guy who frequented my teenage weekends. He sings along to the music with impeccable timing when the lyrics are exercise-relevant (pain, directions, journeys, challenges, distances, heat, thresholds, et cetera), and I'd be willing to bet considerable sums that in his leisure time he wears vigorous aftershave and juts his chin to the beat in dark, flashing bars while clutching a whisky and Coke. I like him, his enthusiasm and the by-the-numbers flirting he no doubt employs with all his female clients. He makes me nostalgic for a simpler time.

"Got the day off, then?" he asks, post-warm-up, leading me to the mirrors for some "floor work." It's a reasonable question at three p.m. on a Wednesday.

"Yeah," I say. Then to discourage further probing, "Is this a busy time for you, usually?"

"Nah, weekday afternoons are pretty quiet. We get some new mums in wanting to lose the baby weight, and some of our older members. The young professionals like yourself tend to come early mornings before work. Try a squat for me, Claire." He guides me down by the shoulders. "Tuck in the tailbone. Lovely." I try not to flinch as he readjusts my pelvis. "Let's have ten of those."

Gavin leans, arms folded, back against the mirror while I hunker down. At the nadir of number six, he twists the knife. "So *what* is it you do?"

I know in my heart it's an innocent question, but right at this moment, confronted with my squatting reflection, thighs quaking in ancient translucent Lycra, the answer *Well, I'm just searching for my purpose* simply isn't an option. "I actually work in finance," I say.

"Awesome." Gavin nods as if this is what he expected—and absurdly, I'm flattered.

We finish the session with a treadmill sprint, and Gavin starts to roar above the music. "I want you! To give me! One hundred! Percent!"

Obediently I thumb up the speed control, puffing and clenching my teeth so he'll think I've hit my limit—but there's no way

I'm giving this my all. It's absolute madness not to hold *something* back: that's just basic common sense.

Contact

An engineer is sifting through the multicolored innards of a green metal cabinet on my street. So that's where all the wires have gone! I hear music, like the strain of a violin, but as I get closer, it turns out to be just one long, mournful note: the dialing tone keeping us all connected.

Co-op

In the local Co-op, I buy some Diet Coke. At the register, I hold up my debit card.

"How will you be paying?" the cashier asks.

"Uh, with this?" I say, waving the card.

"Chip and PIN, or contactless?" he says.

"Contactless."

He picks up a Kit Kat from a pile next to the till, scans it and sets it next to the can.

"I don't want that."

"It's free. Free Kit Kat when you pay contactless." He points to a sign that says this verbatim.

"But I don't want it," I say, and he winces in disbelief.

"Why wouldn't you want a *free chocolate bar*?"

"Because," I say, "I don't want it."

"But why?"

"There is no why. You either want something or you don't. That's what want is." I smell a wave of mint: he's chewing some gum. He can't stop shaking his head. "Everyone *else* has taken it. I've scanned it now. Why don't you give it to your boyfriend?"

"I don't have a boyfriend," I say, to throw him off.

It's going to look bad next time I'm in here with Luke.

Karma

You'd think after all these however-many years I'd have learned to open fizzy drinks at arm's length, just in case.

Beg to differ

"I'm not saying it's not a good job; I just wonder if it's definitely what you had in mind when you quit the old one. The whole *point* was that you'd spend some time thinking about what you really want to do, and I worry you're investing a lot of hope in a role that might not be right anyway—just another quick fix—and you'll end up stuck and frustrated again in a couple of months . . ."

Luke and I are on our way out and I've stopped in the hall to shuffle through months' worth of junk mail in case I've missed something from the blue-plaque people.

"It's the first thing you saw, essentially by accident, and you applied one minute before the deadline—that doesn't scream 'dream job,' to me. Also, by the way, you're not going to find anything there. Who doesn't use email nowadays?"

"Uh, Pizza Palace? Great Wall of China? AAA1Taxi? Domestic Angels? Hollywood Sushi?" I hold up each flyer, then drop them on the floor.

He bends to retrieve one. "Sushi! Let's have sushi. That's *exactly* what I want."

"And you said I wouldn't find anything," I say.

Acceptable

We pass a couple on our street embroiled in a back-bending clinch.

"Is it reasonable to say," I begin, "that it's the least attractive couples who are the most intent on flaunting their sex lives?"

"Hm," says Luke. "I'm not sure it is okay to say things like that."

"But it's true. If I can't say it to you, who can I say it to?"

"Your mum?" Luke suggests.

My mother, if she would only answer the phone, would almost certainly agree with me. Which means Luke is right: I probably shouldn't be saying it.

2

Grandma

I phone Grandma to tell her I'm coming to visit. It rings out three times before there's an answer, and when it comes, the voice is like a cartoon old lady's, creaky and frail.

"He-hello?"

"Grandma? It's Claire!" I say loudly, worried I've woken her.

"Claire," she says faintly, and I wonder if she knows who I am in the moment. There is a pause and a fumble—I guess she is swapping the receiver to the other ear. I picture it, enormous in her bony hand, the same phone she would have picked up when Gum died and she called her children to tell them, one by one. The wait while the rotary dial ticked back round to zero, the silence before the call connected. Grandma's telephone is from another time, when people used the word "telephone" and had important things to say.

"I wanted to check you'll be in later! I'm going to drop by this afternoon!"

"Stop shouting," says Grandma, fully herself again. "I won't be in. I have a date. Mustafa is taking me to lunch." Mustafa is Grandma's Turkish neighbor, a widower whose name is really Erdem, but who tolerates Grandma's lazy racism because he's a good guy who can see what a kick she gets out of it.

"Oh," I say. I had expected her to be delighted I was coming. "How about tomorrow, then?" There is a pause that goes on for so long I say, "Grandma? Does tomorrow work?"

"Tomorrow isn't great, but I can squeeze you in—shall we say half past three?"

"Let me see . . . Half past three could be tricky," I say, though my day is free. "I'll have to move a few things around . . . No, no, it's fine. I'll make it work," I insist above her halfhearted protests.

"You've lost weight," she says the next day, as I stoop to kiss her soft, creased cheek.

"You always say that. If I'd lost as much weight as you claim every time, there'd be nothing of me left."

"Oh, I don't think there's any fear of *that*," says Grandma, heading into the kitchen, where scones are cooling on a wire rack.

"Delicious," I say, reaching for one. "I hope you didn't go to this trouble just for me." She swats at my wrist with a tea towel.

"Indeed I didn't. I'm having the girls round for tea. They're coming at five. That's why I said, if you remember, that today didn't really suit. Here." She hands me the biscuit tin. I open it and peer in at a few sorry digestives lying at the bottom. I take a bite of one; it's lost any crunch it may once have had, and tastes of damp, but I finish it anyway.

We sit at the kitchen table drinking tea from mugs that used to be red but have turned a whitish pink through decades of dish-washing cycles.

"I hear you're having a bit of trouble finding a new job," says Grandma. "How long has it been now—a month?"

"I'm not having trouble."

"Was the old one really so bad you couldn't wait to find something else before you left?"

"I was afraid if I waited, I might never get out. That job was never meant to be my *career*—I was just so relieved someone out there was willing to hire me."

"Mm," says Grandma.

"And then, suddenly, years had passed, and I knew if I was going to get anywhere, I had to leave. I need this time to take stock."

"I see! Well! All right for some."

"It's not like that. I have savings."

"Faye got another pay rise—did you hear? Would you ever think about accountancy?"

"Numbers aren't my strong suit."

Grandma nods. "You must have got that from your father's side. Here." She pushes the biscuit tin toward me. "Have another," she says in a kindly, compensatory tone.

"I'm fine, thanks."

She sighs. "They were your grandfather's favorite. Never liked anything I made as much as those." Along with most of his generation, Gum hated waste. When I stayed with my grandparents as a child, anything I left on my plate would boomerang back next mealtime: gray carrots at breakfast, cornflake mush at lunch, sandwich crusts at dinner. Gum wore the same pair of sandals every summer for thirty-four years, and famously stopped talking to my mother for weeks in the wake of a guerrilla spring cleaning, when she got rid of multiple food items so old they preexisted sell-by dates. Grandma told me at the funeral she knew the end was nigh when he started throwing away tea bags after only one soak. "It was as though a light had gone out," she said.

"So, is there anything I can do to help while I'm here?"

Grandma raises a hand and strikes it dismissively through the air. "You can't do anything. Just drink your tea."

"Are you sure? I could change your sheets, or do some cleaning, or . . . run down to the shops if there's anything you need?"

She's shaking her head.

"Stuart changed the bedding with me this morning. And Faye comes and vacuums once a week. The twins take it in turns to help me with the shopping—you'd be no use: you can't even drive."

"I can drive, Grandma. I passed on my first try, remember? I just don't have a car." I wonder if senility is maybe setting in. In the eyes of the family, passing on my first try has been my greatest achievement to date. My mother failed three times, and Grandma herself took five attempts—and that was in the old days when *everyone* passed.

"Same thing, isn't it? What's the point of having a license if you don't bother to use it? Finish the biscuits, that's what I'd ask you to do."

"Oh, go on, then." I dunk a broken piece in my tea and half of it dissolves and disappears. "Please think about something I can do. Laundry? Some gardening?" I had no idea my cousins were so considerate: I'd always believed myself to be the thoughtful grandchild. I feel bad that I've done nothing, while they've seemingly been running her household between them. They must think I'm terrible.

"You can cut my toenails," Grandma says.

"Yep, yes, sure, okay," I say, straight in. "I can definitely do that. You mean now?"

"Claire," Grandma says, "I'm joking. You don't help out—that's fine; it's how you are. I remember what being your age was like—of course, I had four children under eight then, but modern life is different. You've got an awful lot on."

———

At home that evening, I'm still seething.

"She wouldn't even let me do one laundry cycle! It's not fair, telling someone they don't help when they've just offered to do absolutely anything for you!"

"Speaking of washing," Luke says, "I'm nearly out of clean shirts." He raises a hand when my mouth drops open. "I only mentioned it because I'm putting a load in, and wondered if you had anything that needs washing."

"Please," I say. "You haven't done a single load the whole time we've lived together. This isn't the time for grand gestures."

"I love you," Luke calls, as I storm into the bedroom to gather the laundry for a white wash.

Office life

It's the little things you miss: free pens, notebooks, coffee, the color printer. The incidental conversation.

Girl

On my way back to the flat from another cafe stint, I see a woman around my age sitting on the curb, gripping handfuls of hair and racked with sobs. I think about approaching her to ask if she's all right, but then remember an article I read about someone who was stabbed after asking a teenager to be quiet on the bus. My mother's mantra rings loud—*Don't get involved!*—and for once I listen. As I draw level, I give the girl a supportive half-smile/half-grimace, and she looks at me through red-rimmed eyes, choking on huge, gasping breaths.

———

At home, I feel terrible and ring Luke. He's laughing as he answers; I can hear a female voice in the background.

"Hey," he says. "What's up?"

I tell him about the girl. "What do you think?"

"You left her there on her own?"

I snatch up my keys. "Is that bad?"

"Her parents must be going crazy. Did you call the police?"

I pause on the stairs, one foot dangling midair. "Her *parents*?" Then I realize. "Hang on, she's our age."

"Ohhh. You said *girl*. I assumed child." I sink down onto the stairs, rest my head against the banister spindles. "Well then," he continues, "she's probably fine. Maybe she had a fight with her boyfriend or something."

"Mm," I say, chewing at the skin around my little finger. "Maybe."

"If you're going to lose sleep over it, why don't you go back and ask her?"

"I might get into something too big to handle—I mean, she was *really* upset," I say. "Hey, what was so funny?"

"What?"

"You were laughing when you answered the phone."

"Was I? Oh. Can't remember. Probably nothing."

When we hang up, I run back downstairs to see if the girl is still there, but she's gone.

Unrest

Sleep and wakefulness bicker all night and I think, Why can't you two just get along?

Bowling

My ex-colleagues invite me to a bowling night to celebrate three birthdays that all fall in the same week. There are drinks at the office beforehand. It's the first time I've been back since I left, and the place is different, though I can't figure out what's changed. I go and look at my old desk, which is now immaculately kept by my successor: a young (but balding) gun named Jonathan. His default expression is one of sulky surprise, which I put down to the premature departure of his hair, because he's certainly not at all curious to meet me.

"I'm Claire. I used to be you," I say, holding a hand out to him, "or you're the new me, depending how you look at it."

"You didn't do digital, though," he says, hooking a small plastic bag onto the wrist of my extended hand, before taking my fingers in a limp, damp shake. "Did you?"

"No." I'd spent much of my last year dodging digital, insisting that it wasn't in my skill set. "What's this?"

"You somehow managed to miss all that stuff when you cleared out my desk," says Jonathan, typing so fast he looks like he's faking, though I can see on his monitor he's not. His WPM rate must be insane. I look in the bag, which is weighed down with coppers and small denominations of foreign currency. There are also some bobby pins, a disintegrating *London A–Z*, a bunch of receipts and some pay stubs with my name on them. I notice a few of the latter have been opened, something I never bothered to do.

"You really didn't need to keep this, but thanks anyway," I say. "You could have chucked it." I have so many similar plastic bags at home, full of not-quite-rubbish I can't bear to throw away.

"Do what you need to do. Wait." He reaches over to his cork-board and unpins a sheaf of paper. "Also yours."

I flick through it and my face burns. They're all the personal emails sent in error to my work account since I left: weeks and weeks worth of invitations to brunch and dinner parties, and a thread entitled "Tuesday Drinkies," ten-odd pages of my school friends' plans to meet up for a drink. A glimpse of the final page reveals the discussion has devolved into farmyard-animal puns.

"Wow," I say, "don't you have my new email address? You can just forward this stuff to me."

"Somewhere," he says, resuming his virtuosic typing. "I thought it would be easier this way. Do it all in one go, post them on to you with that other stuff. None of them seemed like they were that urgent."

"Well . . . delete anything else that comes in, will you?" I say, dropping the emails in his recycling box.

At the bowling alley, there's a company tab. I feel bad availing myself of it and end up buying a round for eight people that makes my heart race when I hand over my card. No one even knows I paid for it—they hardly say thank you when I set down the tray.

I open with a half-strike that turns out to be a fluke: my next five balls go straight in the gutter.

"How's the job hunt?" my old boss, Geri, asks, frowning at her bowling shoes while we await our turn. It's the first time I've ever seen her in flats.

"Slow, but it's going, just about. I don't want to rush into anything, end up somewhere I don't want to be."

"We must have been paying you too much," she says, "if you can afford that luxury!"

"I have savings. Anyway, some things are bigger than money."

"Striiiike!" she says, thrusting her index fingers high as Jonathan's ball blasts through the pins. He's turned away already, swigging a beer. "Aw," she continues, patting my knee, "we do miss you! Jono's brilliant, an absolute whiz kid, but between you and me, he can't make coffee for shit."

When I leave, everyone is dancing. The song "9 to 5" has come on the jukebox and I slip away as they all join in with the chorus, feeling like a fraud. On the Tube home, I pull out the pay stubs from my little plastic bag, and see one of Jonathan's has got in by mistake. I'm pleased until I open it and discover he's only making a grand less per year than I had been, even though he's twenty-two and I was in the job for over six years.

Probably nothing

I log in to Luke's emails to see if we've paid the gas bill: I have the gas supplier's reminder letter open on the table as proof. My eye alights on an email dated three weeks ago, from his colleague Fiona: no subject, just a link to some article from a medical journal. She has signed off "xoxo," which makes me think even less of her.

Buddleia

Colin Mason, MBE, has erected some scaffolding outside our building. It doesn't look in the least official or sturdy, and seeing him creaking around up there makes me a little nervous. I hurry past, not wanting to be drawn into conversation, but he's either forgotten who I am or has no further business with me.

The next day, the scaffolding has gone, but the buddleia remains, waving gently in the breeze.

Progress

More than forty years since man walked on the moon, yet still no truly viable alternative to bread.

Déjà vu

As I'm eating lunch with Sarah in a cafe near the school where she works, she talks about Paddy and how happy she is. Her experience of him seems so far removed from the sullen nail-chewer I've encountered thus far that I have to confront the possibility my judgment might be wide of the mark this time.

"I've never met someone who knows so much about everything. The other day, right, I told him about my hay fever and he said I should eat local honey to counteract the symptoms. Local honey." She's shaking her head. "He doesn't even have hay fever himself."

"I've heard that before," I say, and then, "Oh my God, so weird: *this* has happened before. You and me, sitting here talking about this, me telling you I've heard about local honey before."

"No," says Sarah firmly, leaving absolutely no room for debate. "It definitely hasn't happened. I'd never heard of it until Paddy told me."

"I know," I say, annoyed. "It's called déjà vu? This is the second time it's happened to me this week."

Sarah looks at me and grips my wrist, interrupting the rise of my salad-laden fork.

"Claire, I don't want to freak you out but I think you should maybe go and see a doctor. Do you smell burning?"

I sniff the air. "No? Maybe? *Is* something burning?" I say. "I can't tell if I only think I can now because you mentioned it. Why?"

"Talk to Luke," she says. "It's probably nothing at all to worry about, and I might not have got this right, but I'm pretty sure I read somewhere that frequent déjà vu is linked to brain tumors. And the smell of burning."

"So there's a little bit to worry about," I say, certain I can feel something hard expand inside my skull.

Pathology

I call Luke to sound him out.

"Start from the beginning. Forget about anything you've read online and give me the facts."

I tell him about my lunch with Sarah, about Paddy and the local honey.

"Right . . ." I detect a twist of impatience.

"You did say to start at the beginning," I remind him, but to keep him onside, cut to the déjà vu. "What do you think? Be straight with me: I can take it."

"Second time this week?" He doesn't sound even slightly concerned.

I say, "At *least*. Part of the issue with déjà vu is the feeling itself being so uncanny: it's hard to separate it into different instances."

"Okay, let's back up a bit. Have you had any headaches? Problems with your vision?" I consider this carefully. "Hangovers don't count," he adds.

"Well . . . there's a general sort of background throb, but I've always put that down to, like, life."

"We'll talk more when I come home," says Luke, "but in the meantime, don't worry."

"Don't worry, we'll get through this, or don't worry, there's nothing to worry about?"

"The latter," he says, gearing up for a yawn.

"And is that your personal or professional opinion?"

"It's both."

"Ignore the email I just sent you, then," I say, referring to the dossier pulled together from my afternoon's online research.

Free time

When I had a job, I used to fantasize about what I'd do if I didn't have to work anymore. Go to the gym every day, get really fit, train for a marathon perhaps. Finish *Ulysses*, read *Moby Dick* and one of the big Russian guys. Get to grips with the economy, also modern art.

Second opinion

I still haven't registered with a doctor in London, despite Luke's incredulous nagging and the fact I've lived here for nearly eight years. Luke remains entirely unperturbed by Sarah's diagnosis, but just to be finally, unequivocally sure, I make an appointment to see our family doctor.

"Claire," says Dr. Patterson when I enter, "it's been a while. What seems to be the problem?"

I say, "It's probably nothing. I don't really know why I'm here."

His bedside manner hasn't changed: an off-putting blend of amusement and skepticism. His smile deepens when I get to the déjà vu, via a number of arduous caveats.

"First things first: are you pregnant?" he asks.

One hand flies to my stomach, the other to my head. "I don't think so. Is this a symptom of pregnancy?"

"Well, no," he admits, "but a woman of your age . . . Let's say it doesn't hurt to rule it out as part of any health conversation. You're sure?"

"Certain. I can't be. My boyfriend—*partner*—and I are very safe."

Dr. Patterson chuckles. "You'd be surprised how many times I've heard that from women who turn out to be some way along."

"Is that true, then, about déjà vu being linked to brain tumors, or . . . ?" I ask, trying to sound not bothered either way.

"Been consulting Dr. Google?" He swoops in without warning, flashing a light in my eyes. "I think you'll be absolutely fine," he says, and as an afterthought asks, "No headaches? Dizziness? Sickness?"

I shake my head. "I just wanted to be on the safe side."

He presses his lips together. "We all want to be reassured from time to time, don't we? Often these worries can be brought on by stress. Are you having a busy time at work?"

"It's . . . it's a bit complicated," I say. "I'm between jobs at the moment. By choice, I mean. I haven't been fired or anything."

"Ah." He takes off his glasses and sits back in his chair, huffs on the lenses and thumbs them with a hanky. "Sometimes, when we have *too much* time, we worry unduly about our health. If we don't have the daily distractions of, say, a job or"—he gestures to my stomach—"a family to look after, we might find our focus becoming quite . . . narrow." He blinks nakedly a couple of times, then replaces his glasses. "Insular," he adds, in case I've failed to recognize that this is the talk he gives the lonely people who find excuses to come in for the company.

"It's just temporary," I say. "I'm waiting to hear about a few things." Though I've heard nothing since the blue-plaque deadline weeks ago, I remain optimistic about my chances.

"Was there anything else?" he asks.

I decide against telling him I wake in the night convinced I feel lumps in my armpits and breasts.

"Not a thing," I say, smiling widely as I get up to go.

On my way to the train station after my appointment, my mother's car goes by: I'd know that slow-rolling Beetle anywhere. I raise my hand at its tail end, on the off-chance I've coincided with her once-in-a-journey check in the rearview mirror. The blinker flashes, and as the car heads right, her face turns to me before she trundles out of view.

Cryptic

"I never thought I'd be a mother, and then you came along," she has said on more than one occasion.

Failure

An email, at last, from the heritage people informing me my blue-plaque application has been unsuccessful. They do not say why, but do say why they can't say why ("overwhelming response") and express a friendly hope that my interest in heritage will nonetheless "continue to thrive." They have misspelled my name.

When Luke gets home from work, it's nine thirty. He's startled when he turns on the light to see me at my laptop in the near-total dark and I imagine how I must look: hunchy, lemur-like, crazed.

"You okay?" he asks.

"I didn't get the job."

"The—Oh. I'm sorry. That sucks," he says, and other platitudes I don't listen to as I turn back to the fruits of my post-
rejection research: resume tips, information about funding
grants for niche post-grad studies, Wikipedia articles about those
niche post-grad studies subjects, nannying jobs, bar jobs, admin
jobs, expensive intensive residential cookery courses, fast-track
routes for law, medicine, the civil service, agencies specializing
in ski-season placements in Canada, Europe, New Zealand,
Russia, programs for living and working abroad in Japan, South
America, China, the UAE. I have more than twenty different
windows open, each displaying so many tabs my computer has
taken the executive decision to file the overflow in cumbersome
sub-tabs.

"Do you want to talk about it?" Luke asks.

"Nothing to talk about," I say, hitting the power button and
signing out with the electronic shutdown chime.

How hard can it be?

Throughout my working life I've had emails addressed to: Clare,
Clair, Clara, Cara, Kate, Louise, Catherine, Carol, Cleo, Caro-
line and *Derek*.

Canal

A lunchtime walk down by the canal, which lies flat and still as
glass. There is no one around and for one tiny second I consider
taking off into the water. The afternoon shivering as I'm swallowed up.

Lists

I've been keeping a list on my phone of business ideas, should I chance upon an adventurous millionaire. So far it reads:

1. *Black milk (for goths?)*

Local library

The standard-issue public-library smell—musty pages, instant coffee—still holds the promise of knowledge and new worlds, so I can't be all that jaded yet. Besides me, there are three other users: a Rastafarian man poring over the bookies' betting odds, a woman in a burka, shoulders shaking as she watches something on one of the computers, and a huge bearded white guy wearing long shorts, cruising the shelves with plastic bags bunched hemorrhoidally from both fists.

While waiting for my ancient laptop to load, I pick out a title from the shelf next to me called *Surviving in the 21st Century*, a compendium of disorders and syndromes, which range alphabetically from ADHD to schizophrenia, via depression, Internet addiction, IBS and perfectionism. I open it and read from the chapter on hoarding:

Early signs include a tendency to group things into piles, with the intention of coming back to them later. These can often be a manifestation of emotional blockages: sadness, defeat, confusion or sometimes even ambition or hope. The Hoarder often struggles to distinguish between what is important or useful and what is not.

My computer's labored whimpering has given way to a grinding gurgle, which means it's ready to use, so I slap the book shut and slot it back on the shelf.

Communication breakdown

"Darren, it's Clive," the librarian is saying into the phone. "I wanted to check if Michelle knew whether Jeff Jones had left his new mobile number with Angus? We've lost a digit, so we're a bit stuffed."

Four a.m.

The evening's wine has left my bladder full, my mouth dry, a thump in my temples. There is a pain, like something turning, in what might be my liver—possibly it's paranoia, or it could be my appendix. My heart is going a little too fast, and I am suddenly beyond certain that I have carbon-monoxide poisoning. My father was right: we should have bought a detector. I didn't listen all these years, and now it's too late.

This week—if I survive the night—will be different. No wine, except maybe a glass, or two, absolute tops, at the weekend. Cut back on the coffee. Start taking some care, I think, gripping the covers. Really, *properly* start looking for a job. Get past this thing with my mother once and for all.

I turn onto my side and make out Luke's dark shape beside me. I love him, and one day he'll be dead. He starts to snore.

"Stop. Snoring," I say firmly, and he does, without waking.

Tube

A family of Orthodox Jews gets on: improbably young parents with seven—seven!—children. In the dingy, yellow-lit crush their clothes are a fabulous anachronism amid all the hoodies and jeans. In the middle of the carriage, the father stands, hands clasped behind his back, keeping himself upright with core strength alone, while beneath the wide felt brim of his hat his ringlets bounce and drift. His wife, boosting a child on her hip, in glossy wig, thick tights, dark skirt, white shirt, makes me almost nostalgic for school uniform: the tribal day-in-day-out safety of it. When after a few stops the family file off, the space left behind is quickly absorbed; but their presence lingers, like incense.

News

"Which bits of this do you want?" Luke asks of the paper.

"Crossword," I say, pen already poised.

"Never any interest in the main section. Don't you want to know what's going on in the world?" He holds up the front page, which looks full of blood and flames.

"I know what's going on: terrorist threats, terrorist attacks, shootings, food shortages, drought, floods, women being raped and killed. No, thank you." I shake my head. "Don't you know the expression? No news is good news."

"Not what that means."

"And yet true," I say.

Liquid meal

Ever since someone told me milk is technically a food, I've all but abandoned my latte habit.

No change

The doorbell sounds while I'm still in my pajamas; retiree-style, I peer out of the window to see if I need to answer it. There are two children standing there, floppy-haired boys, maybe eleven years old.

"Yes?" I say when I open the door.

"I was hoping to speak with your mum if she's in?" says the freckle-faced redhead, with such supreme confidence I wonder for a second how he knows my mother.

"She doesn't live here."

"Oh," he says. "Then may I speak with the person in charge?"

"That would be me. How can I help you?" I fold my arms and lean against the doorframe. "Young man," I add, fooling no one.

"We're raising money for charity. I'm doing sponsored stand-up, and Liam's doing a sponsored swim." He's well spoken, a nice-seeming kid, but I wouldn't have pegged him for funny.

"Good for you," I say. "Tell me a joke."

He shakes his head firmly. "I'm still working on my material."

Liam is hanging off the railings, suspended forward like a diver ready to jump.

"And how far are you swimming?" I call over to him.

He shrugs.

"So will you sponsor us, then?" the redhead asks. "It's for a good cause." From his pocket he hands me a wad of slightly damp, grubby paper.

I unfold it. *Tom and Liam are raising money for the Humane Society* is written across the top. There's quite a good sketch of a dog in one corner. Underneath are a series of names, and to my mind, staggeringly generous donations: someone named Pippa Jackson has promised thirty pounds; the de Courcy-Pitt family fifty pounds. In my day, fifty pence was considered generous.

"You know, I don't generally give money to animal charities," I say. "I'd rather the money went to scientific research "

"Animal testing?" interrupts Liam, disgusted.

"You didn't let me finish. Scientific research into cancer and other illnesses."

"My dog had cancer," says Liam. "That's him in the picture."

"*Human* illnesses," I say.

"Are *you* sick?" asks the redhead, who must be Tom.

"No. Why?" I say, slightly alarmed that he's sensed something, in that eerie way children in films have of seeing right to the quick of things.

"Pajamas," he says, pointing, and fair enough—it's four in the afternoon. "Are you not going to sponsor us, then?" he demands. Liam, meanwhile, has hopped off the railing ledge, preparing to move on to more munificent households.

"Listen, I'll make an exception this time because you guys are doing a good thing. I admire your get-up-and-go. Wait here."

Because you can't be too careful, I shut the door on them while I find my purse. I used to think being a grown-up meant having an abundance of loose change lying around—in pockets and bags, on the kitchen counter. Not small fry like coppers, but the big fellas: fifty pences, one-pound and two-pound coins. But all I can scratch together is about a quid, not even. When I open the door again, Liam is kicking the bin with moderate force.

"Stop that," I say, and to my surprise he does. "I'm afraid this is all I have." I offer my handful to Tom. He looks at it with undisguised disdain.

"We could go to an ATM?" he suggests, brightening for a moment.

"I don't think so," I say, and his face falls again. He picks his way through the coins, counting out loud. It's painful.

". . . forty, fifty, fifty-five, sixty, seventy, seventy-five, eighty, eighty-two." He looks up as if to confirm that this is my final offer. "Eighty-two p," he repeats. I nod, a little sheepish. He pockets the cash and carefully writes, £00.82, on his creased piece of paper. "What name shall I put?"

"Oh, don't bother with that," I say, stepping backward and starting to close the door.

"You have to. Our teacher said. Oh yeah, and do you pay tax?" He hands me the pen and paper.

"Excuse me?" I scribble something illegible, too embarrassed to put my real name.

"If you're a British taxpayer, we can get extra money. Uh . . ." He looks at Liam.

"Twenty percent," says Liam. He gets out an iPhone and prods the screen a few times, calculating. "That would bring you up to . . . ninety-eight point four p."

"No, I'm sorry, I'm not. I was, and I will be again, but you've caught me between jobs, I'm afraid." I wonder how it has come to pass that I'm apologizing for my life choices to strange youths on my doorstep. "By choice. I wasn't fired or anything."

"Never mind," says Liam.

"Yeah, not to worry," says Tom. The coins in his pocket crunch musically as they saunter off up the street.

Those who can

"What about teaching?" I ask.

Luke is shaving at the sink; I'm perched on the edge of the bath, imagining myself—long skirts, low bun—reading from a huge storybook to spellbound children gathered on a sun-flooded carpet.

"What about it?"

"As a job. For me."

He lifts his chin to scrape underneath. "What would you teach?"

"I don't know. Primary?"

"You need to know math."

"I know math!"

"What's thirteen times fifteen?" he asks, meeting my eyes in the mirror.

I don't even try. "They only go up to twelve in primary school."

"Hm." I flinch as he cruises the Adam's-apple bump.

"Think of the holidays—how great that will be when we have kids of our own."

He frowns in the glass, enhancing top-lip access. "I'm wondering where this teacher thing has come from. Feels a bit sudden."

I look into the bath, at the grayish flotsam stranded at the far end. "So, do you *not* want to have children, then?"

"I never said that."

"Just not with me."

"Didn't say that either."

"Oh. 'Kay." I turn on the tap, batting the flow toward the debris, trying to rinse it away. "And . . . when . . . *do* you think you might want to?"

He turns his face one way, then the other.

"When you've worked out what you want to do, we'll talk," he says, fluttering his razor in the water.

Honesty

Stop saying "great" so much. Also "wow!" "interesting" and "amazing."

Hm

So, I think, watching our Good White Towels blush slowly pink in the washing machine, that really *is* a thing that still happens in this day and age, after all.

Time

"I'm just trying to understand what it is you do all day." Luke has a knuckle in one of his eyes, and I can see he's really trying. On the table are a check I told him I would cash and a parcel for his sister I told him I would mail.

"I know it sounds strange," I say, "but the more time you have, the less time you have. Every moment becomes so precious." He's looking up at the ceiling, inflating his cheeks. "I'm sorry. I'm sorry. I'll do it tomorrow," I say, and he nods and blows the air through his teeth.

It's good of him not to mention his own job, which—when it comes down to the nuts and bolts of the thing—is all about giving people more time.

Give and take

Just after we started going out, Luke got shingles and was wiped out for a week. I bunked off work for two days to watch daytime TV by his side, play Scrabble and prepare nourishing invalid food (chicken broth, whole wheat toast, orange wedges, grapes)—except one evening when he hit rock bottom and I ordered Domino's as a special treat.

Sick-Luke was wretched and ashamed: he had the tragic air of a disgraced politician. "But you don't understand: I'm *never* ill," he kept insisting.

"Good. Because I'm never this nice," I'd reply, easing him into a warm bath or fluffing up his fever-flattened pillows.

Of course

"Listed and historic buildings are particularly vulnerable to structural damage from buddleia, with annual maintenance costs estimated at nearly £1 million."

No wonder the heritage people didn't embrace Adam Buddle, or by extension, me.

Reassurance

"Let's try looking at it another way. What do other people say your strengths are?" inquires Ann, the enormously patient "Career Genie" I found online and phoned at a very low ebb.

"I really can't think of anything."

"What about Mum and Dad? I bet there are things where they would say, 'Oh, Claire's *really* good at that.'"

When I was growing up, my parents held an unwavering, blanket belief in my abilities that I took for granted; lately, though, I've been plagued by the sense that I've failed to deliver on all those high hopes.

"Um, sometimes they'll phone me for help with the crossword?"

"Logic, communication, language skills," Ann says, clacking her keyboard. "That's a good start. Come on, something else." There's a long stretch of silence. "It can be anything, no matter how small or silly."

"I've . . . I've had compliments about my scrambled eggs."

"Well, that's all about good time management," says Ann, proving *she* at least has found her vocation.

3

Rush hour

Maybe I haven't been working all day in the traditional, office-bound sense, but I'm still a person trying to get somewhere too.

Conflict resolution

I meet one of my uni friends, Rachel, for a drink after work (her work). She's spent ten minutes analyzing a string of texts from a human rights lawyer, which are by turns flirtatious and brusque.

"What should I say to this?" she asks, showing me a reply that's just come in.

Not too bad. Yours? it reads. (The original question, which I helped her to draft, was, *Hey, how's your week going?*)

"I'm not sure I'm the right person to ask. I've been out of the game so long, I'm more likely to say something that will scare him away."

"How *is* Luke?" Rachel asks. "Is he still being difficult?"

It takes me a moment to work out that she is referring to the last time we met, when I told her Luke and I had been fighting. I only said this because she'd been saying how lucky I was to have him, and I didn't want to seem smug or complacent.

"It's a bit better, thanks," I say, and warming to the fiction, add, "I took your advice. It really helped." Her suggestion was to set some time aside each week to discuss our relationship frankly.

"That's so great," she says, squeezing my hand. "Always happy to help."

I ask her about work, in the vaguest terms possible to obscure the fact I'm not entirely sure what she does. It has something to do with Africa, I want to say an NGO, but couldn't be certain without checking her email signature, and inwardly curse myself for not doing this before we met. As she talks, I cling to a few key words, which in any other realm would be awful jargon (conflict resolution, mediation, dialogue), but in Rachel's world—which is actually the real world—are literal and vital.

"I wish I had your conviction," I say. "You're so passionate about what you do. You're making a difference. That must feel amazing."

She jerks a shoulder. "I don't think about it that way. Believe me, a lot of it is very boring paperwork. You know," she says, "not everyone can be a hero, or live the dream—we just need to contribute what we can. Pull our weight, earn a living. There's no shame in that."

I sense a lesson intended for me there, doused in disapproval. It's a tone I'm becoming more familiar with the longer my state of voluntary unemployment lasts.

"I totally agree. Well said," I say, squeezing her hand this time, and she extracts it delicately to compose a reply to her hot-and-cold lawyer.

Self-expression

"Never really got the point of sorbet," I say while an advert for a new brand is playing. "It's neither kitten nor cat."

"What?" says Luke, grinning.

"It's not delicious and luxurious like ice cream, but it's still full of sugar so it's not even healthy."

"What was the other thing you said?"

"Neither kitten nor cat?"

"Yeah."

"What about it?"

"It's not a saying."

"It is!"

"No, it isn't."

"Luke, I promise you it definitely is. Neither kitten nor cat— neither one thing nor the other. Falls between two stools."

"Yeah, *that's* a phrase. The cat one is not."

"I've said it hundreds of times and you've never batted an eyelid."

"You've never said it. It's not a phrase. Where did you get it?"

"Er, the English vernacular? I can't believe you haven't heard it before. *You're* the weirdo here."

His grin grows even wider: I'd be furious if I wasn't completely certain I'll be having the last laugh.

"Name one person who uses that phrase other than you," he says.

"That's ridiculous. It's like me saying, 'Name someone who uses the word "the."'"

"No, because 'the' is a word, which you just proved by using it yourself. Come on: one person."

"My mum. She says it all the time."

"Ohhh," says Luke, smirking. "Okay."

"You said name one person!"

"Humor me: one more. Anyone who isn't your mum?"

"Everyone else!"

"There's a very simple way to find out who's right," says Luke, pinching his phone from his shirt pocket with a smug flourish. "'Neither . . . kitten . . . nor . . . cat.'" He taps it in and turns the screen to me, triumphant. "Not a phrase."

I snatch the phone and click through the search results: pages 7, 8, 10, 19, 22. He's right: there are endless mentions of kittens and cats, but not a single hit for my phrase. "Well . . . it's a saying from the olden days. It's been passed on verbally. It wouldn't need to be written down anyway."

"Claire," says Luke, "that doesn't sound very convincing out loud."

"Ring my mum. Ring her right now: she'll tell you."

"Oh, there is no doubt in my mind that your mum uses that expression," Luke says. "But I think you'll find no one else does."

"Fair enough—I'd say that too, if I was scared of being proven wrong. Don't call her."

"Your mum isn't talking to you. I don't think she'll appreciate me phoning at half past ten at night to quiz her about a phrase she made up."

I click through a few more search results pages at random: 34, 42, 45, 59. Nothing.

I've never felt so alone.

Tube

This man is staring at someone down the carriage with such open desire and longing that I turn to see what the fuss is about.

No one has looked at me that way, ever, not even Luke, who's *in love* with me.

Identify

In the cafe, the barista smiles warmly.

"Back so soon?" she says, and I laugh, though I haven't been in for a while.

"Can't keep away!" I say, and already at the end of my banter reserves, immediately place my coffee order.

Now it's her turn to laugh. "Fallen off the decaf wagon? That didn't last long!"

"Ha!" I say as I go to sit down, because it's less awkward than asking what she means.

I open up my laptop and take a career questionnaire, my new strategy to discover the perfect job I've never heard of. I find a check-box affair asking me to identify with one of three options in response to each statement: "1" = "very skilled" and "3" = "not as skilled as I'd like." Any to do with math or computers are easy: I select "3" with something close to pride. Others—"move and turn objects" or "make very small finger movements"—are so bafflingly vague yet specific I can only assume they relate to a particular field far beyond my experience. I submit my answers with a tiny thrill of excitement.

The results are diverse and surprising: hypnotherapist, customs officer, technical writer, forestry professional. I picture myself, clad in hard hat and high-visibility vest, wandering through dappled woodlands, but the image fades when the barista says, "Oh my God!" as though she's seen someone returned from the dead. She is looking from me to another customer who is standing at the counter. "I thought you were her!" the barista says, laughing.

"You're the spitting image of each other! Are you twins? You must be sisters, surely!" The girl turns around, confused and smiling, but when she sees me, her nostrils flare.

"Really?" she says, turning back to the barista. "I don't see it."

I'm with her—I don't either—but I'm pretty put out she finds the notion so repellent. I shrug and shake my head apologetically. I'm not sure if I'm sorry for having deceived the barista or for being such a letdown of a doppelgänger.

Comfort

Paul and I meet for an after-work pint. Work today for him meant writing grant applications, and doing Skype interviews for his new exhibition about to open in Reykjavik.

"And how was *your* day?" he asks once we've covered his.

"Good!" I say. "By which I mean, obviously, entirely unproductive. But on the way here I had the most comforting thought: I'm one day closer to knowing what I'm going to do with my life."

Paul gulps down a couple of inches of beer, belches tenderly onto the back of his hand. "Sounds encouraging. So, what, have you narrowed it down to an industry?"

"No: what I mean is, even though *mentally* I'm no clearer, I'm still *technically* closer."

"What? How do you figure that one?"

"Well, I can't be any further away, can I? Time doesn't go backward," I say.

He laughs. "Yeah, but—and I'm sure this won't be the case, but *in theory*—you might never work out what you want to do. You might just settle for something like last time, or take a corporate job for the big salary. I stress: *theoretically*."

"Okay, but . . . even if I do that, either way I'll have made a decision, and thus will know what I'm doing." My eyeballs are burning: I haven't blinked in a while. "So either way I'm one day closer. Right? I'll drink to that!" I tilt my beer in for a "cheers."

"Yeah . . . I mean, I guess . . ." he says, clinking without feeling. "In the same way we're all one day closer to death."

Saturday morning

This park is full of twentysomethings heading to brunch, the price of which will make their visiting parents (who struggle to keep up with their offspring's strides) triple-check the bill, but remain insistent that This Is Their Treat as they reach for their wallets.

Groceries

Luke and I are in the Co-op buying dinner. We've been here for twenty minutes, done three circuits of the shop. It's part of a new two-pronged initiative: to expand our culinary horizons and cook at home more.

"What do *you* want?" Luke says, not for the first time.

"Anything," I say. "You tell me."

"What are the options again?"

"Limitless!" I say. "Imagine a dish and I'll cook it."

"Pasta, then," says Luke.

"Except pasta. I already said I don't want pasta. But anything else, you choose."

"Pizza," he suggests, and I wrinkle my forehead.

"I thought we said we'd try new things. Go wild, be creative."

He says, "I give up. You decide."

I pick up an eggplant and put it in the basket.

"With what?" Luke asks at my shoulder.

"Please. Don't. I'm shopping on the spot here. I need a bit of space." Extending my arm, I sweep him away.

Without a word he goes and stands by the flower buckets at the automatic doors, watching my every move. I pick up some tomatoes, some cheese, some chicken, put back the eggplant, pick up a cabbage, a pepper, put back the cabbage, put back the cheese, and then abandon the basket in the toiletries aisle and the two of us slope off to get takeaway.

Crosswalk

You don't get to wave me across; the law says you should stop, and I don't have to thank you.

End matter

As a kid, I watched a lot of videos. If I was on my own, I would keep watching after the film had finished, past all the credits to when the screen went blue, right up to the point where auto-rewind kicked in, certain I'd be rewarded with some special private message for persevering where no one else would. With books, I'd read from cover to cover—acknowledgments, lists of titles from the same publisher, the forms to fill out for overseas orders.

I think about these things while I have the very last of the bran flakes for breakfast: cereal dust, which suits me just fine. It thickens the milk and makes a nice paste: porridge without the effort. I wonder if this commitment to the dregs is something that should be celebrated, or if it means I have trouble moving on, letting go.

Job description

Words like "maestro" and "superstar," twinned with "administrator" and "volunteer."

Body politics

"Whenever I'm naked, you seem to see it as an invitation," I say to Luke, who has helped himself to a handful of breast as I undress for bed. "I wonder why you think that's okay."

"I'm sorry that you feel that way," says Luke, kissing me now. "Maybe it's because I only ever see you naked when we have sex? Anyway, I see it more as an opportunity."

"Oh," I say, "so it's *my* fault we don't have enough sex? If I was naked more often, would that help?"

"I never said that," says Luke, but after a pause he adds, "It would be an interesting experiment."

Pillow talk

"You're *beautiful*," Luke whispers—as though to remind, or convince, himself.

Reaching out

I ring Grandma with the express intention of undercutting her claim that I "don't help out." I've decided to become her confidante: I'll invigorate her with youth and liberalism, and in return she'll impart homespun wisdom and teach me how to *really* cook—elixir-like stocks, the fluffiest sponge cakes—bequeathing me her kitchen utensils when she dies many years hence, at peace and fulfilled.

"Yes?" she says, answering the phone after barely one ring.

"It's Claire . . ." I'm caught off guard by her speed, "your granddaughter. Flannery," I add, throwing a hand up at my idiocy.

"Yes. What can I do for you?"

"Is this a bad time?"

"No." She sounds insulted at the very suggestion she'd ever be less than ready for anything.

"Good! So . . . how are you?"

"Fine. Claire, is something the matter?"

I wish I'd prepped myself for this, written down a few conversation points, the way I used to when calling boys in my teens. "No, not at all. I was only . . ."—there's a pause while I flail for a topic—"wanting to . . . uh, ask your advice about something."

"Oh?"

"It's a gardening question."

"Oh."

I tell her about the buddleia and the conflicting information I've read.

"We had one of those years back: it came bursting through the back wall. The 'bastard buddleia' we called it," she says.

"Really? What did you do?"

"What didn't I do! Let's see—I tried cutting it back with shears, but that only made it worse. Went at it with an ax. Poison."

"Wow," I say. "And did anything work?"

"Yes: we moved house. I fell pregnant with your mother and we needed more space. Left it for the new owners to worry about. But it was, I suppose, quite pretty in its way—in the right place, they can be lovely, you know."

"Yeah, I've grown quite attached to ours."

"Well, and you might find actually that it's holding everything together. Give it a tug and the whole building crumbles!" She cackles. "After the war, they were everywhere—sprang up in the rubble overnight. Rather like a poultice on a wound, I always thought. Nature's balm."

I take this rare poeticism as my cue to move things up a gear on the confidante front.

"It must have really changed the way you looked at life. Going through the war, I mean. Made you think about how fleeting our time on earth is." She's quiet; I fear she's nodded off. "Grandma? Hello?"

"Yes, I'm here. I was only thinking: you might want to set fire to it."

But I was thinking I might want to leave it be.

Season's greetings

An email from Dad. Subject heading: *Christmas.*

> Mum said what about a cruise. 7 nights Canaries with her mother. Something different. We thought you wouldn't be interested—you'd want to spend Christmas with Luke. Let me know as I'll need to book asap. Love, Dad

I reply:

> OK, seems you have it all worked out. Don't worry about me. I'll look after myself. C

Half an hour later, he's back in my in-box:

Great—all booked. James Bond theme Christmas Dinner,
five courses including Champagne. Lobster supplement
£15 extra per head. Mum and I may do this but will
decide on the day. Grandma won't want to get bogged
down with the claws. I will have to pack a tuxedo.
Love, Dad

Hair

There is nothing on this earth I can do to my hair to make it look
better than fine. My younger self had no idea how much of my
life would be spent despairing about it: how limp and flat it lies on
my head, how abundantly it sprouts elsewhere.

"You had a great head as a baby," my mother said to me. This
was last Christmas, before Gum died, back when she was still talking to me. She's always been big on hair, big on big hair, the bigger the better, and mine can only be a disappointment to her.

"A great head of hair?" I asked, surprised, because in all the
pictures I look pretty bald.

"No," she said, "a great big head. Huge. I had to get six stitches!"

And the two of us screeched and gasped so long my father was
moved to come down from his office.

"Share the joke?" he said in the doorway, and with tears standing in our eyes, my mother and I shook our heads and smiled,
exhausted.

Second chance

I ring Sarah, in need of a friendly voice, but Paddy answers instead.

"Oh, hi, Paddy. Is Sarah around?"

"She's in the shower."

"Could you tell her I called?"

"Okay."

I decide this is the perfect opportunity for him to prove me wrong about my poor early impression of him. "How are you doing? It's Claire, by the way."

"I know."

"Work going well?"

"Yeah."

"Any nice plans for the weekend?"

"Not really."

I *knew* I was right, I think—never doubt yourself. But for Sarah's sake I press on.

"Sarah said you guys might go up to Hampstead Heath. I love it there."

"Really."

"Maybe the four of us could go together sometime. You guys and Luke and me. There are ponds you can swim in. We could take a picnic."

"Yeah . . . I'll have to check with Sar." His tone conveys grave misgivings about this plan.

"Not this weekend. I meant in the summer. No rush. Whenever. It was just an idea."

"Okay."

"Well, listen, Paddy, it's been great catching up. I'd better not keep you—see you soon, I hope."

"Bye."

Sisters

We're having friends round, so I'm in the big supermarket and naturally join the wrong checkout line. Ahead of me are two wild-

haired women whose groceries, excepting a six-pack of beer, con-
sist entirely of orange-stickered items: yogurts, sliced turkey, meat
pies and coleslaw, all past their best.

"That's 9.76," says the checkout guy, and the women launch
into a livid debate about who should pay.

"I lent you a tenner for the bookies!" says one.

"No, no, no, no!" the other shouts back—an unconvincing but
heartfelt defense. This back-and-forth continues for some time,
and behind me, the growing line sighs.

"You pay!" shouts the first, walking away with the bags. "I've
had enough! You owe me! I'm done here!"

Muttering, the other one pulls a fistful of cash from her coat
pocket and slams it in the bagging area.

The checkout guy gives a rueful smile as they traipse off. "Sisters. Always in here, always fighting."

At the bus stop, I see them across the road, settling into a doorway. From their coat pockets, they produce real metal cutlery and
tuck into their picnic, chatting away. Before the approaching bus
obscures them, they clash their beer cans in a sloppy toast and I
find myself wishing that I had a sister to grow old and mad with.

Entertaining

Luke gets in as I'm prepping the starter for dinner, smoked trout
on brown bread.

"Yum," he says, kissing me on the cheek. He stays watching as I
try to fit fish slices to bread squares: an exact and fiddly operation.
"Why are you doing it like that?" he asks. "Why didn't you put the
salmon on whole slices first and cut them into squares after?"

"Trout," I say. "Shows how much you know."

It isn't fair that he's spent the day saving lives and gets to come
home and be right about this too.

———

"Everyone should learn the Heimlich maneuver! It should be a legal requirement!"

The meal is done, we're four bottles in, and passions are running high.

"So how do you do it, then? Teach me," says someone.

"This is my point! I don't know!" I say.

"I'll show you," Luke offers, stacking the plates.

"You shouldn't have to! This is what I'm trying to say! You don't listen; no one is listening to me!"

My feet are soaking wet: there's water everywhere, but the dishes at last are done.

"Do you think they had a good time?" I ask.

"Sure," says Luke from the kitchen table, head in his arms.

"Was I too much? I think I might have been too much."

"No." This said on the exhalation.

"Did you like the dessert? I liked it. There's some left. We can have it tomorrow."

"It was fine," yawns Luke.

"Only fine," I say, and march to the fridge, take out the cheesecake and dump it—dish, spoon and all—in the bin.

In the morning, my blood is charged with regret and bad feeling.

"I'm sorry," I say to Luke. "I'm a horrible person."

"No, you're not," he says into his pillow. "Go back to sleep."

"I am. I'm sorry. I love you," I say, kissing his head, his warm neck, his velvet-smooth back.

Problem

I used to think the problem was I didn't like my job; but now I see the problem is that wasn't the whole problem.

Multitasking

Today's mid-afternoon game-show contestants include a marketing executive for a Web development company, a business analyst for a stockbroker, a body-combat teacher and a statistician for the pharmaceutical industry. So by the end of the episode I've learned not only the capital of Lesotho (Maseru) and the key ingredient in a sidecar (cognac), but also the existence of four more career paths I don't think I want to pursue.

Dawn to dusk

Coffee, coffee, coffee, coffee, wine, wine, wine.

Collateral damage

"Do you want to know the worst bit about my mum not talking to me? I've run out of hand cream and can't go home to restock." My mother has been buying luxury hand cream in bulk for years, ever since hearing a rumor at book club that her favorite brand was about to be discontinued. The fact it has remained widely available is, she insists, due to the change in *her own personal* consumer behavior, so substantial and dramatic as to have falsely inflated the perceived demand. I've been in no hurry to explode her theory, since the ever-replenishing supply meant I could help myself every time I went home, assuaging any niggling guilt with the knowledge that, if anything, I actually saw *more* of my parents than I would were moisturizer not a factor in the timing and frequency of my visits.

"See?" I rub the back of my hand against Luke's cheek.

"That's rough," he says.

"This one *bled* the other day. Look, I have scales."

"So buy some more."

"I can't. Do you have any idea how much one tube costs?"

I tell him and watch as he blanches with shock.

"Maybe you should try calling her again," he says, handing me my phone. "I think it's high time you two worked things out."

More time

"Hi, Dad."

"Is that Claire?"

"Obviously. Unless I've got a secret sister you haven't told me about."

"What?"

"I'm the only person who's going to phone and call you 'Dad,' is what I'm getting at."

"I don't understand," he says. "What's this about a secret sister?"

"Never mind. How are you?"

"Fine, thank you." There is a pause, which under ordinary circumstances would be filled by him calling unprompted for my mother. "Was there anything in particular . . . ?"

"I was hoping to speak to Mum, if she's there." I listen for her in the background during another silence; picture her vehemently mouthing, "No," shaking her head and slashing the air at her throat.

"She's still not ready," he says at last. "She's . . . *We* are sorry, Claire, but she needs more time."

"But I need to explain," I say. "How can it get better if she won't let me explain?"

"What is there to explain?" her voice comes, shrill but distant. Dad must have me on speakerphone.

"Could you tell her I'm sorry for upsetting her?" I say, pretending I haven't realized, and then take a breath because my voice is about to split. "That I really didn't mean to, and that I miss our chats?"

The line is quiet, like a vacuum.

"You could have been a wrong number," says Dad.

"Huh?"

"Just now, when you said, 'Hi, Dad,' and I asked if it was you. It could have been a wrong number, another woman phoning for her father. *That's* why I checked it was you." He sounds pleased to have squared this one away.

"Okay," I say. "I guess that makes some sort of sense."

"I hear you have a buddleia problem—you need to get that removed immediately. They can cause a lot of issues if you don't act quickly."

I'm touched that this information must have filtered down from Grandma via my mother, but his tone makes me want to plant a thicket in the walls.

"It's not that straightforward, actually: I've been looking into it."

"Tell Luke I can recommend someone if you need scaffolding."

I close my eyes. "Oh, I'll be sure to pass that on."

"Claire, I'm just trying to help."

"Sorry—and thank you, honestly, for the concern, but I've got it in hand."

"I'd ask how's work, but . . ." says Dad. "Any news on that front?"

"Not yet. A few possibilities, nothing concrete."

"Well, all the best, now," he says. "Unless there was anything else?"

"No, just goodbye. Bye, Mum," I say and hang up before she has a chance to say nothing in reply.

Good and bad

"As a nation we need to reassess what is objectively 'good' and 'bad.'"

"Mm." Andrea nods, eyes fixed on the device in her hand. She's not really a friend, more a friend of a friend, but as a free-lancer (something in social media), she's available to hang out during the day, and together we tour interchangeable cafes peopled exclusively by Mac-users.

"This morning, right, the weather woman—weather forecaster? Does she forecast the weather or just tell us about it? Anyway, she said, 'This fabulous weather is set to continue.' But what about dying crops? What about shrinking reservoirs? I don't think climate change is fabulous."

"Ha," says Andrea to her device.

"I mean it," I say. "Why is it presumed to be the case that warm, sunny weather is good, when we know for a fact that rising temperatures are causing all kinds of mayhem? Do you think Somali weather forecasters are as upbeat about sunshine as we are?"

"Well, bad weather is linked to depression," Andrea says. "Seasonal affective disorder—there's a scientifically proven link between sunshine and happiness, and between gloomy weather and sadness."

"You're doing it too," I say. "Bad weather, gloomy weather. We've just been *conditioned* to think that way. If we were taught to love the rain and the cold, we'd be a much happier nation."

"Just imagine if you put all this time and energy into an actual job," says Andrea. "Seriously, you're wasted in . . . doing nothing."

Mistletoe and wine

"What are you doing for Christmas?" I say, counterfeiting a yawn to suggest nonchalance, which in turn sets Luke off on a genuine one.

"I think I'll be working—my parents and sister might come down to London, rent a flat nearby or something. Why?"

"What about if I spent it with you?"

He looks up. "This is quite the change of heart."

I gnaw on a thumbnail. "We've been together seven years. If not now, when?"

"Wait," he says, "is this about your mum? Are things really that bad? You've always said you could never leave your family at Christmas."

I shrug. "I think she just needs some space. I'm sure they'll work it out—they can have Grandma instead, go on a cruise or something." I move in close so our noses touch. "Anyway. *You* are my family." His face crumples into a silly, soppy smile—for which I would mercilessly mock him, if it weren't the very mirror of my own.

That's the spirit

In the park, a tiny dog trots by. In its mouth, a branch four times its size.

Destiny

In a fit of bored nostalgia, I Google a childhood friend with whom I've long since lost touch. She seems immune to the social-media pandemic that's claimed most of my generation (or perhaps she's wisely avoiding it), but at last I find her several pages into the search results. She's working in Aberdeen, involved in the disposal of radioactive waste. Granted, when I saw her last, we were eight years old, but nothing—not her love of tomato ketchup, nor her peerless Sylvanian Families collection—gave the slightest indication *this* would be her path. Radioactive-waste disposal! Aberdeen! I try to imagine her life now and see: an office in a trailer, tea breaks with a gruff bearded colleague (the two of them like astronauts in their protective suits), air dense with drizzle, the dark drive home, a warm carpeted tract house tucked inside a cul-de-sac, a tabby rescue cat, husband in the kitchen with dinner in the oven, takeaway on Saturdays in front of the TV.

Out there

We're reading in bed. Luke's propped on an elbow with the sports pages from the weekend; I'm still deep in *Ulysses*.

"Have you ever thought about living somewhere other than London?"

"Where?" says Luke after such a long time I thought I'd imagined having spoken.

"This is what I'm asking you." Another long pause. "Luke."

"Give me an example."

"Wherever appeals. Devon or Bristol or Yorkshire or Jersey. Aberdeen. The Outer Hebrides. Iceland, Nova Scotia, Newfoundland. Somewhere else."

"No," says Luke.

"Would you consider it?"

"*Ulysses* not going well?"

"Shut up." I knock him on the head with it, losing my page, which isn't a terrible outcome. "I don't mean move *now*—though I could be convinced, if you wanted to."

"Nah," he says.

"That's that, then, is it? 'Nah.'"

"Yup." He turns back to the paper.

I pick up *Ulysses*, weigh the huge heft of it on my palm. "You know, I never actively *chose* to live here—I came because that's what everyone else did. But there isn't any reason why I'm still here."

"Bit harsh."

"No, no, of course you're why I stayed. But it's not as though *I*, *personally*, need to be here. Think about it: if you wanted, or needed, to relocate, I could go tomorrow. It might actually be easier on the job front—I could be anything I wanted somewhere else, like a dinner lady in Cornwall, or a receptionist in Fife. A librarian in Gloucestershire. For example."

"You could be those things here." Luke throws me a glance, a vague and lazy imitation of an interested person.

I put the book down and uncurl my legs. "No, *here* it would be weird. *Here* I'd be seen as eccentric. London is great, but it's exhausting . . . The work culture here is so ambitious. Okay: name one of our friends who just coasts along in a middle-of-the-road job." Luke reconfigures the paper with much thrashing and rustling, then settles down and keeps reading. "Exactly. You can't, because there isn't one. It all has to be really interesting, or creative or meaningful or prestigious or well paid or ideally *all* those things. Even the ones who went into shitty grad internships are making serious money now."

He turns to me with a serious, sympathetic furrow, places both hands on my shoulders and finds my eyes with his. "Claire. I'm going to be honest. I feel it's time." He takes a deep breath. "I think . . . I really think you should give up on *Ulysses*. It's okay: I won't judge you. You'll feel so much better."

It's tempting. Things have got so desperate recently I've taken to stroking the spine of *Moby Dick* when I pass the bookshelves, craving the wide majesty of the ocean, and even the lengthy technical passages about whaling, which rationally I know I'll hate but right now hold a raw, anorak-ish appeal.

"Where are you up to, anyway?" asks Luke.

"You made me lose my page. Two hundred and something."

"What's happening?"

"It's hard to explain. There's no real *story* per se."

"Try me," says Luke. "I've read it."

"You have not."

"I have! When I was in Sri Lanka."

"The whole thing? You read it all?"

"Of course the whole thing! It's a masterpiece. Honestly, though, if it's too much for you, I promise I won't judge. It's a challenging read and maybe you're not in the right frame of mind for it. You could try *Dubliners*. It's more digestible."

I claw the book back open, but even as I start reading again, my attention's already wandering off to tiny windblown villages crouching by the sea.

Tube

On the last train, a woman grimly chomps her way through an entire bag of gummy bears. I've been there, my friend, I think, taking in her rumpled office-wear and sallow, tired skin.

Admin

It's been two months since I renewed my driver's license—only eight months late—and I still feel a fillip of pride whenever I remember this achievement.

Next stop, the dentist, I tell myself most days, but have yet to show any sign of following through.

Rhetoric

The buddleia has been variously described (over the course of today's online research) as stubborn, self-sufficient, a rank opportunist, overbearing, dazzling, a nuisance, undemanding, charming, munificent, a home-wrecker, a butterfly bonanza.

Butterfly effect

When I was six and playing in the garden, a butterfly landed on my arm and remained there for ten proper—i.e. Mississippi—seconds. I held my breath as it flexed its wings, preparing us both for its imminent departure; for every (Mississippi) second it stayed, the more important and chosen I felt. But when it flapped away, and I ran inside to tell my mother, I found that the right words would not come, and so instead I kept quiet.

Trying

"Hello?"

"Mum, it's Claire." There's a long silence.

"It came up as 'unknown number.'" She sounds peeved to have been so easily duped.

"I know. You won't answer my calls. I wanted to try and . . . Are you still angry with me?"

She sighs, which I take to be a good sign. Low-key resignation I can handle.

"I'm not angry. Hurt? Yes. Confused, about why you'd make a joke in such poor taste at my father's funeral—"

"Okay, right: this is why I'm calling. I mean, I should say first it wasn't strictly a joke, but—"

Another sigh. "I don't have the energy for this at the moment."

"Please wait—it wasn't a joke, *but* neither was it meant to be a big thing at all. And I'm sorry about the timing: I agree it wasn't perfect."

"Is that an apology?"

"Yes." I hold my breath. *Could* it be this simple?

She laughs. "Oh, well then, everything's *fine!*"

"Mum . . ."

"I don't know what you want me to say, Claire, really. That it's okay to sling around accusations about my father, so long as it's *not* at his funeral?"

I try to keep my tone level. "I really think you're overreacting: if you'd heard it at the time, you'd have understood it wasn't an *accusation*. It wasn't meant to be a serious thing: I honestly thought everyone else knew what I was talking about."

"Well, it sounds pretty serious to me. And, Claire, come on: you *just* apologized about the timing!"

"That isn't— Stop twisting everything I say! Can you please fucking *try* and understand?"

She doesn't speak, but I don't know where to go from here.

"I think we should leave it there for now," she says eventually. "I don't think this is doing anyone much good."

Tube

A few seats down, I spy the former love of my life. He's gained some weight, and his clothes aren't the best, but here comes that old familiar throb, regardless. I redirect my gaze to the floor and stare at the gray linoleum in a poetic, intense way, to suggest he couldn't be further from my brilliant mind.

"It's you," he says, crossing the car, and I take a moment to stir myself from my deep reverie.

"Oh!" I say. "Hi." He stands above me, holding the rail above his head. He's wearing the same aftershave he always did—intoxicating and popular, I've smelled it a hundred times since on passing strangers.

"I must have walked right past you."

"No change there, then." I was intending a lighthearted riposte, but the words come out strange and bitter.

"You have," he says. "Changed, I mean. In a good way: you look great. You really . . . You look really well. Not that you didn't look good before." He has positioned himself so that his feet lightly touch either side of mine.

"What are you up to these days?" I say, eager to take the heat off me.

"Bit of research, bit of advising. The band takes up most of my time." He nudges my foot with his. "Hey, you should come watch us play. We're on tonight in Camden—I'll put you on the guest list. It would be great to have a drink after, catch up." His tongue gleams, caught between his teeth in a way he might think is playful. "Just you and me."

"Oh," I say, "tonight, I can't. Some other time, I'll look you guys up."

"Coffee, then?" he says, smiling his wide, joker smile. "Surely you can spare half an hour for a coffee—for old times' sake?" His knees now gently press into mine. Such immediate, easy intimacy!

"Sorry," I say, with Herculean effort, dispelling dizzy scenes of emotional free fall in some glowing, foggy-windowed cafe. "I have plans. This is my stop."

"It was great to see you," he says as I stand up. He places a hand lightly on my waist, leaning in so his lips skim my ear. "You seem really happy."

"I am," I say. "I'm really happy." And as I disembark—five stops from where I need to be—I realize that in some deep, lonely way I'd been waiting for this moment for too many years.

Signal

"Wi-Fi's fucked." Luke is in boxers: barefoot, bare-chested.

"It comes and it goes," I say.

He steps hopefully around the room, cradling his laptop like a colicky infant he's lulling to sleep.

"You're going to make a great father," I say, and because he's opened his mouth to protest, I add, "When the time is right, I know, not yet."

Dream

I'm carrying a baby in my bag, but not in any careful way: just another thing tossed in there with my phone, my hairbrush, my purse and my keys.

Friday night

I'm at Sarah's—the same flat I shared with her before Luke and I bought our place, five years ago. She's had a series of quiet PhD-student flatmates since, but tomorrow Paddy's moving in, so tonight I'm here to mark her last night of freedom with wine and a dinner of potato chips.

"The TV was a deal-breaker." Sarah nods at the huge, sleek flat screen sitting in place of the tiny ancient box on which we used to watch *Friends*. "I was a bit sad to get rid of the little box."

"No antenna issues with that beast, though, I bet." We had been obsessed with making tiny adjustments to the antenna to get the picture spot on. "Remember when we'd got it just perfect and then Luke came along and ruined it?" On his second ever visit to the flat, Luke had seized the cable, asking what it was for, and Sarah and I cried out in horror as it fell from his startled fingers.

"Bloody Luke. It was never as good after that," says Sarah.

"He's lucky I didn't end things right there and then. So"—I lean forward to press up some chip crumbs with a fingertip— "how are you feeling about living with Paddy?"

She smiles. "Don't laugh, but I'm ridiculously excited about all the stupid little things you probably take for granted. Like cooking a big pot of chili together and freezing it in batches."

I nod energetically, dosing our glasses with wine. "I know exactly what you mean. There's something so appealing and . . . primal about that: stirring a bubbling pot with your mate, storing up food for the winter. You know that bit in *Little House on the Prairie*—or was it the one in the woods? When they smoked and salted the deer meat?" Sarah nods, but I think she's indulging me. "That was my favorite part. The first summer I read it, I begged my dad for weeks to build me a smokehouse in the garden. He refused."

"I can't imagine on what possible grounds."

"I know. So unreasonable." I take a sip of my wine and sigh. "Luke and I have tried all that batch-freezing business, but we cannot seem to get it together. We'll forget to put in a crucial ingredient, or leave it in the freezer so long it becomes completely inedible. We have some fish pie in the bottom drawer that I swear is more than three years old."

Sarah looks forlorn. "Claire! You're killing my dream!"

"No. Hey." I put down my glass and take her face in my hands. "Listen to me. You will be fine. You have a pension. And a car. You and Paddy will do the chili thing: I believe in you, okay?" She nods, and I release her, returning to my glass, which I press to my cheek. "It still amazes me sometimes that I'm allowed to live on my own without proper adult supervision. Isn't it sort of incredible we can do whatever we want, whenever we want? Have potato chips for dinner."

"Not go to work."

"Ouch."

"Sorry, sorry, that came out wrong. I'm just jealous you get to lie in."

"Actually, I get up earlier now than I ever did when I had a job."

"Really?"

I nod. It's not a *total* fabrication: maybe two days out of five I'm out of bed by seven thirty if Luke's had an early start, and as far as I'm concerned, that's good enough to make the claim. "Figuring out what to do is *way* harder than my old job. I cannot believe how quickly the days go."

"Dare I ask . . . where have you got to with it all?"

"Um, nowhere?" I say, tipping two more bags of chips in the bowl—paprika, and chicken and thyme—shuffling them gently to let the flavors mingle. "I feel as if every decision I've made has *cut off* possibilities rather than broadened them. What if I'd make an amazing potter but will never know because I never tried it?"

"We could take a class? I'd be up for that."

"But the same goes for everything: photography, gardening. Butchery! I can't take a class in everything."

Sarah sloshes her glass toward me, managing somehow not to spill a drop. "I really think you have to believe in yourself. Trust your instincts. None of those things ever appealed before, so why would you want to take them further now?"

I consider this. "But you didn't always know you wanted to teach. Did you?" I look over. Sarah's frozen at the coffee table: eyes wide and cheeks bulging, trying to gain control of a huge clutch of chips between fingers and mouth. "Good *God*," I say. "If Paddy could see you now."

She shoves in the remainder, laughing.

"That is why I can't allow potato chips in the house," she manages once she's recovered, dusting off her hands against her jeans. "With teaching . . . I don't know. I've always loved kids. I enjoyed school, and I suppose I liked the fact I'd been through it myself."

"You make it sound so simple and logical. Why can't I make those sorts of connections? Do you think there's something wrong with me?"

"Of course not."

"Maybe I just don't like anything enough. This dick, right, Jonathan—who replaced me at work? He *loves* the job; he's obsessed with the agency—get this: he's even started organizing a networking drinks thing himself."

"How do you know?"

I know because I check his social-media accounts almost daily, not to mention my old employer's online activity. "I get wind."

"So, good for him! He's found his thing. Doesn't that prove it's possible?"

"But why wasn't it *my* thing? It's not just Jonathan. My old colleagues, my boss, Geri—they all care so much more than I did. They would *scream* whenever anything good happened at work."

"Maybe you're just not the screaming type. You liked it when you started there."

"Not the way they did. I always felt like a fake."

"I remember you getting excited about stuff," Sarah insists. "That graffiti festival you did for the vodka company. That was great."

"Street art," I correct her. She's right: it had been a coup, and led to my promotion from "assistant account manager" to "account manager." "That was fun. But at the end of the day, I got some people talking about vodka. I mean really, what difference does that make to anyone?"

Sarah pulls the band from her ponytail. I can smell the shampoo as her hair tumbles down: Herbal Essences, the same brand she's used since we were fifteen. "But it was fun! That's fine. You don't *need* to change the world."

"I know. But don't I need to think what I do is worth something? That was great for my early twenties; isn't it time to get serious now?"

"Didn't you want to be a psychiatrist when we were younger? That seemed like a good fit," she says.

I set down my glass and stretch out on the sofa, looking up at the ceiling. "I did, before I realized it was medicine, which meant I'd have to do science, so I ditched it." I'd got the idea from an American young-adult novel about a girl whose parents were both psychiatrists. It must have sounded precocious coming from a twelve-year-old, and got a guaranteed laugh from adults, so became my stock answer for a number of years.

"And nothing's appealed since."

"Well, not specific jobs. More like a general lifestyle idea. Glass corner office, sushi and coffees delivered to my desk, great clothes, poring over something—photographs?—spread out on a table."

"Okay. I think I see where you went wrong. All those vague, title-less jobs have already been taken by characters in New York–based romcoms."

"This might sound very naive, but I really didn't think when I took my old job that I was embarking on a path that could be my career. I was still a child! I just wanted to pay the bills and make the most of wine o'clock on Fridays. I thought I had all the time in the world to study more, retrain, travel."

"Oh my God, you sound just like my mother, Claire."

"I've always thought Ruth talked a lot of sense. You should listen to her more."

"Yeah, but she's sixty-four! You have so much time!"

"No, I don't! What if I want to have a baby in the next few years? So I start something new, barely get a handle on it, then have to go on maternity leave while people five years younger zoom past me?"

"You could have stayed and zoomed. You need to recognize that you've made a choice."

"More and more I find myself wishing my parents had been farmers," I say.

Sarah closes her eyes, shakes her head. "No."

"It would've solved everything. Think about it: I'd have land, security. And skills! I'd have so many good skills. Milking cows, planting crops, raising hens."

She relents. "It's not too late. Sell your flat and buy a few acres somewhere. Luke can retrain as a vet—there's got to be some overlap."

"Why don't you come? We'll need to have lots of babies to run the farm when we get old—you can teach them!"

"I'm in. What about Paddy?"

"Of course Paddy too. He'd be perfect for, um . . ."—I do my best, but it's tough finding a use for "industrial interior designer" in this bucolic setup—"building barns . . . ?"

"I know: he can convert the old outbuildings into a B and B! For an extra income stream."

I point at her. "Perfect."

Sarah clasps her hands, beaming—mission accomplished—and I decide to try and set my Paddy-doubts free. She clearly thinks the whole world of the guy.

Saturday morning

Two a.m.: three bottles down, we've cracked into the amaretto, and reached the end of our fourth potato chip salad (salt and vinegar plus cheese and onion—the unbeatable classic)

"I should go," I say, making no effort to move.

"Do you want to stay?" says Sarah. "I can pull out the sofa bed in your old room."

It would be so easy. All evening I've been flooded by a tender wistfulness for our early twenties years in this flat: dinner parties on the sofas with plates balanced on knees, endless cups of tea, gin and tonics while we got ready to go out, hobbling home many hours later barefoot to devour round after round of peanut butter toast . . .

"I'd love to, but I'd better not," I say, struggling up and sending a shower of potato chip crumbs to the rug. "Imagine poor Paddy arriving with all his stuff tomorrow to find me passed out in your spare room. That's not how you want to start your new life together. Anyway, the night bus goes right to my door."

Sarah stretches her arms up for a hug.

"There's always a bed for you here if you want it, Clairie." She hasn't called me that since we were about twelve years old and I feel a sting of sadness—but also gratitude, that she is still by my side after all this time.

"You're the best," I say, gripping her to me in a soft, fragrant hair-and-cardigan bundle.

Saturday morning II

I wake up and lean my forehead against the cold window. In the dark, I make out rows of parked double-decker buses: big, silent beasts like sleeping whales.

The doors are open, though the driver's nowhere to be seen, and dazed, I make my way out of the depot to the road, where I wait fifteen minutes on the pavement for an unlicensed car service to drive me across the city to my flat, and charge forty-six pounds for the privilege.

Hairdresser

Six-plus months and who-knows-how-many split ends: I can defer this haircut no longer. Though I've been going to the same place for five years, my visits are so infrequent and my presence clearly so insipid, I'm greeted like a new client every time.

"Tell me," demands my stylist, Giulia, a fierce, tiny tattooed person whose asymmetrically cut hair is bleached white and buzzed so her scalp shows through on one side. When I release mine from its ponytail, it drips forlornly down my back.

"Well, it's clearly a disaster. *Look* at these ends," I say disloyally, like an embarrassed parent siding with a disapproving teacher. I take a random section between my fingers and hold it up for inspection. Giulia agrees with a frowning nod, and under the too-bright lights and ubiquitous mirrors, the ambitions I had for a big change desert me. "So . . . I guess just tidy it up, take off however much you need." I karate-chop a hand to my chest. "Here? What do you think?"

She pouts. "Do you want all one lengse, or do you want the layer?"

"What do you think?"

A shrug. "All one lengse is easy for me."

"Right, but will it *look* better? In your opinion?"

She peers at her watch and then at me in the mirror. "I sink so. *Hell*-see-er. Come." She ushers me over to the sinks, snapping on a pair of latex gloves like a rebuke.

Back at the mirror, she sets to work, making frequent, brusque corrections to the position of my head. Meanwhile, a few stations down, another stylist and her charge animatedly compare notes on a series of implausible common passions: martial arts, Ethiopian food, a Bulgarian electronica festival. When it turns out they share a favorite book—an obscure-sounding Scottish novella from the eighties—it's only fear of fanning the flames of Giulia's ire that stops me looking around for hidden cameras, to check I'm not the subject of some cosmic, highbrow gotcha.

The magazine I was offered hasn't arrived, and after a brutal stretch of silence, I ask in desperation, "Busy afternoon?" to distract from the moonlike pull of my reflection.

"Yes. Please, down," she says, pushing my skull forward so all I can see is the soft indignity of white middle flesh oozing through my bunched shirt.

I look up in surprise when not much later she sets down the scissors and reaches for the hair dryer.

"You've finished already?"

"Yes. So. Do you normally blow it a-dry?" she asks.

"Oh, no, I don't normally bother."

Until I was twelve or so, my mother insisted on drying my hair for me, convinced some indeterminate Olden Day malady would carry me off if she didn't. No doubt the stories we read together at bedtime, about kindhearted invalid children doomed to die tragic deaths in dark winters didn't help. But when puberty hit, I found myself on the lookout for low-risk, high-impact ways to rebel and—too proud to let things slide at school, too scared for cigarettes or boys—I seized upon our morning hair-drying ritual. I would storm off to school with soaking shoulders, slamming the door against my mother's bitter protestations.

"I sought so." Giulia puts a hand on my shoulder, and her face next to mine. "But the heat and the movement? For you, it's good. Even just-a fast blast. To make it less . . ." She affects an expression suggesting flatness, limpness, despair, with impressive eloquence. "It make it better. More . . ."

"Thicker?" I suggest.

"Alive!" she cries happily over the hair dryer's roar.

Perspective

Hurrying past my old office building, I can't help myself looking in the window. Geri and Jonathan are crowded round a phone receiver, gesticulating excitedly. The office has been decorated for Christmas—*how* is it December already?—with the usual lopsided artificial tree garlanded in colored lights and way too much tinsel. On the windowpanes I note a new touch, white tissue-paper snowflakes and red tissue-paper letters stuck on to spell out "ho, ho, ho"—though to anyone on the outside, like me, it reads, "oh, oh, oh."

The most wonderful time

Luke and I return home at nine p.m. on Christmas Day, from the flat his family have been renting nearby. I'm exhausted from non-stop eating and small talk: Luke was called in to work for several hours before dinner, and I kept up a bright stream of chatter in his absence, hoping it wouldn't become apparent to anyone else that without him there, I was effectively gate-crashing some strangers' sacred Christmas traditions.

In our living room, we sink into the sofa and I pull on my gift from Luke's mother: a pair of novelty pig slippers, which make an oinking sound when you press the snouts.

"Hard to know how to take these," I say. "They're so clearly not your mum's style. Is this how she sees me?" I paddle the pigs up and down.

"I really wouldn't overthink it if I were you," says Luke, but then, *he* got an iPad mini.

At around ten p.m., I get a phone call from my father. The line is crackly and barely audible.

"Ship to shore! Ship to shore!" he keeps repeating, clearly possessed by the festive spirit. My mother is conveniently engaged in the final round of a heated charades tournament along with some of their table companions.

"It's her turn right now, so she can't speak," he says.

"Literally!" Grandma crows in the background, then screams, *"THE EXORCIST!"* several times before the line goes dead.

Lights out

"I loved spending Christmas with you," says Luke, wrapping himself around me.

"I had a great day."

"Hope you didn't miss your parents too much."

I think of them and Grandma out on the dark sea, listing gently in their cabin beds.

Compromise

"We always do what you want to do," I say. It's late afternoon on New Year's Eve. Fanned out on the duvet is a selection of DVDs, all with subtitles, from some best-ever list Luke is making us work through.

"Yes, we *do* always do what *you* want to do," Luke says.

"Simply not true. I do loads of things now that I never did before you."

"For example?"

"Watch boring films. Foreign! Sorry, I meant foreign. Watch *foreign* films—I never used to do that."

"Anything else?" he asks.

"Leave parties early."

"Anything good? Any positive things?" he says, climbing on top of me, bracing his knees to my sides.

"Eat more veg? That's a good thing. And wrestling. Before you, I hardly wrestled at all." I grab his wrists and attempt to topple him, but we both know that's not going to happen.

"Do we have to go to this thing tonight?" he says. We're supposed to be going to a New Year's Eve party with my school friends in a bar charging twenty pounds for entry alone. "Can't we stay in and hang out instead?"

"Only if I get to choose what we watch."

"Done!" he says, rolling off me, triumphant.

I get up to draw the curtains on what's left of the day, and like outlaws lying low in a scuzzy motel, we crawl back under the covers to watch *Sister Act*, followed by *Sister Act 2*.

4

Make yourself heard

Behind the bus stop, one of the local eccentrics hammers on the shuttered door of a closed-up shop with an actual hammer. As always, he wears his silver lamé suit: a relic of a future that never came to pass (or—to be absolutely fair to him—a future that hasn't happened *yet*).

"It's the only way," he explains, shouting above the terrific noise of his own making. "It's the only way they'll answer me, you see."

Wednesday

I spend the morning planning an elaborate meal for Luke, composed of recipes from five different websites.

At the meat counter, I take a ticket and wait for my number to appear on the digital screen. I'm about to step forward when I feel a tug on my elbow.

"May I go next?" says a small, anxious woman in a beige rain-coat and thick glasses, which magnify her eyes adorably. She shows me with shaking hands a screwed-up ticket saying, "47." The screen is displaying 79. "I must have missed mine."

"Know the feeling," I say, stepping to one side as she places her order for a single lamb's heart.

"So, what have you been up to today?" Luke asks through a mouthful of Slow-cooked Pulled Pork and Super Zingy Slaw, breaking off a chunk of the Best Jalapeño Cornbread to mop up what's left of the sauce from the Mac 'n' Cheese With All the Bells 'n' Whistles.

Call

On the table, my mobile twitches like something in its final throes. "DAD" is lighting up the screen and I already know what this is about: my mother is suddenly dead, or dying, or waiting for tests to confirm she is dying; or *he* is dying, or has found a lump that he is sure is nothing, but is having checked out just to be safe.

"Dad, what's up?"

"Nothing's 'up'—just giving you a call to see how you are."

"I'm good," I say. "No news my end. And yourself? And Mum? You're both okay?"

"Fine," he says. (He doesn't say, "Mustn't grumble," his erst-while stock response, which vanished from his vocab when, be-tween flats years ago, I briefly moved back home, and said one evening in the fluorescent kitchen gloom, "Ugh! It's *insufferable*, that phrase!" with a spiteful passion neither one of us saw coming, or quite comprehended; and he, turning red, drew his mouth downward and blinked in a sort of sad, surprised defeat.) "And Luke?" he asks. "He all right?"

"Luke's good," I say. "Working hard as always."

"Yes, well . . ." The implication hangs: a cable loose in the wind. *Yes, well, someone has to.* "I'm going to be in London to-morrow," he says suddenly.

"Oh? How come?"

"A meeting."

"With who? For work?"

"Yes."

"Right," I say. "So . . . you were calling to . . . ask if I would like to meet up?"

"Would you?" says Dad.

"I would. Would you?"

"I would . . . if you would."

"I would."

"Good."

Definition

We're watching a documentary about the Missing Persons Bureau.

"On average, a missing persons report is filed in the UK every two minutes," the voice-over explains. "Only a very small fraction of these cases ever make the headlines." On the screen, a police officer calmly inputs vital statistics into a database.

"I wonder if I'd make the news," I say to Luke. "You definitely would: 'Promising Brain Surgeon Vanishes.' They'd love that. Hey, that reminds me. Will you do me a favor?" I dab his leg with my foot. "If I ever disappear, please could you tell them to put me down as 'medium build'? I'd take 'slim' or 'slight,' obviously, but understand if that might be a push."

"Medium," he says. "I'll try and remember."

"I should pick out some photos just in case," I say. "They have to be flattering yet true to life. I don't think I trust you not to unearth some red-eyed double-chinned horror." I prod my stomach mournfully. "I can't imagine anything worse than being described as 'heavyset' on the ten o'clock news."

"What about 'heavyset' *and* 'unemployed'?" asks Luke, going right for the jugular.

Serves me right

The same, single article—"How to Find Your Dream Job"— advises me to: burn all my plans, tear up the rulebook, shop around, try on different hats, count my blessings (and gifts), be kind to myself (yet realistic), listen to my dreams, follow my heart (ditto the path less traveled), move the goalposts, change gears, consider my options, watch out for signs, test the water with a toe before diving in headfirst, take the economic pulse, listen to my elders, ignore all advice.

Dad

I see him before he sees me, hoving into view on the escalator and frowning vaguely into his wallet. Buffeted by end-of-day commuters, he looks totally conspicuous, and causes a small commotion at the barriers by inserting the wrong ticket into the machine.

"Dad," I call, waving when finally he is freed. He looks everywhere except at me, so at last I stride forward to take his elbow.

"There you are," he says, a little cross. I hook an arm round his neck, and he pats my shoulder in a manner that might be reciprocal, or to signal Time Up on the hug.

"Lead the way," he says, pushing me gently, irksomely into the evening rain.

In the restaurant—a reasonably priced chain disguised as an authentic trattoria—we study our paper-menu placemats in silence. I look at him every so often and realize with a small jolt that his hair has turned completely gray. I wonder if this is a recent development, or if it's that memory has been supplying the old hue from habit. He's reading with the same absorbed but skeptical expression he wears for the Sunday papers.

"What'll you have?" I ask.

"Artichokes: now, are they the long green things?" he says.

"That's asparagus. Artichokes are sort of beige and bulbous." A brisk nod, as though I have passed his test. "That's right. And zucchini is . . . rocket?"

I laugh. "Courgette."

"Is that funny?"

"No, it's just I think I understand why you were confused. Americans call rocket 'arugula' and courgettes 'zucchini.' Maybe that's where the mixup came from."

"So why doesn't it say 'courgette' on the menu? We're not in America."

" 'Zucchini' is Italian for 'courgette'—this is supposed to be an Italian restaurant," I point out, and Dad shakes his head and tuts, as if this confirms a long-held suspicion about the state of the world. A waiter appears, a young skinny guy, fully mustachioed and sprightly of air.

"Are we ready to order?"

"I don't know about *you*," says Dad to the waiter, "but I think we are. Claire, go ahead."

I order salad and risotto and, though I told myself firmly I wouldn't drink tonight—glancing at my father to confirm he wants in—a bottle of the house red.

"So did you have the thing looked at? The problematic growth?" asks Dad once the waiter's gone, and there's a kick in my chest: have I some kind of mole or tumor I've forgotten about? Am I not only dying but also losing my mind?

"The . . . ?"

"The weed? Coming out of your wall."

"Oh, the buddleia. No, no, that's all fine," I say and direct him away from further questions by gesturing toward the incoming Chianti.

"So, you enjoyed the cruise?" I ask, as it's poured.

"We did," says Dad. "They had an absolutely outstanding singer who performed in the evenings. Large body mass, like the fellow who died."

"John Candy?" I guess. "Richard Griffiths?"

"No, no, singer. Italian. Beard."

"Oh, Pavarotti?"

"Exactly. This individual"—he shakes his head—"absolutely outstanding. Good enough to be on the London stage." He says this with the authority of a seasoned West End hit-maker.

"Well, he probably *wasn't*," I say, "hence performing on a cruise."

Dad purses his lips. I feel a bit mean, and quickly move on. "It was strange not spending Christmas with you. The first time ever." I trace my knife along the restaurant slogan on my placemat-cum-menu: *Mangia bene, vive felice!*

Dad nods. "Well. Good to try something different."

The wine is anemic and sweet, and I've been drinking it like juice: with frequent, thirsty sips. "I think they water it down," I say, partly because I believe this might be true, and partly to mitigate the stark fact of my already half-empty glass versus his untouched one. "So, anyway, how was the meeting?"

"Fine," he says.

"What was it again?"

"Oh." He stops to take a long, noisy pull of his wine. "It was, ah . . . to do with potential changes to the way things are run. Restructuring."

"Really," I say pointlessly.

"Yes," he confirms in kind.

"What . . . sort of changes?"

He enters into a lengthy explanation, and though I really do try to listen, I'm already lost a few acronyms in. I nod and crease my brow, and squint at my glass, trying to gauge how long is long enough to wait before refilling.

". . . a possible redundancy package."

"Right," I say, nodding more vigorously now to make up for the fact I'm reaching for the bottle. "Wait—redundancy? Redundancy package for who?"

"Nothing's definite," he says. "I said *if*."

"If what?"

"If these new measures come in."

"If these new measures come in, what?"

"Here we go!" says the waiter. "Who's having the lovely salad?"

"Dad," I say, leaning back as the plate is set down. "Could you please repeat the bit about what happens if the new measures come in?"

Without tasting his soup, he picks up the shaker and salts it with vigor. "There may be redundancies. I might be affected, but it's early days."

"Oh no! I mean, okay. So . . . how are you feeling about it?"

In the gurning, strangled voice he reserves for moments of high hilarity or stress, he says, "It doesn't really matter how I feel."

"Hey!" I put down my fork. It feels forced and false, an overdone gesture. "It matters to me." He shrugs as he slurps up a steaming spoonful. I return to my fork and waltz a slice of tomato through the vinaigrette.

"They want to be careful about mice," says Dad, nodding toward the flour sacks piled haphazardly in corners, part of the rough-and-ready vibe.

"Probably stuffed with straw," I say. We eat without speaking for a while.

"Don't tell your mother what I just told you."

"Couldn't even if I wanted to." I watch as he scours the bowl of every last smear with some bread. "Why won't you tell her? Don't you think you should?"

"She won't understand. I wouldn't get a moment's peace."

Though this is probably true, I feel a karmic need to stick up for her. "She might surprise you?" He shakes his head and we sit looking into our empty dishes. "How was the soup?" I ask.

"Bit salty."

"Any sign she might be thawing—you know, on the me front?" I ask, after another silence.

"How was everything with the starters?" says the waiter, seizing our plates.

"Fine, thank you," we say in accidental unison as he glides away.

"Who wants a little something sweet?" Our friend is back with some smaller menu cards.

Dad looks to me to answer, which makes me briefly, unbearably sad. I check the time: somehow we have only been here for less than an hour, so although I really don't want dessert, I say, "Sure, we'll take a look."

"Ooffff," says Dad, rubbing his belly, which has grown a little fuller than seems healthy for the wrong side of sixty. "I don't think I could have a whole one. Maybe we could share?"

Via an onerous process of elimination ("What do you want?" / "What do *you* want?" / "I'm happy with anything." / "So am I." / "Maybe not the panna cotta?" / "Agreed. Not the panna cotta." / "The lemon tart—was that a face you made?" / "Happy to have it." / "Oh, I was going to say not that? But if you want it, we can . . . ?" / "Very happy not to have it." / "So that leaves three—go on, you choose." / "Honestly, they sound equally good to me. I couldn't choose between them. You choose. Any. But not the tiramisu." / "And apple crumble's boring, so shall we go sticky toffee?" / "Fine." / "You're sure you don't want lemon? I think you wanted the lemon, and when I said I didn't, maybe you were just agreeing to be polite." / "I'm happy with anything. Lemon is fine. Sticky toffee is fine." / "Sticky toffee, then?" / "Sticky toffee it is. / "Sure?" / "Sure. I only want a taste anyway.") we order the sticky toffee pudding. While we wait, I try again to broach the subject of my mother.

"I don't know how to fix it," I say. "There doesn't seem to be a way to make it all right."

"She's a strong-minded woman, Claire," he says. "She's still grieving. I think you'll need to wait this one out."

"Could you try talking to her for me?" I say.

"I have. I am. I will," he says.

Dessert appears. In less than a minute of frenzied gouging and scraping the plate is practically spotless, and our spoons gleam brighter than when they arrived.

"Do you think he's a homosexual?" says Dad in a stage whisper, leaning in eagerly, hands clasped under his chin. The look in his eye says, *I know I shouldn't, but* . . . His lips are crusted, dark from the wine. I scrape at mine with a fingernail.

"What?" I say, although I heard full well and know he means our waiter.

"Never mind," says Dad, falling away.

When the bill arrives, I root for my purse and say, faintly, "Can I . . . ?" safe in the knowledge he will say no.

———

On the walk back to the Tube station, I practice saying, *I love you, Dad. Don't worry about work. I'm here for you no matter what happens,* over and over to myself.

"Huh?" says Dad.

"What?" I say. Then, quickly, "Thanks so much for dinner."

"Take care now, Claire. Send my regards to Luke."

I offer a kiss up to him like a question; he bows his head to accept it, and as he pulls away, there is the sudden burn of his coarse shaven cheek rasping mine.

Approval

When I told him I was handing in my notice without a new job lined up, my father didn't miss a beat.

"There might be something for you here. One of the administration girls, Karen, is leaving soon to retrain as a beautician."

I imagined commuting from the city to the suburbs, bonding with my dad over office politics while we ate sandwiches and drank bad coffee. It was, in a strange way, tempting.

"It's a really kind offer—"

"Now: it's not an offer. You'll have to go through the official channels. I can't make any guarantees."

". . . but I have savings. The plan is that I'll be okay without earning for a few months. A stopgap job might just be a distraction."

"It isn't a stopgap for Hilary," he said, referring to his PA of fifteen years, sounding faintly indignant on her behalf.

"I know. But I think maybe I'm more of a Karen."

There was a pause while he computed. "You want to become a beautician?"

"A Karen who hasn't found her niche yet."

"I'll email HR just in case you change your mind."

"You honestly don't have to do that, Dad—"

"It's no problem. But remember: no guarantees."

My mother, on the other hand, was much more encouraging.

"Oh *good*," she said. "I never thought that place was right for you."

Having spent the past two years complaining about it, I immediately leaped to the company's defense. "They're very highly regarded in the industry. You know they received more than a hundred applications for my job within twenty-four hours of advertising it?"

When I first started there, in an effort to help my parents understand what I did, I'd email them articles from the trade press that mentioned my employer in a positive light. *Fantastic, well done, Claire*, Mum would reply. *Yes, very good*, Dad would add. I stopped when, at a family party, I overheard my mother patiently and repeatedly explaining to a deaf great-uncle that I worked in "COMMERCE!"

"It was a good first job," she said, "but it was never really you."

"How do you mean?"

"I don't know why you're being so defensive. *You* said you handed in your notice because it wasn't right."

"Okay." She had me there. "If that wasn't 'me,' though, then what would you say is? When I was little, what did you think I'd be?"

"Well, a mother for one thing. You always loved looking after your dolls."

I picture my womb, dark and empty. "I meant as a career."

"Claire, you know I've always said you could do anything you wanted." She sounded like she still believed it too.

"What if I don't know what that is? Don't you have any ideas?"

"Ooh. Now. You're putting me on the spot there. Let me have a think and I'll get back to you."

But she didn't. And then she stopped talking to me.

Tube

A man in paint-spattered jeans and Reeboks, holding a newspaper wide open, moves his lips as he reads, like an actor committing lines to heart: lines of devastation in the Philippines, public executions in the Middle East and a review of the latest fried-chicken food truck patrolling a far-flung corner of the capital.

Lunch

"What did you have for lunch?"

"Turkey sandwich."

"From the cafeteria?"

"Yeah."

"Dessert?"

"Apple."

"Any biscuits or snacks?"

"No. Well, a yogurt. Are you out for a run?"

"What flavor? No, I'm walking. Why?"

"Forest fruits. You sound out of breath."

"I walk very fast." I hold the bottom of the phone away from my face to mute the offending breathing. "You know, you never ask what I had for lunch."

"What did you have for lunch?" Luke says in a monotone.

"I'm not saying you have to ask. Just pointing out that you're more than happy to say what *you* had, but when it comes to me, you're not so interested."

"To be honest? In this instance, that's true."

"Fair enough." I'm quiet for a moment. "But it's polite to return the question."

"Did you have something really exciting? Is that why you asked? Now I'm actually curious," says Luke.

"No, I asked because it helps me to get a sense of your day. It's nice for me to picture what you get up to."

"I drilled a hole in a human skull this morning," he offers.

"Yeah, but don't you do that most days?"

"I have lunch *every* day."

"Hey, me too!"

He gives a (surely affectionate) sigh. "Go on, then, what did you have?"

"Guess."

"No, I don't want to guess. Fine: goose."

"I'm not going to tell you if you're going to mock me."

"Oh my God."

"Okay, I'll give you a clue: think fish."

"I said I don't want to guess! Tuna," he says.

"Bingo. Tuna salad. That wasn't so hard, was it?"

"What happened to cutting back on fish?" (Last night, over our cod-fillet dinner, I suggested that we should pledge to buy fish only once a fortnight, and then always to be sure it's sustainably sourced. "But you were the one who forced me to start eating fish in the first place," Luke said, bewildered. "Now you want to take it away?")

"It was canned tuna. We had it in the cupboard already. That fish had been dead for a year or more. Plus, I've been thinking about our plan to cut down, and on second thought I wonder if we shouldn't just make the most of it while stocks last."

"No pun intended," says Luke.

"No: pun *intended*," I say.

Post

On the doormat, an envelope addressed in Grandma's gnarled, knotted hand. Years ago, she would send me treats in the post, a roll of Life Savers or Jolly Ranchers. Swaddled in bubble wrap and brown paper, they had the vague thrilling feel of contraband, and I would savor them with rare self-restraint, eking them out for a week or more. Sadly, all that stopped when I graduated, and this particular missive looks flat and unpromising. When I tease out the letter, some newspaper clippings waft to the floor. I pick them up and scan the headlines:

300+ APPLY FOR STARBUCKS JOB

LATER PREGNANCY INCREASES BREAST CANCER RISK

CALL TO CURB SPREAD OF INVASIVE SPECIES

(The latter does not, as I feared, refer to immigration control, but instead her local council's proposed treatment of buddleias. When it comes to Grandma, you never can be too sure.)

> *Thought you might be interested in the enclosed.*
> *Forearmed is forewarned, as they say.*
>
> Fondest,
> Grandma

The letter is written on the personalized stationery she and my grandfather have always used; now, however, she has crossed out Gum's name in a single, thick black stroke.

TV dinner

The fridge has nothing more to give than this packet of old stir-fry veg, marinating in its own brown seepage. The tangled bulk slithers into the wok and I drench it in some sweet, glossy sauce, to disguise its true colors and taste. In the background, a once-charming TV chef is cooking for a man named Gary, and slinging leading questions over his dish-toweled shoulder.

"How often, Gary mate, do you wake up the next day to a pile of greasy takeaway containers and wish you'd had something a bit healthier for dinner?"

"If I'm honest," says Gary, meek and miserable as though his Internet browsing history has just been published for the world—and his wife—to see, "if I'm totally honest, every time." The chef smiles knowingly, shimmies his frying pan, tossing cubes of meat high in the air.

Clothes

Now it's three o'clock, well into Dead Time: the meal-less stretch of empty hours that span the afternoon. Every minute I've spent on today's job-hunt strategy—a series of impassioned speculative letters explaining why I would make, variously, the perfect literary manager at a theater, projects coordinator at a museum, picture researcher for a fashion magazine and (anomaly among wildcards) resettlement officer for a prison—has been matched by the same frittered away on semi-skimmed, half-digested articles and the live-blogs of an entire TV series I've never watched, including all 391 below-the-line comments (which at one stage turned into a heated argument about a different, equally unfamiliar TV series).

For a change of scene, I head into our bedroom. While Luke folds and puts away his clothes each evening, with the conscientiousness and foresight that propelled him through medical school, mine accrue in a dune at the foot of the bed.

"Do you think you're going to deal with that soon?" Luke asked last night, watching a sock spontaneously scud down one side of it.

"Sure," I said, with the best of intentions.

Now I pick up a T-shirt at random and sniff the fabric, then, deciding it'll survive another wear, drape it carefully on the bed. Next, a top I have owned for years but never worn. Every so often, on it goes, in the hope I've developed the brio to pull it off; but each time, after a grimacing, tugging spell at the mirror, I end up actually pulling it off and dropping the thing back into the pile. I hold it up by the shoulders, considering whether to hang it up or fold it away in a drawer, or get rid of it, finally, altogether; and unable to decide, sink down in despair at where all these things will *go* and how they will ever get there.

Name-calling

I say, "Would I be Clarence, then?"

Everyone's moving lasagna around their plates, forking up mince a granule at a time and giving the pasta a wide berth.

"No. It's not the masculine version of your name; it's the male equivalent, the way it feels. For example," Rachel explains, pointing, "if Lauren had been a boy, her parents wouldn't have called her Laurence, but they might have called her something like Joshua."

"Him, surely," I say through a mouthful of salad I've picked from the bowl.

"And Francesca would be Raphael."

"Okay, I get it. So I would be something like James?"

Lauren considers this, shakes her head. "James is regal. *Kings* are called James."

"John?" I try, and everyone choruses, "No."

"John's timeless. Claire's kind of—no offense—eighties."

"Yeah! Or . . . a flight attendant name," says Rachel. Everyone murmurs agreement in a quick, muted way that makes me certain they've discussed this before, behind my back, probably in the pub near Fran's flat, when I had other plans, or wasn't invited, shouting over each other in their eagerness to list my many flaws. *Crap hair! Bites her nails! Awful posture! Eighties name! Yeah, no, wait, flight-attendant name! Yeah! Yeah! Shit clothes! No job! Lacks ambition! Just . . . really annoying!*

Fran weighs in. "I think yours would be more like . . . Rod. Or Ken."

"Yes!" says Rachel. "Exactly!"

"Absolutely not. You don't get to be Raphael and lump me with *Rodney* or *Kenneth*. No *way*."

"It's just a bit of fun, Claire," says Rachel.

"I know that! I am having fun! Who wants seconds?"

Words like "stuffed" and "delicious" are muttered as they push away their plates.

"How was the girls' dinner?" asks Luke, sitting down at the lasagna dish.

"A disaster: they hardly ate anything. I've already seasoned that," I say quickly as he picks up the peppermill. He sets it down unwillingly, digs in.

"Well, they're idiots. This is delicious."

"You don't have to tell *me*. Get this: Fran said, 'Claire, your cooking is always so hearty.'" I wait but see no reaction from Luke. "Hearty!"

"What's the problem? It's a compliment. Satisfying. Comforting. Hearty's my kind of food."

"No: it's code for heavy and stodgy. The implication being that I'm fat."

He rolls his eyes and shovels down a forkful. "I *really* don't think it means that." His fingers creep back round the peppermill and he begins to grind faux-gingerly, teeth clenched as though braced for a blow.

"I know these people—she meant I'm a fatty with an awful diet and I'm trying to make everyone else fat too. Your palate must be really jaded: I got the seasoning spot on."

"Hey, I've just had an idea!" says Luke urgently, still grinding. "Instead of taking everything everyone says to you, or does *near* you, as a personal attack, why don't you just . . . not?" He wipes the orange glow from his lips with two quick licks.

"I've just had a better idea! Why don't *you* hop on over the fence, try spending a few minutes on my side for once?"

"I so wish I could, but"—he shakes his head—"no can do. There's this crazy lady over there shouting totally wacko things whenever I try to get near." He bugs out his eyes. "She's extremely deluded and insane. It's quite tragic because she's actually allright-looking, and I've heard her cooking's real hearty—"

He yelps, doubles over, limbs a-jerking as I set myself on him, tickling hard.

24/7

Trying to conceal the monster within is an arduous full-time job in itself.

?

I phone Grandma to say thank you for the HEADLINES OF DOOM.

"I wondered if you'd got it, when I didn't hear from you," she says. "I asked your mother the other day—she said she couldn't remember the last time you phoned her."

My mouth falls open. "She actually said that?"

"Claire, I can't talk long. I've got the little girl from next door coming in to do my hair."

"You mean Sharon?"

"Of course." Sharon is in her mid-thirties, a mother of three.

"Okay," I say. "Did she . . . Did my mum say anything else? About me?"

"To be honest, Claire, I do think you might lift the phone to her more often. She has rather a lot on her plate at the moment. This bowel business: tell me, what's *your* take? Your friend, the doctor—what does he think? *Should* we be worried?"

Panic stirs, a tiny lick.

"What?" I say.

"Well, I've heard it's one of the better ones . . . but she keeps telling me there's no point going there until we *know* it's that for sure and it's just a question mark at the moment."

"A—"

"But it's a worry all the same. I never get the full picture: I know she thinks she's protecting me, but I'm no fool. Did I tell you about poor Wynn? They found it in hers, secondary, and she's only a couple of months left."

"Wait, but *whose* bowel—"

"Wynn, my Canadian friend. You've met her. Mind you, she's pushing ninety, so—"

"No, I mean, before that, when you first—"

In the background comes the prim trill of her doorbell. "Oh! Listen, I'd better go—that'll be Sharon."

"Grandma!" I say.

"Don't *worry*, Claire. I'm sure your mother's right and it's nothing. Bye now!"

?????????????????????????????????????

I ring "MUM," then "HOME," and getting nowhere, try "DAD," but no one's picking up. "This is why people should have more than one child!" I shout as the rings go on and on.

Reassurance

"How bad is bowel cancer?" I say, when Luke finally answers two hours later.

"Depends," says Luke. "Why? Who has it?"

"I don't know! My mum, maybe, but she won't answer my calls!" I tell him, or try to, what Grandma said, but it was so elliptical it doesn't make much sense; plus in my frantic state, I've developed hiccups.

"I couldn't even ask who she meant! Because I didn't want Grandma to think I didn't know! I'm! A terrible! Daughter!"

"Shh, it's okay. Calm down."

"It might not be okay." I try to steady my breath. "How bad is it? Is it one of the bad ones?" I've spent the last two hours Googling frantically, and have so far been able to counter every rational, medically sound reassurance with three grisly firsthand horror stories.

"It depends when they find it, but honestly, until you know more there's no point in getting so worked up."

"Will you try her? Please? She might answer you."

"Of course I will," says Luke, my shining knight.

He calls back about five minutes later—during which time I've been contorted at the sink, trying to drink water from the wrong side of the glass, while also keeping one eye on my phone. The front of my T-shirt is drenched, but the hiccups seem to have dwindled.

"Okay," he says, all business, "so firstly, it isn't your mum—it's your grandma's bowel." I look up, mouthing vague words of gratitude. "And it sounds as though everything is probably fine. She'd eaten beets for lunch, forgotten and got a fright the next day when she thought she saw blood in the toilet. So she called herself an ambulance and they took her in for tests."

"But she said there was still a question mark," I say, feeling bad about how much less I care now I know it's only Grandma.

"There were shadows showing up on the scans," he says, "which the doctor thinks are probably just benign cysts, but they're waiting on results to confirm. She didn't sound worried at all."

"Good. Phew. Okay. How *did* she sound?"

"The way she always does. Normal."

"Really? Good. That's good. Did she ask about me?" He doesn't reply straightaway. "Luke?"

"She asked how you were."

My heart leaps. "And? What did you say?"

"I said you were well, that you were keen to sort things out."

"And? Luke! What did she say to that?"

He hesitates. "She . . . said she'd prefer to . . . She said *she* would be in touch."

"When?"

"When she's ready, was the implication."

"Don't call her, she'll call me?"

"Something like that."

"Well. Thanks anyway," I say, gulping back a straggling hic-cup.

Pity

There goes another great song, ruined by the ad man to sell a fancy car.

Dependency

Chugging my way around the park, I pass a blind lady and her guide dog out for a stroll. Who is walking who? I wonder—and then—isn't that true of all dogs and their owners?

Starbucks

"Blah! Blah! Blah?" shouts the barista, competing with the milk steamer's vicious hiss while holding a paper cup aloft, Statue of Liberty–esque. I laugh, delighted, at this strange mutiny, before it dawns on me that what she is holding is my double-shot macchiato, and what she is shouting is my name.

Ditty

I've found the solution to the rising clothes mountain: everything-goes-in-the-washing-machine.

Bed

Some nights our bed feels much too small: hot and hard with el-bows and knees, and the cloying stickiness of flesh against flesh, not just Luke's skin on mine, but my own on me, inner thigh cleaving to inner thigh, arm to armpit, breast against breast, and I long to be alone and stretch out asterisk-like; but then, of course, there are also the nights when the space between us is chilly and wide, and my reaching fingertips yield no response, or sometimes a slight shrugging-off.

Optimism

This tiny brown tidbit on the living-room floor: mouse dropping or . . . peppercorn?

Math

If I can just digest enough TED talks, self-improvement podcasts, overviews on the Aristotelian sense of purpose and firsthand ac-counts of former city workers who set up artisan businesses from their kitchen tables, then *surely* the answer will reveal itself to me, in its own time and own way?

Waiting game

"But what do you do to *fill* your time?" the quiz-show host asks the retired lab technician from Worcester.

Drive

"Why are you dressed like an unwell teenager?" says Luke when I enter the kitchen.

"I need to be able to focus on the road. I can't have my hair falling into my eyes or my sleeve getting caught on the emergency brake."

We are hiring a car to visit Luke's parents; therefore my attire (headband, tracksuit bottoms, thin-soled tennis shoes—no laces) has been carefully chosen for maximum comfort and minimum hazard.

"Time I dusted off my driver's license," I said when I first had the idea. "Take control, be bold. Brave new world."

"You go, girl." Luke had snapped his fingers to and fro, though his eyes remained faithful to the soccer game.

Now he says, "Are you sure you're okay to do this? I'd be really happy to drive."

"Thanks, but I'll be fine. I really *want* to," I say.

In the car, I puff out my cheeks a few times and slowly release the air. I pat the gearshift, grip the steering wheel, tweak the mirrors, grind the seat back and forth on its rails.

"Ready?" says Luke, thumbing the sat nav.

"No," I say. "Give me a minute. I need to get my bearings."

"We're heading that way," says Luke, gesturing behind.

"I meant my bearings *inside* the car. Wait, I thought north was that way?" I point to the windshield.

"You do know north isn't always just straight ahead of you?" says Luke. I shake my head in faux-disgust, faux because his assumption was right on the money.

———

"Bear left." I slap on the blinker. "*Bear*, bear left, not turn."

"What does that mean? I can't go left: it's just straight road. Luke! What am I doing?"

"Never mind—keep going. You're doing fine." His hand floats out and knocks the signal light back to neutral.

A bit later, he says, "You could swap lanes now. There's nothing behind."

We've been sitting pretty in the slow lane ever since I first edged, terrified, onto the highway.

"Quite happy here, thanks," I say, daring to tap my fingers on the wheel in time to R.E.M. on the radio.

Luke's phone buzzes. He looks at it and swiftly returns it to his pocket.

"Who was that?"

"Work."

"Who? Danny?"

"No."

A pause. "Who, then?"

"Hm?"

"Who was the text from if it wasn't Danny?"

"Fi?"

"Fi, as in Fiona? I know who Fiona is." He shrugs. "You *know* I do. What did she want?"

"It's . . . too boring to go into."

"Okay." I check the rearview and side mirrors, think about changing lanes, think again. "Does she have a boyfriend?"

"Who?"

"Who do you think? Fiona. Does your colleague Fi have a boyfriend?"

In fact, I already know the answer to this from a recent online binge, starting innocently enough with a cursory scan of her Facebook page; but the curiosity soon slithered into dark, oily fascination, which eventually saw me, at some point long past midnight (Luke must have been in bed or at work), clicking through a series of bikini shots from a 2010 trip she took to India, while lifting up my sleep T-shirt to pit her abs (taut) versus mine (disappointing). The boyfriend is a relative newcomer named Pete, who is, in my professional opinion, slightly too good-looking for her.

"Um," says Luke. He flicks open the glove compartment and peers in, flips it shut. "Sort of, I think. Guy sounds like a douche. Why do you ask?"

"Pass me, then, if you're going to," I say to the Mondeo that's practically kissing my bumper. "*I* think she might have a little crush on you."

"What? Fiona? No," he says. "No way. Where did you get that? You've never even met her."

"I can tell," I say. "If she's got any kind of taste, she'd have a crush on you."

"Well, that's true," says Luke, turning up the music.

I raise my voice. "Why do you think he's a douche, then?"

"Ugh, Claire, I don't know! I get the impression she likes him more than he likes her, that's all."

"The opposite of us," I say. "Just joking. Luke. That was a small joke." I continue, "Why don't we double-date with them? I'll be able to suss what's going on."

"Might be a bit weird," he says.

"Why?"

"Wouldn't you think it was strange if *she* suggested that we double-date?"

"No." (I would.) "I think it's strange that *you* think it's strange. You spend more time with this person than you do with me and yet I've never even met her. What does she look like?" Obviously, I already know this too: she falls into the petite, slightly plain category that a lot of men seem to find irresistible, and which makes me mistrust her even more than I did when she was just a blank canvas.

"I don't know," says Luke. "Normal-looking?"

"You'd make an awful witness. Let's break it down: hair color? Bigger or smaller than me?"

"Are we still talking about this?"

"*We're* not talking about this; *I* am and you're refusing to answer perfectly straightforward questions. For reasons I can't quite grasp."

"What were your questions? Hair is sort of . . . brown?" His palms are pressed together, clamped between his thighs.

"Light or dark brown? Long or short? Would you say she is bigger or smaller than me?"

"I don't know, smaller—turn here! Turn here, this is your exit, go, now, go!" We sail past the junction. "Claire! That was our exit!"

"You didn't give me enough warning! I told you I needed plenty of time to respond to directions. I've said that right from the beginning!" Our voices fill the car, hit the roof. "What are we doing? Tell me how to correct this!"

"I don't know!" says Luke. "I'm waiting for the fucking thing to reroute!" He hurls the sat nav into the footwell and picks it up straightaway, to examine the damage.

"That'll help."

"We'll need to get off at the next junction," he says, suddenly neutral. This is his tactic of old: to make me seem irrational by contrast. "Take the next left, then follow the road back to the highway."

"I need more than that—where do I get off at this traffic circle, for example? Luke!"

"Mum, it's me," says Luke, and I turn to see him on the phone. He shrugs at me and shakes his head as though he had no choice in the matter, as though *he* hadn't phoned *her*. "Yeah, no, everything's fine. We're just going to be a bit late . . . No, closer to five. Sorry about that." I see him slide his eyes toward me. "She is, yeah." We orbit the traffic circle once, twice. "That's right. Crazy traffic . . . Okay, bye."

"I am what?" He doesn't answer. "The traffic is fine."

"Third exit," says Luke. "Would you have preferred that I say you missed the exit?"

"But I didn't miss the exit; you did. How am I meant to turn when I don't know there's an exit? And it's only added five minutes to the journey. You didn't need to call her."

"Sorry—clearly I failed to account for the fact that you would have us creeping at forty the entire journey. I'd said we'd be there by four."

I check the clock; it's already twenty past.

"If you hadn't been so busy drooling over Fiona, we'd be there five minutes sooner than we're going to be," I say, almost, but not entirely, in jest.

Luke laughs, horribly. "Can you actually hear yourself?"

I jab at the radio, trying to find the off switch while keeping my eyes on the road. It blasts unbearably, then buzzes with static before I manage to find the right knob. Luke turns the sound up on the sat nav and for the rest of the journey our silence is punctuated only by its terse, robotic instructions.

Pressure

Luke's parents are standing in the driveway when we approach.

"How long have they been waiting out there?"

Luke unsnaps his seatbelt and reaches for the handle.

"Could you please at least wait until I've stopped the car?" I ask, and he sighs and slumps against the headrest. "Great, they're going to stand there and watch me try to get into this tiny space. I

NOT WORKING 123

can't park under pressure!" I say, stalling, grinning and waving all at once. Luke's father, Bob, steps forward and starts to direct me with broad whole-arm gestures that bear little relation to the negligible space I have on either side. After numerous unsuccessful attempts, I back out, flustered, and yank up the emergency brake. Bob steps forward, knocks on the glass and motions winding it down.

"He needs to update his mime," I mutter, pressing the button. "Hi, Bob! Hello, Jan!" Jan, clutching her cardigan together at the throat, waves vaguely with her free hand, balled around a tissue. "Shall I park on the pavement? I think that might be easier."

"No, no," says Bob, "we don't park on the pavement. There's plenty of room. Let me guide you in."

"Okeydoke!" I cry.

"I'll get out, then. There won't be enough space on my side once you're in," says Luke, bolting out and pushing the door shut with gusto.

After fifteen or twenty minutes of maneuvers—each micromanaged by Bob—I finally manage to wedge the car beside Bob and Jan's old red sedan. There's barely enough room for *me* to get out, and I slide with some trouble through the tiny gap between car door and wall, and sidestep around to the front.

"Come here, you!" Bob draws me to him, jiggling our embrace a little in a playful way that feels a bit much, like he's trying out a new way of being with me.

"Oh dear, are you poorly too?" asks Jan, gesturing at my getup. Her nose is red and streaming.

"That's Claire's driving outfit," says Luke.

"I need to be comfortable behind the wheel."

"Claire doesn't drive much," Luke adds, pulling me to him. His hug binds my arms so I can't shrug him off. "But she did a *great* job getting us here."

When he releases me, I move toward Jan, but she holds up a

hand in warning. "Better not get too close," she says, pressing the tissue to her nose. "Come in, out of the cold."

"I'm sorry to have kept you waiting out here. Parking isn't my strong point," I say.

"You got there in the end," says Jan, closing the door behind me.

Dinner

The four of us go to the local Chinese, where Jan and Bob are regulars. No sooner have we sat down than a waiter appears and removes our chopsticks, replacing them with knives and forks.

"Oh, I'm fine with chopsticks," I say quietly when he goes for mine, unsure which faux pas gets precedence: flagrant cultural insensitivity or drawing attention to the same in Luke's parents.

"Have both," says the waiter, helping me out with a gentle smile-and-bow.

"Everyone happy with house red?" Bob says, simultaneously giving the waiter the go-ahead.

"Absolutely," I say, with a touch more enthusiasm than feels appropriate. I didn't want to drink this evening, but if I don't, Luke's parents might think I'm pregnant, and it's really not good to get their hopes up.

Bob turns to Luke and starts to ask him about work, so I lean in close to Jan, all-girls-together. "Do you know what you're having?" Another waiter passes bearing aloft a noisy, steaming griddle dish. Several heads at other tables turn in her wake.

"What is that?" says Jan, scanning the menu.

I point. "Sizzling garlic prawns, must be. Smells great. I think I might go for those, actually. What about you?"

"Oh no," says Jan. "I wouldn't want the attention."

"So, Claire," says Bob, before I can think of a response, "we haven't seen you since Christmas, when you were on a mission to—as I think Luke described it—find yourself?"

"That's one way of putting it." I look at Luke, who is staring intently at the menu.

"Then my next question comes in two parts: a) have you succeeded in finding yourself? and b)—which is of course contingent on a)—where had you been all your life?"

"Ever the logician, Bob! Well. If the answer to a) is 'Sadly no, not yet,' the answer to b) must be 'I'm still looking.'"

"But what do you think you'd *like* to do?" asks Jan. "You must have *some* idea."

"Honestly," I say, "this is what's so hard. I know this is going to sound very vague but I'm keen to do something that means something. Not just glorified admin, as so many jobs seem to be nowadays." They're nodding, waiting for more, faces straining with the polite desire to understand, but there's nothing else to come.

Then Jan breaks the silence, slapping her hand on the table. "Police force. There you are. Excellent benefits, job for life, making a difference to society."

I'm about to laugh but catch myself when I see she's not joking. I look to Luke for some assistance, but he's enjoying himself too much. His head rocks in slow, delighted agreement. "It's perfect, Mum. Claire loves *interrogating*, to really get in there and sweat the small stuff." His eyes flicker to mine for the briefest second, and though the tone is light, there's a private sting. "I can't believe I didn't think of it."

Bob weighs in. "I can see you in the uniform. Yes, very smart. You'd look most . . . dependable."

He means fat, I think sadly, picturing myself, dumpy in the trousers, chin bunched around the hat strap.

"Thank you," I say. "Plenty of food for thought. Speaking of which, what's everyone having?"

"I see what Luke means about interrogation!" says Bob, gaze roving to check everyone's laughing.

The waiter arrives to take our order. I chicken out of the flamboyant prawns—opting for chow mein instead—and spend the rest of the meal steering the conversation as far from policing as possible.

"How's the painting going, Bob?" I ask. Bob is an amateur watercolor artist—and serial gifter of his output to Luke and me.

"Good! Thank you for asking, Claire. I'm about to begin a series of local buildings, with a view to putting on an exhibition, hosted by the Historical Society."

"Fantastic!" I say. "That sounds wonderful! Are there . . . any criteria for which buildings you choose, or do you just . . . go for the most attractive?" Sometimes, my resourcefulness really takes me by surprise.

While Bob answers, I keep flicking my gaze to Luke, who I suspect, despite the surface appearance of civility, is totally shutting me out. To confirm, I put my hand on his knee: no response.

"Claire's very interested in heritage," Luke says with sudden enthusiasm. "You applied for that job, didn't you?"

"What job's this?" says Jan, shooting forward in her seat.

"Oh"—I press my fingers hard into his leg—"it's nothing. I mean, it was just a last-minute thing on the off-chance for . . . You know in London they have those blue plaques?"

"Of course," says Bob. "We have them here too. A wonderful scheme. Well, that sounds terrific! Good for you. When will you hear?"

"No—I already found out. I didn't get it," I say, sitting on my hands to try and stop squirming. "It was ages ago, before Christmas—just a stupid spur-of-the-moment application. I don't know why Luke mentioned it."

"Well, I'm sure you've got plenty of other fingers in the fire," says Jan.

"I hope *not* . . ." says Bob, shielding his mouth with his hand, stage-whispering out of the side of it as though Jan can't hear.

"Irons, rather," says Jan, cross with herself for the mistake. "Fingers in pies."

But having set up his punch line, Bob won't be put off. "Fingers in the fire! *That* would be a bit painful!"

"Are you waiting to hear back from lots of other places, or . . . ?" Jan asks.

"Well," I say, wrenching apart my wooden chopsticks, "not as such. Applications are so time-consuming, and if I'm not sure what I want, it feels like a waste to go through all the stages for something that might not be right anyway. I'm mainly doing lots of reading and research at the moment, into different avenues I could take."

"Right," says Jan distantly.

"Hey—what sort of frame did you guys end up choosing for the lake view?" Bob asks, no doubt sensing my discomfort. He's referring to our Christmas present, a muddy scenic piece of his that went straight on top of the wardrobe. I look to Luke, ready to comply with his story, glad of the opportunity to be reunited, however briefly, in benign deceit, but he doesn't yield an inch.

"Sorry, Dad, we haven't got round to it yet. It's been a bit crazy this year between work and exams. I'll take it in next week to be done," says Luke, then adds, "or Claire might if she has a spare moment."

Back at the house, we drink tea at the kitchen table.

"Would you give me a hand setting up the new DVD player next door?" says Bob to Luke. "It's defeated me so far, I'm afraid."

Luke stands, nodding, draining his mug.

"How are your parents, Claire?" asks Jan when they've gone.

"Oh, they're . . . both well, thanks. Nothing to report really. My mum—" I stop, not knowing where I'm going with this. *My mother isn't speaking to me, and my father may be about to lose his job.* "She sends her regards. My dad too. They both do, to you and Bob."

"Well, give them our best," says Jan, plucking a fresh tissue from the box on the table and hooting into it before settling into a middle-distance stare.

I clear my throat, looking around the kitchen for something to say.

"Basil plants always die on me." I nod at the thriving one on the windowsill. Jan doesn't look surprised to hear it.

"You mustn't be afraid to prune," she says. "Pinch off any flowers immediately—sounds brutal, but that's how to make it thrive."

"Noted," I say. Through the glass doors I can see Luke and Bob in the living room. Bob stands and intones like a priest from the manual, which rests on his open palms. Luke kneels by the television; his face and forearms glow blue in its light. "I give him a hard time sometimes, but he's all right, really, isn't he?"

"Who, Luke? Of course," says Jan. "We're all very lucky to have him."

Sick

In the night, I wake and two things are wrong: I'm alone in the bed and need very much to be sick. I grope for the light switch, and when I find it—certain I won't make it to the bathroom on time—I kneel over and retch into the bin by the door, leaking tears of strain and self-pity. When I'm done, I take a grim inventory of my output: one glistening serving of chicken chow mein. The sight provokes a few more fruitless heaves, until weak with relief and clammy with sweat, I curl up on the carpet to recover.

The bin, I see now, is actually more of an ornamental tin

bucket, featuring an illustration of cats dressed as Victorian humans. One in a top hat reads a newspaper, perched on a fireside armchair. Another—the wife?—in a pink dress is brandishing a lorgnette in its paw (I summon "lorgnette" with surprising ease from the mists of childhood books featuring stern schoolmarms and Alpine boarding schools), and looking down on me through it with such haughtiness that I find myself nearly *glad* I was sick, if only to have answered this creation with the contempt it deserves.

In the bathroom, I clean the bin with toilet bleach, and on the way out exchange a woeful look with myself in the mirror, impressed by how pale and wretched I look. In the guest room, softly groaning, I crawl back under the covers, and as I fall asleep, my mother appears to me, holding my hair away from my face and rubbing my back, saying, "Poor pet, poor love."

Disagreeable

"Where did you sleep? I missed you."

"My old room," says Luke, setting out knives and forks.

"I'd have been happy to sleep there too." I follow him round the dining-room table, laying dessert spoons in his wake.

"I didn't want to disturb you. Dad and I stayed up late." He embarks on another lap to correct the direction of my spoons.

"Probably for the best, anyway. I was sick."

"Really?" says Luke, turning back to look at me. I realize I'm still following him. "Are you all right now?"

"Fine," I say. "A bit shaky, but okay. It was the chicken chow mein: we did not agree. Nor did I get on with that cat bin in the guest room."

"What?" he says in a tone that suggests he doesn't want to know. "Look, if you need to go upstairs and rest, I'm sure my parents won't mind."

"Luke, is something wrong?"

"What do you mean?"

"You've been acting weird with me ever since we got here."

A hand lands *splat* on his chest. "*I've* been weird? What are you talking about? You're the one who was chipping away the entire drive about some insane bullshit."

"You treated me like a stranger all through dinner last night. You didn't even want to sleep in the same bed! How do you think it makes me feel? You're the only reason I'm here."

He's pinching the bridge of his nose, head tilted back as though stanching a bleed. "I just wanted to come and see my parents, forget about work and have a relaxing weekend—but now I'm under siege for not paying you enough attention. I'm not your babysitter, Claire."

This last comment—as Luke well knows—keys into a deep-seated, long-held, only-child fear that I'm needy and high mainte-nance. "Not fair," I say in a low voice. "I don't know if it's work stress you're taking out on me, or something else, but please don't treat me like one of your teenage girlfriends."

"What does *that* mean?"

On the drive home from the Chinese last night, Bob and Jan reminisced about what a ladies' man Luke had been at school. "Who was the little blonde, Bianca or something? Followed him around everywhere!"

"Called him *Lukie*," Jan added dryly.

"She went to every single one of his soccer games, came around all the time with cakes and cookies she'd made. Hint, hint, Claire!" His eyes found mine in the mirror. "No, I'm only joking. And Luke hardly said a word to her! Never called her back . . ." Luke had pretended to be embarrassed, but even in the glancing shadows of the backseat I could see he quite enjoyed this image of himself: aloof and irresistible.

"She's a solicitor in London now, her mother tells me. Very

good money apparently," Jan said, twisting round in her seat to nod at me conspiringly.

"You know what? Never mind," I say to Luke. "Whatever."

He draws a hand down over his mouth. "I can't talk to you when you're being like this."

"Yeah, well, I can't talk to you *at all*." Suddenly, mortifyingly, everything gushes. My face is in hot, snotty chaos. "It's as though you're a different person! It's . . . it's like you can't even bear to be *near* me." I pull out one of the dining-room chairs and sink into it. "Argh!" I say, trying to laugh between sobs, but my breath catches and a hiccup comes out. "It's so unfair that this never happens to you!" Luke comes around the table behind me and stacks his head on mine. He reaches his arms around my waist and clasps them in front of me.

"*Please* don't *cry*," he says. Through the open door we see Jan scurry past, head turned discreetly away.

Reparations

On the drive home, we are polite and cautious.

"Is that too loud?" Luke asks of the music, and I say no, seesawing my shoulders to the beat. For my part, I give life in the fast lane a try, passing perhaps three or four cars, before a bullying Mercedes puts me back in my place.

At the service station, I buy sweets: jelly beans, Luke's favorite, though I'm not such a fan. Luke picks out all the greens for me and holds them cupped in his hand so I can help myself without having to look away from the road.

"What have you got on this week?" I ask. We both know the answer already, but he plays along.

"Working nights until Sunday," he says. "How about you?"

"Oh, you know. More of the same."

"Are you . . . making *any* kind of progress?" he asks.

I suck too hard on a jelly bean and tut accidentally. "Honestly, I don't know."

"Maybe you just need to dive in and try *some*thing."

"But if I do and hate it, all this will have been for nothing. Plus I'll have lost another crucial few years."

"Okay," says Luke. "I'm not trying to rush you. I only want to make sure you're not losing perspective."

"What?"

"That this isn't becoming about more than a job."

"Meaning?"

"A job doesn't have to define you."

"Yours is literally part of your name."

"Well . . . that's the exception that proves the rule," he says.

"Reverend, professor, sergeant," I say. "And that's before I even look at Wikipedia."

On the radio, a hectic procession of jingles: windshield replacement, cash for gold and a legal claims service for accidents sustained in the workplace.

5

Money matters

For the last few weeks I've been diligently avoiding my bank balance, but after six days of careful spending (no cafe trips, meals
entirely composed of cans and fridge staples) I'm confident I've
restored sufficient order, and log on to my online account. Com-
bining savings, my last bonus, plus a small, borrowed portion of
Luke's salary, I'd originally calculated I could just about manage
a frugal six months without earning, but what confronts me now
is so shocking I shut the laptop lid.

I phone Geri, my ex-boss, to follow up on a possibly too-breezy
email I sent her, asking if she knew anyone in need of a free-
lancer.

"Actually, I'm glad you called. We could do with someone here
to help get a new campaign up and running. Jono's totally
swamped with his own stuff at the moment, and you already know

how we work, so it would mean I wouldn't have to waste time explaining every little thing to someone new. Does that sound tempting?"

"Definitely. How long would it be for?"

"Well, as long as it takes. Six to twelve weeks? Don't worry, I'm not going to trick you back into a full-time contract or anything."

"It sounds perfect, thank you," I say.

"Great. Start Monday?" she says, and names my fee. Pro rata, it's nearly double my old salary.

"Wow. Really? Are you sure?" I say.

"Hey, that's freelancing for you," she says. "Happy to reduce it, if it would make you more comfortable."

"I think I'll manage. See you Monday."

And so to square one

"I think we're popping you . . ." says Geri, resting her fingertips lightly on a surface adjacent to the intern's desk, "here for the moment." Her eyes scan the rest of the office, perhaps in the hope that by being so vague, I won't notice my new desk looks an awful lot like the mini filing cabinet where the printer used to be. An old monitor sits there instead, shrouded in dust but with fresh claw marks at the corners where it's been manhandled out of retirement.

"We need to get you something to sit on," says Geri, shuffling a hand through her hair. Last time I saw her, she wore it cropped pixie-short; now, it's almost at her chin. On the way in, I noticed other big changes: Conrad from operations has grown a serious beard, and Seema, the business manager, is extremely pregnant. It feels heavy-handed, like on TV when bad prosthetics are used to indicate elapsed time.

"I'll go," says the bare-shouldered girl at the intern's desk. She is very pretty, very young, and when she stands up, reveals herself to be wearing a black evening dress.

"Bea, you don't need to do that," says Geri, but the girl has already drifted off, her bare feet soundless on the wooden floor. "Her father is Martin Warner," Geri says meaningfully. The name is vaguely familiar, from company press releases, I think. "It's important that we're all Very. Nice. To. Her." She waggles the mouse and logs me on to the system. That the passwords haven't changed since I left is at once comforting and depressing. Bea returns with a stool that has MAIL ROOM. DO NOT REMOVE!!! emblazoned on the seat.

"What an amazing dress," I say, taking the stool from her.

"Oh, thanks." She flops into her swivel chair and readjusts the fabric. "James won a thing last night."

"James is Bea's boyfriend. He's a music producer." Geri steps in like the cheerful PR rep of a charming-yet-wayward Hollywood starlet.

"So you guys had a big night celebrating?" I say.

"We didn't so much go to bed as *not* go to bed," says Bea, and Geri laughs her client-facing laugh: tremulous, musical and woefully affected.

"Feel free to use the sofa in my office if you want to take a nap later," she says with a discreet wink. "Or if you need to go home early, just slip away."

"I'll be fine—I'll just drink shitloads of coffee," says Bea, and Geri lets fly another arpeggio as she heads off into her office.

"I think she's fucking my dad," Bea says to me.

"Ohhhh no. I don't think that can be true. Geri's very happily married." I perch sidesaddle on the stool, which has uneven legs and is a fraction too high for my filing-cabinet desk.

"Well, if she isn't, she wants to," says Bea, tipping back her head and pushing the floor away with splayed toes, spinning round in her ergonomic chair.

In passing

I arrive home just as Luke's leaving for work.

"Hi."

"Hi."

"How was it?"

"Fine. Weird to be back. Weird how not weird it was, I mean."

He nods and reaches for the door. "Well, bye, then."

"Kiss?"

"What? Oh yeah, right." With his hand on the latch he leans back toward me but doesn't quite make it.

"Try again?" I say, and we connect this time. "See you tomorrow, I guess. Same time, same place?"

"It's a date," says Luke. "Night, night."

Solitude

If I was single, it might all be so much simpler: there would only be myself to disappoint.

Yoga

"Lift your fingers to the stars," the instructor says, and a silent forest of arms grows up, reaching for the polystyrene ceiling tiles.

Co-worker

In the kitchen at work, I coincide with my replacement, Jonathan, who leans over me to open a cabinet above my head.

"It's Jonathan, isn't it?" I say into his armpit. "Claire — we met before at the bowling thing. I used to — "

"Sit at my desk. I know. What are you doing back?"

"Geri asked me to come in and help out. It's sort of a favor. A paid favor."

Jonathan spoons out not enough coffee. The kettle struggles to boil. "What exactly is it you're doing again?"

"I don't know how much I'm allowed to say. It's a campaign for a new client — a clothing brand? Still confidential, even in-house, I think."

"Oh right, that, yeah." He nods, sagely, though I doubt he has a clue. "So still no proper job, then?"

I sigh. "No. Nothing feels right. Maybe I'm destined to be here forever. The signs seem to be pointing that way."

"But you're just temping. There's no permanent role for you here." He checks himself at the last second. "Is there?"

"Don't worry, I'm not here to take back my old job." He snorts, but I can't gauge the tone: defensive or derisive, it isn't clear. "So how are you settling in?" I ask.

"Well, I've been here a while. So I'm pretty settled now. Developed quite a few new projects myself."

"Sure," I say, "learning the ropes."

"Tied up a lot of loose ends, if that's what you mean. Things were in a somewhat chaotic state when I arrived." He holds up his hands, warding off the intended offense. "Observation, not a criticism." The kettle clicks and he fills the French press; the grains flounder in the water. "Want some?" he asks, taking me by surprise with a question that isn't a challenge. Unless, it hits me, perhaps it *is* a challenge to see if I'll accept his undrinkable offering with grace.

"Love some!" I crouch sportingly at the fridge, hooking up the milk in the crook of my thumb. "Milk?"

"Please," he says.

"Say when."

He does only when it's about to spill over. The contents of his mug are nearly white: hot, milky water with the barest hint of coffee. He stirs in three heaping tablespoons of sugar, tapping the rim officiously when finished.

"Huh. I would have had you down as a no-frills kind of guy," I say. "You know, as it comes. As in black, no sugar. Basic. Straight up."

Jonathan jabs at his glasses, which have slipped down his nose. "I need to get back to my desk," he says.

"Observation, not a criticism!" I call after him, tipping my coffee-water down the sink before I start to make a proper pot.

Tube

A small boy with slicked-down hair wears a large talent-show sticker on his buttoned-up shirt. Someone (his mother or his grandmother, or perhaps even his great-grandmother) offers him a packet of potato chips, but he places a pudgy hand to his chest and shakes his head, eyelids fluttering. I smile and he hunches his little talent-burdened shoulders, sighs and kicks his box-fresh Nikes, which swing several inches above the floor.

Survival of the fittest

Not proud of the fact that when crossing the road, I use fellow humans as a buffer from the oncoming traffic, but there it is: that's the sort of person I am.

Crisis

Over breakfast, Luke idly drops a bombshell, claiming the mirrors in the gym locker rooms are warped to flatter the beholder.

"But why would they make you look thinner?" I ask, dropping my spoon in a panic that the wide reflection I'd dismissed only yesterday as grotesquely distorted might in fact have been *slimmed down*, and therefore several degrees more forgiving than the reality.

"To make your workout seem immediately effective," he says. "You see results, you keep coming back."

"No, no, that doesn't make sense. If you look *fatter*, you'll keep coming back, to lose weight. If you look thinner, you'll quit: job done."

"Why don't you ask them?" says Luke, hands up. "I'm just a humble brain surgeon. What do I know?"

"*Trainee*," I say, "and I'm not sure snipping aneurysms or whatever qualifies you as an expert in consumer psychology."

"*Clipping*," he corrects me. "Shit." His eyes zigzag across his laptop screen. "There's been a massive earthquake in Chile. Three thousand deaths and rising."

"Oh my God. That's terrible." I allow enough seconds to pass, stirring my porridge. "Maybe . . . maybe it's different for men and women. The men's locker-room ones make them look thinner, and the women's ones fatter."

"We should donate," Luke says, tapping quickly, so I shelve the subject, pending further investigation.

After-work drinks

I go to a nearby bar with some of the other "young people": Bea the intern and two recent graduates, long-limbed, large-eyed girls like gazelles, with masses of hair and lovely clothes I can't believe their salaries cover. Because I am the oldest by some years, I feel obliged to buy the drinks.

"You know how it goes," Bea, on her third nine-pound martini, is saying, and I nod, although I don't, really. She's spent the past half-hour talking about her ex-boyfriend Fox (not a nickname), who's been sitting outside her new guy's house for hours in taxis that must, though I'm the only person concerned by this detail, cost him a medium-sized fortune. The current boyfriend isn't at all pleased. "I reckon he's more worried about his *daughter's* safety than mine," says Bea indignantly.

"Wait," I say. "The music producer has a *kid*?"

"Two. Marlie's three, and Rhys is sixteen."

"Sixteen! How old are you?"

"Nineteen," says Bea, sucking on an olive, "next month. Rhys is not my biggest fan. I'm very much the evil stepmother."

I smile into my house wine.

"And James is how old?" asks Jemima, one of the graduate girls.

"Forty-two? I can't remember exactly."

"What do your parents think?" the other one, Lara, asks.

"About what?"

"About the fact your boyfriend is more than twice your age."

"Mum flirts with him. She does with all my boyfriends. Dad and him go hunting together." Bea shrugs. "They think he's great."

"What do you two *talk* about?" I ask.

"Music, obviously. His psycho ex, my psycho ex. Therapy, parenting, our screwed-up families." She frowns, suddenly defensive. "Why? What do you and the doc talk about?"

"Oh, all kinds of things," I say, playing for time. My mind has gone blank, save for this morning's gym-mirror tussle. "You know, normal stuff."

"Such as?" Bea insists.

"I don't know! Health. Science. Fitness. World affairs." It gets worse the more I say, so I stop. Meanwhile, Bea and the graduate girls exchange round-eyed looks of naked pity.

After after-work drinks

When the lights get brighter, I'm finally forced to accept everyone's refusal of *one more* and gather together all my many things: so many layers and tote bags to wrestle onto my body.

"Text me to let me know you got home okay, okay?" I say, first to Bea, hugging her, then to the other two, Jemima-and-Lara, whom I also embrace in what I hope comes across as a big-sisterly way, seizing their narrow, elegant shoulders, repeating, "Promise, promise you'll text me when you're home safe?" and they say they will.

At my Tube stop, I wait for the lift up to ground level behind a crowd heaving with the same intent, and somehow miss out on two separate loads before I manage to get inside. At the entrance to the station, passing through a quiet, hard-hatted cluster of men ready to begin their night's work underground, I am briefly and passionately appalled that they have to wait for the straggling pub-dregs to leave before getting on with the vital task of keeping London running.

Breaking into a jog through the dark, my bags (always so many bags) lift and pound at my sides, while in my earphones an anthemic song swells, a favorite from years ago, when, fresh out of university and new to the city, all my burgeoning hope and ambition seemed totally reasonable and absolutely achievable.

Table for one

In the kitchen, I hack clumsy hunks from the block of cheddar I find in the fridge, then inspired by a craving for more salt and fat, smear each crumbling piece with lumps of peanut butter. Stuffing down my improvised dinner, I fix a solemn stare on my phone and wait to hear from my young colleagues, until it occurs to me that none of them have my number.

Cracks

"Has that crack always been there?" I run my eyes along the hairline streak bisecting our bedroom ceiling like lightning. It's barely visible, and the effort of tracking its path has the disturbing effect of watching it grow in real time.

"That's what you've been thinking about?" Luke, on top of me, says into my neck.

"I just noticed it now, this second," I say, squeezing him tight.

He flops over onto his back. "Show me." I point. "Yes, definitely. Or no, hang on. Maybe I'm thinking of the one on the landing."

"You mean the one on the stairs?"

"There's one on the stairs?"

"There's one on the landing?" I'm struck by a terrible thought. "Wait—do you think it's the buddleia? The roots—is this why we should have got rid of it?"

"We didn't get rid of it?" Luke asks, up on an elbow, brow pinched, tone sharp and disapproving. I feel like a child, a failure, an utter waste of space.

"Hold on. I made an *informed* decision not to." I look up again. "No, I'm pretty sure that's been there since we moved in," I say with more authority than I feel. "Let's keep an eye on it and get someone in to take a look if it gets worse. Okay?"

Luke looks at the crack and then at me. "If you say so," he replies.

Let it flow

Giving blood might well turn out to be the best thing I can do with my life. In which case, it's time to stop talking about it and start getting it out there.

Query

"I was wondering whether you'll be in on Saturday . . ."

"For another one of your visits, I suppose," says my doting grandmother.

Say it with flowers

Weighing up the pros and cons of this small, dusty plant versus that bunch of pink dahlias, I fast-forward a few days to the flowers dead and brown, and take the plastic pot to the counter.

"Isn't that thoughtful?"

In the dark hallway, Grandma turns it this way and that in both hands to examine the stubby growth from all angles.

"The lady in the shop said it wouldn't need much looking after: just stick it by a window and water when it's looking dry."

"Like me," she says, and I wonder if flowers would have been better after all.

Bag for life

"Tell me," says Grandma, now settled in the kitchen, pushing a mug in my direction, "whatever happened to that nice doctor you were seeing?"

"Luke? We're still together. Why do you ask?"

"Oh, I haven't seen him for a while; I suppose I assumed he'd left the scene. He didn't come to your grandfather's funeral, of course." She sniffs, picking at something on her skirt. "That was poor form, we thought."

I decide against prodding the hornets' nest "we."

"He was working. He sent you a card, remember? Saying how sorry he—"

"And what *about* a wedding, then?" she interrupts, as if returning to the main business from which I'd willfully put her off course.

"Luke and me? Not in the cards. It's not really us: all that fuss and expense."

"Mm." Grandma cocks her head. "I suppose if there aren't any children, there's no real rush. Besides, it keeps you on your toes."

"Well, ha, yes, but no, and, also, you know, if there *were* children, a wedding isn't . . ." I start again. "It's totally fine not to, for my generation." Her eyes slide down to my stomach, but I ward them off with folded arms. "Not that there are any children, yet. We're waiting until he's fully qualified." I hold the tea under my chin, bathing my face in its warm, wet breath. "I *think* that's what we've agreed," I say, more to myself than to Grandma.

From her throat comes a noise like a roosting pigeon. "Be careful, Claire."

"About what?"

"I'm sure it feels very free and New Agey living together like that, but these institutions exist for a reason. You're not getting any younger—you need to be sensible and think about it: two years down the line, no children, no marriage certificate or anything concrete to bind you together—what's to stop him taking a young Polish bride?"

"I don't know—love?" Grandma raises a come-off-it eyebrow. "We own a flat together: that's pretty concrete. Anyway, I don't think Luke would know where to start finding himself a 'young Polish bride.'"

She snorts. "He doesn't need to look; the place is crawling with them—hospitals are the worst. Attractive blond Poles everywhere he turns." She stabs a knobbly finger at me. "Wait'll you hear *this*: I read a piece in the paper saying *British employers* are having to learn Polish now because none of their staff understand them. Imagine!"

"Don't you think it's wonderful they'd go to that effort to communicate with their employees?"

She turns her face away for no other reason than to cast me a sidelong look. "And what about *your* job? Have you sorted that out at least?"

"Actually, oddly enough, I'm sort of back where I was. At the old place."

Grandma's eyes bug out as she swallows her tea. "No! They took you back? That was good of them."

"They *asked* me back, on a short-term contract, and I agreed. I'm freelancing really."

"Oh." She sits back in her chair. "Well, I suppose it's better than nothing."

"It's a good thing. The best of both worlds: I can make some money—quite good money, actually—while I figure things out."

She shakes her head. "You know, Claire . . . I don't know. I can't keep up. One minute you couldn't get out fast enough, the next you're back there and thrilled. Though I shouldn't be surprised—you were always this way, even as a very young child."

Leave it, I think.

"What way?" I say.

"Not *jittery* exactly." She screws her eyes shut and flutters her fingers. "Wait'll I think now. Fuh, fuh, fuh, it's an 'f,' I think."

"Flighty?" I hear myself saying. "Flaky? Fickle? Feckless?"

"No, no, none of those, no. *What* is the word? It's on the *tip* of my tongue. You know what I mean."

"Frivolous? Flibbertigibbet . . . y?"

"No!" She looks incredibly annoyed. "Fuh, fuh, not fanciful, not fickle . . . I suppose you *could* say flaky, but not quite—"

"Fearless?" I say, on the off-chance I've misread the signals and she's trying to pay me a compliment.

"No, that's a different sort of thing *entirely*."

"Finicky?"

"Yes! No! Nearly. It's coming to me." Her eyes spring open. "Kinky!"

"Kinky?"

"Kinky."

"Mm." I chew on the inside of my cheek. "Might you mean *kooky*?"

"No."

"Quirky might work too?" I try. "Though it's a bit, you know, patronizing. Quirky: it irks me." I smile, pleased at the rhyme, but it fails to register across the table.

"Kinky. The word is kinky." Her chin snaps to her chest with satisfaction. "Such a funny, *kinky* thing you were—and you really haven't changed at all," she says almost fondly, "except you've lost the weight, of course." She reaches for the cookie tin and twists the lid, lost in thought. "A lot of women lose their looks with the pounds, but if anything, yours have improved. It's aged you, perhaps, but on balance it's worth it." She pops the lid and wedges a chocolate-chip cookie between her teeth. "Suppose you won't be wanting one of these," she says, crunching down, crumbs flying.

———

Another cup of tea in and Grandma's really found her stride: arms akimbo and eyes gleaming. I haven't seen her this way since well before Gum died. She looks ten years younger.

". . . and he pushed in front of me as if he was royalty! I'd say he thought he *was*, mind you—they have a tendency to make these grandiose claims: king or prince of such-and-such a . . . tribe? The same thing happened to Pauline, you know."

"Someone cut in line at the grocery store?"

"Oh, you're being *purposefully* difficult. It was the drugstore, and *her* fellow was making a big song and dance about something or other, so the cashier had to call security—you know the way they get very aggressive—"

"No, I do *not* know, nor do I like where I think this is heading."

"Well, neither do I, Claire. It's a disgrace. The government needs to start clamping down. So much talk, yet in they flood. Your mother agrees, that I know. What's the matter with you?"

"Where to begin," I say thickly to the flesh of my palms.

As I'm preparing to leave, Grandma disappears, and returns with a heavy-looking bag for life. Attached is a sticker bearing my name, biroed in wobbly capitals.

"Here." The contents clank as she hands it over.

I look inside and then at her. "Do you want me to . . . clean it?"

"You can do whatever you wish. I've done one for each of the grandchildren."

"One . . . ?"

"Bag of wedding silver. Stuart got the tea set, being the eldest, but"—she takes my free hand and jogs it up and down—"you got the candlesticks; I thought you'd like those."

"I do, very much, but won't you miss all this stuff?"

"I'm too old to entertain now; you young ones will get much more use out of it. I was going to give it to you when you got married, but all *my* grandchildren are far too modern to bother with such tedious tradition, so I thought I should do it while I'm still here, to avoid any bickering over my dead body!"

"Okay. Well. I'm not sure what to say to that."

" 'Thank you, Grandma, for all this lovely silver'?" she suggests.

"Thank you, Grandma," I say, leaving it there.

"Crystal next time!" she calls as I walk down the drive, flapping both hands above her head in farewell.

Clarification

At home, I clean the silver, the first time I have done this since I was small, when my mother lighted upon child labor as a means of keeping me entertained during the school holidays. I loved the ritual of it: laying everything out on a towel, and gently buffing with greasy polish and soft cloths to transform the murky, finger-smudged pieces into gleaming treasure. Mum would let me do her wedding rings too, and back on her hand, they looked foreign and bright, and I'd resolve to monitor their reversion to dullness (a vigil that never lasted beyond that same day).

"How was Grandma's?" asks Luke when he gets home. "Did you *rob* her?"

"She's off-loading my inheritance early," I say, "starting with the precious metals."

"And what," says Luke, picking up a tiny, hollowed-out oblong with clawed feet, "might this fellow be?"

"That item is, quite obviously, a very fine example of the classic . . . mustard bath? And this is the mustard-bath ladle." I place a tiny silver spoon on his palm and start to rub a tankard. "It's technically 'wedding silver,' but she's given up on us ever getting married. She is onto you, my friend."

Luke laughs. "This should be good."

"She knows all about your plan to wait till you're fully quali-fied, then leave me for a twenty-year-old Polish nurse."

"Busted," says Luke. "What did you say to that?"

"What is there to say? We're happy how things are. We don't need to get married."

"Oh. Okay."

"Is that not how it is?"

Luke shrugs. "That's how you feel, is it?"

"I thought we both did. If it isn't, we should talk about it."

"Your plan sounds fine."

"It's not *my plan*. It's my understanding of our situation. If you think differently—"

"You don't need to shout."

"I'm not shouting." (I'm really not.) "I'm just trying to establish where you stand." I go hard at a dark spot on the tankard handle that won't budge.

"Let me put it this way," he says. "I'm not in any *rush*, but I wouldn't rule it out."

"Neither would I! I don't think we have."

"But it sounds like you can take it or leave it?"

"Only because I thought *you* didn't care either way," I say. He moves behind me, but I can still see him: many tiny Lukes re-flected in my silver empire. "I'm not sitting around waiting for you to propose, if that's what you're asking."

"You could propose too, you know," he says.

"Hang on, let's back up a bit: *you're* the one who's always said it's just a bit of paper, that our commitment to each other is what counts. You already know this is it for me, love-wise. You are, I mean."

"So you're saying you *wouldn't* ever propose?" he asks.

"Why does one of us have to? We could decide together. Like equals."

"All right, yeah," he says. Then quickly adds, "Let's revisit this at some point in the future. Two years? No—three?"

I clap my hands. "Oh, *Luke*! We're engaged to be engaged! Grandma is going to be so thrilled to hear this! Kidding, kidding, kidding," I say, watching multiples of his shoulders visibly tense, and then relax in miniature.

Skin

"Did you *want* any help?" asks a white-coated, broad-bosomed lady, topped by a large, flawless bun. Her makeup is dense and meticulous, her scent powerfully sweet. I grimace no, and attend to the glowing bank of products, squinting the way I've seen shrewd consumers do. "Maybe there was something in particular you were after?" she wonders aloud.

"I'm fine, really, thank you," I say, but now it's as though all that censored helpfulness is bubbling away like toxic waste, and unable to bear it, I cave and confess. "Well, I was thinking about looking at maybe buying some anti-aging cream."

"Certainly," she says. "What was it you had in mind?"

"Um. Anti-aging cream? I don't . . . know how else to say it."

With a pleasant sigh, she rattles through the options, batting densely frosted lashes with impressive speed: "Day cream, night cream, serum, double serum, extra-firming, tinted?"

"Right. Oh. I see. Yes. I wanted, well, wondered, really, what would *you* recommend?" I jut my chin forward and smooth my brow, giving her ample opportunity to praise my skin, its youth and dewy suppleness. Instead, with Mary Poppins-ish efficiency, she marshals a crowd of tubes and pots on the counter.

"Six separate items?" I press the pads of my fingertips under-

neath my eyes. My mouth hangs open as I consider my complex-
ion in the magnifying mirror: a vast, banal iteration of *The Scream*.
"The eyes are that bad? They need their own special one?"

She beams. "It really is a super gel. It'll do wonders for the issues
you have here"—she waves an illustrative pinkie—"and here"—
the other pinkie appears; together they sweep in broad arcs. "I'd
recommend you also think very seriously about the daily youth-
renewal moisturizer. I guarantee you the years will tumble away."

Miracles do happen

It worked! I'm fourteen again! The cream has awakened a long-
dormant gland, restoring my chin, my forehead, my nose, my
cheeks to adolescence in all its greasy, pimpled glory.

Strategy

Geri's invited me to join today's breakfast strategy meeting. I
wanted to decline, but it seemed a bit rude—plus there's free fruit
and pastries.

Jonathan, sitting at Geri's right hand, looks triumphantly re-
sentful, as though my presence is the last bit of proof he needed
that I'm here to pry my job from his efficient, clammy grasp. But
he needn't worry about me, unless he wants a chocolate croissant:
there's only one left, and I plan to make it mine.

Awkward

Now we're into the thick of the general meeting, and I've fallen
into my old waking nightmare: that it will never end and I'll be
stuck in here forever.

Bea keeps making faces at me, and I'm struggling to find an expression that humors her without alienating everyone else. She's also brought her phone in—which isn't allowed, but no one says anything—and every so often she takes a break from texting to pipe up with off-topic ideas.

"My mate Angus is an indie coffee supplier: we should use him for the office. That stuff is—no offense—crap," she says, when someone asks her to pass the French press. "He only does one blend, but it's perfect. He's a coffee prodigy."

"Ooh," says one of the graduate girls, "I think I read about him in *Metro*. He's hot!"

"Give his details to Claire," says Geri, trying to wrest things back on track. In addition to my freelance duties, I seem to have become the intern's PA. I write *Coffee* on my notepad.

Bea leans over. "And what about getting a fruit crate delivered? My god-sister owns an organic orchard in Somerset. You can get apples and . . . other fruits. Whatever's in season. Plums?"

"What's a 'god-sister'?" asks Jonathan.

"Claire, make a note," says Geri, nodding at my pad.

Fruit crate, I write. *God-sister. Plums?*

"Okay, so! Accounts! Over to Justin, please, with the figures from the second quarter." Geri passes a sheaf of spreadsheets around. I don't bother taking one: I never got to grips with the accounts bit, and certainly don't plan to start engaging now.

"I think we should order the Bumper Scrumper box." Bea passes her phone to Geri, who flashes a smile of acknowledgment, and dispatches it immediately back down the table. "Shall I just order it now," says Bea, "while I've got all the information here?" She turns to Justin the accountant with an outstretched palm. "Jasper, please may I have the credit card?"

He looks at her, appalled.

"Doesn't 'scrumping' mean 'stealing'?" I say, to try and defuse the swelling tension.

"Bea, my love," says Geri, "Claire's going to look into it *after* the meeting and we'll discuss and come back to you later, okay?" The phone comes whizzing down the table to me.

I write, *Bumper Scrumper,* and note the cost, which justifies the "scrumper" bit: twenty pounds for "an average of 15 apples" is pure daylight robbery.

"Look! The farm's called B. Organic," says Bea.

"Take it away, please, Justin!" says Geri.

Justin clears his throat.

"It's a pun, like as in 'be organic.' But also, guess what the B is short for? Claire," Bea persists in a stage whisper.

I shake my head—*Shut up*—but she takes it to mean *I give up.*

She points to herself, and beams. "B-E-A."

"Column one: you'll notice gross profit is down on the last quarter," Justin begins, glaring at *me,* which is preposterously unjust.

"Isn't that cool?" says Bea, and I give her a desperate thumbs-up.

"Claire, *please,*" says Geri. "*Sorry,* Justin, go ahead."

At her side, Jonathan's printout rises too late to disguise his smirking mouth.

Experience

This lunchtime crowd of suited male youngsters teeming from the entrance of my bank's HQ had better be schoolchildren on a field trip. I may not be sitting on a vast fortune, but I do think it's fair to expect that the people entrusted with my entire worldly savings are old enough to, at the very least, shave.

Love in the city

Today it seems as though every person I pass is trying to lock eyes with every person they pass, in the hope they'll recognize the One among the masses; also, that the One will recognize them too.

Baby talk

In a new bar with a halfhearted and confused theme (light-up globes, old wooden tennis racquets, oversize keys) comes bottle after bottle after bottle of white wine, which started off sour and stringent but has developed a mellow pineapple-ish flavor in the drinking. The conversation has tacked this way and that, growing more confessional as sobriety ebbs.

"I'll tell if you do," Rachel says.

"No way!" says Lauren. "All right, fuck it. Fifty."

"As in fifty *thousand*?" I clatter my glass down with more force than intended, soaking both hands and cuffs with wine. To save money, I skipped dinner and the inevitable consequences are now taking their toll. "As in that's what you, personally, earn: fifty thousand pounds. To yourself, every year. *Wow*."

Lauren clarifies, "Before tax. What, does that seem a lot to you?"

"Are you kidding? Why? What do you make?" I ask Rachel.

She twirls her glass by the stem. "Not as much. Forty-seven."

I wring my hands to dry them. "Forty-seven!" My voice, shrill with shock, can't get any higher.

"I earn way less than my school friends, though," she adds. "They're all making sixty, seventy plus. Actually, Fran's raking in seventy, aren't you?"

Fran nods, blushes, sheepish.

"I don't want to say what I was making," I say. "Where did I go so wrong?" I turn to Lauren. "I thought you got paid a pittance like me. When did *you* start raking in the big bucks?"

"I suppose I just stuck around long enough. Don't get me wrong—I don't love it there, but it's nice to know these years haven't been wasted, that I'm actually worth something tangible. Does that make sense?"

Later (one bottle, two, whatever: keeping track is *pointless* and *boring*) the talk turns, inevitably, to babies.

"Rob and I are trying," Lauren says and clamps a hand to her mouth. "I shouldn't have said that. We're not meant to be telling anyone!" she squeaks through her fingers.

I dutifully join the oh-my-God chorus, then Fran leans in. "So are we! I'm not meant to tell anyone either, but"—she clutches fingers with me and Rachel—"I have to tell my girls!"

There follows an onslaught: Since when? How often? Was it weird the first time? How did you know you were ready? et cetera. It's like virginity all over again; now, as then, I have little to contribute. I don't even know the right questions to ask.

"You're very quiet, Claire," says Rachel. "If you weren't knocking back the wine, I'd wonder if you were already on the way. When do you think you and Luke will? This could be the perfect time without a job to worry about, no?"

"Except a job is *precisely* what I'm worried about."

"Okay, so here's what you should do: get a job in management consultancy, put in a year or two max, then get pregnant just in time to enjoy your corporate maternity package. Problem solved!" says Fran.

"How does that solve my problem? The whole *point* is that I want to find a job that *means* something—and please, before anyone says anything, I know motherhood is meaningful, and I know it's a job. But is the best use of my skills and time really producing another human who will only grow up to disappoint me the way I've clearly disappointed my parents? Aren't there enough *people* already?" I exhale and cover one eye with one hand, stare at the table, dab at stray grains of salt with the other. "Oh God, I've totally hijacked this. Sorry, sorry, I think it's lovely you're ready to start families, honestly. And I don't *not want* to have children. I just . . ." I take a few breaths. "How can I bring another life into the world when I don't know what I'm doing with my own?"

"Babe," breathes Lauren.

"Anyway, I'm barren."

"Oh *what*?" says Fran. "Shit, sorry. We didn't know."

"Well, not officially, but I *know*. You know? Isn't it *exactly* the sort of thing I'd be?"

Someone puts their hand on mine, strokes the back with their thumb.

"We love you, Claire. We're here for you—you know that," says Fran, as more hands pile on.

I feel ludicrous, like a sad Disney princess consoled by a coterie of cheerful woodland fauna.

"So, to sum up: babies! Yay!" I shake my fists by my shoulders and look up to a trio of lopsided smiles: everyone's too far gone to disguise their concern. "Hey! What are you all still *doing* here? Go on, go home and get procreating!"

Sisterhood

Perhaps these two beautiful Italian women chatting with their backs against the toilet mirrors would be so kind as to step aside so that the less naturally fortunate among us might have a chance to disguise our many flaws.

Boy

Now all my friends have left, but I'm still here and have somehow slipstreamed into a conversation with a young man, a poet and play-wright. (He tutors wealthy children for money.) He is twenty-three years old, with eyes so big and intense I can hardly bring myself to meet them, and a name I can't get right, no matter how many times he tells me—Calum or Caleb or Conrad; it becomes a running joke in which he keeps changing it to confuse me. He's earnest, idealistic, and his hair curls perfectly, as though for me alone, and he's listening to everything I say with something that feels close to *awe*, as though he's never met anyone like me before; and he laughs at all my jokes with his head thrown back so that I can see the baby-pink ripple of his palate, and he touches my shoulder, my elbow and (once) the small of my back with feather-light fingertips—as if he wasn't really touching me at all, but rather wanted to show the impulse was there, one I understand because I've felt it too; not *romantic*, of course, because I have Luke, who I love and who I only haven't mentioned because it simply, honestly hasn't come up, nothing more sinister, however, being equally honest, there is nonetheless an attraction in the purely *scientific* sense of two dis-crete entities drawn together; but when he mentions a film by a di-rector from Hong Kong, a film Luke made me watch, about yearning and forbidden love, I go, "Oh! That's my—" and I'm about to confess, about to say *boyfriend's favorite film*, but I so don't want this boy's attention to curdle, because when do I ever get to feel this good, this charismatic and this *un-monstrous*? So, I say like a traitor, "That's *my* favorite film," though I found it in truth a little slow, but no, credit where it's due, still beautiful; and right now I love that he loves it. I love that he loves it more than I care that Luke loves it, because this boy is *new* and full of possibility, he is a poet who thinks I am "rare" (it glows like a coal in the pit of my stomach), and he thinks I *know* things, such as WHO I AM and WHAT I WANT, whereas Luke, good, old, devoted Luke, knows I don't know anything, and not only that, he also knows all my faults and bad habits—he has seen me on the toilet, seen me squeezing my pores at the mirror, kissed me despite putrid morning breath, *made love* to me despite all the horrors of my body, heard me say mean, bitter things about people, about himself, to his *face* for nothing, less than nothing—for being supportive, patient, constant, *too* loving, *too* accepting; for simply sticking with me even when he knows what a hollow person I am, and, "Um . . ." I'm saying to the boy, daring to look into those huge bovine eyes, to steady myself with a hand on his shoulder, "um, just . . . I'll be . . . Give me one minute," and then I get out of there, plowing through bodies, and tumble into the first taxi I can find, my insides humming, disappointed but grateful, ultimately, that I never did get a proper handle on his name, so that I can't spend tomorrow, or next week, or next month Googling him and in turmoil about what might have been.

Taking advantage

"Good morning! Seemed you had fun last night."

"I did," I say, struggling for specifics, beyond the where and the who (noisy bar, girlfriends). "Sorry I was home later than I said."

"You certainly made waiting up worth my while," Luke says, grinning.

"Shit." I throw my arm across my eyes. "I'm really sorry."

"I hope you're not," says Luke. "I was on *fire*. 'Best ever': that's a direct quote. You do remember the excellent sex, don't you?"

I can't tell whether he is having me on and look at the bin for a condom wrapper. The bin isn't in the corner where it should be, but by the bed—no wrapper and, mercifully, no vomit.

"I'm not falling for that," I say.

"Which part? Best ever, or that it happened at all?"

I nod at the bin. "Where's the condom wrapper, then?"

He freezes. "Claire, are you kidding me? You said you were ready to stop using protection—in fact, you *insisted* that we didn't! Please tell me you weren't so drunk you can't remember making that quite-major life decision."

Everything is tingling and not in a good way. "Yeah, no, of course I was *kidding*. That was a *joke*. Of *course* I remember." But now he's openly laughing, so I whomp him with my pillow. "You're such a dick! Don't *do* that!"

"Sorry, sorry, that was mean," he admits.

"Ugh. I must have been in a complete state."

He laughs. "Are you going to tell me the great epiphany now?"

"The great epiphany . . . Is this another joke?"

"You said you'd understood something fundamental about life, but when I asked you to tell me what it was, you wouldn't."

"'Couldn't' might be more accurate," I say. Now that he's mentioned it, this does sound awfully familiar. I *do* recall a state of vivid revelation, a sense that the fabric of the world had burst open and exposed some essential truth about human existence. That, I do remember.

"What a tragedy," I say bravely, "to have come so close to the meaning of life and yet have nothing to show for it."

"We are indeed much the poorer," agrees Luke, nuzzling my shoulder.

Moderation

I wish I liked myself a bit more, and wine more than a bit less.

Spinning

Dismounting the exercise bike post-class, heaving and dizzy, I vow to myself it's the last one I'll take. All this energy into going nowhere is starting to take its toll.

6

Fast

I get an email from Sarah at work: *Can you meet tonight?*

Everything OK??? I ask, but she only confirms the time and place, and for the rest of the afternoon I speculate about what could possibly be wrong. Paddy's moving out, he's seeing someone else; she's pregnant; one of her parents is gravely ill . . .

She's already at the bar when I get there, sipping Prosecco. She slides a glass across to me as I sit down, and I strike *pregnant* from my mental list.

"How are you?" she asks.

"How are *you*? Are we celebrating? Have you got a new job?"

She holds up her left hand, where a diamond ring now sits.

I smile, shaking my head. "What?"

"What do you think?"

"You're engaged?"

"I'm engaged!"

"To Paddy?"

"Of course!"

"Oh my God!"

"I know!"

"Oh my God!"

"Yeah!"

"Oh my God." I say it more quietly this time, glass at my lips. Her forehead wrinkles a little. "And, of course, congratulations!" We both look at the ring, the way it glitters when she moves.

"What do you think?" She bites her lip.

I take her hand. "It's beautiful."

She smiles. "About the whole thing. I thought you might be a bit . . . unenthused."

"What? No! I *love* Paddy!" I say with maybe too much zeal.

"I know *that*," says Sarah. "I was worried you'd think less of me or something. Because you're anti-marriage."

"I'm not anti-marriage. Why do people think that?"

"Not anti. But you can take it or leave it."

"I mean, it's *fast*," I say.

She looks confused. "We've been living together a couple of months already, and going out for nearly a year."

"Seven months," I correct her. "It's not that long."

"My parents got engaged after two weeks. Seven months isn't fast. Okay, it's not seven *years*, but I don't want to wait seven years before I get married." She chips at a drip of wax on the table, eyes locked on the task. I wonder if she's referring to the fact Luke and I have been together for seven years.

"I don't know." I take a long sip of Prosecco. "It's just happened a bit sooner than I expected, that's all. I think it's great—if it's what you want."

"It is!" She looks like she might cry. "You're the first person I've told. Not even my mum knows yet."

I seize her arm. "I'm so happy for you, Sarah, really and truly—

I'm sorry, I needed a moment to catch up. Just because *I* wasn't mentally prepared for this doesn't mean *you* aren't. Please tell me everything: how did he propose?"

She blots her nose elegantly with the back of her ring hand as she relays the details. The diamond goes berserk in the candlelight. ". . . Then he came out with this incredible, emotional speech—about me and how he's finally found his soul mate . . . Honestly, I can't do it justice, but we were both in floods of tears by the end of it."

"That sounds amazing," I murmur, and I *am* amazed, not only that he's capable of such moving rhetoric, but also that he's comfortable pouring out so much feeling, unbridled. I feel a newfound admiration for him.

"And yeah, I *was* a bit surprised when he asked, but it feels . . . It does—it just feels right."

"Maybe I shouldn't say this"—I knock back the rest of my Prosecco, and flag down the waitress for another round—"or maybe I should wait until we've had a few more drinks, but what the hell."

"Go on . . ."

"Early on, I had a few reservations about Paddy." To be fair to my acting ability, this does seem like news to Sarah. "In the beginning."

"Why? What's wrong with him?"

"This is my point: I don't even remember!" I try to silence the voice in my head, reeling them off without any difficulty: *monosyllabic, sullen, boring* . . . "You're my best friend: any guy you ended up with was going to have a hard time impressing me. But the *moment* I saw how important he was to you, I was there: on board, one hundred percent. So what I'm getting at is, if Paddy ever needs anything—and I mean *anything*—a kidney?" I segue into a gruff mobster voice, pointing a thumb to my chest. "You send him over to Mama. Ya hear me?"

"I hear you," says Sarah, looking relieved. "Thank you, that honestly means a lot."

God, I hope Paddy looks after his kidneys.

Checking in

It's Saturday, Luke's working, and I'm home alone trying to advance my career plans. I've designed a new color-coded spreadsheet delineating companies to target, application deadlines and training programs that might be of interest. My formatting skills, though, are not up to scratch and I've spent much of the morning resizing columns and truncating text to fit inside boxes that simply won't expand, for all the troubleshooting solutions I've tried.

I scroll through my phone and realize I haven't been in touch with my parents for a while. Calling them feels a bit much, too involved, given I haven't spoken aloud yet today, so I fire off a text instead.

> Hi, Dad. How are you both? Any news re: work? Hope all OK. C xxx

> No.

> No = no news? Everything OK? xxxxx

> Fine claire just in town having a muffin witH MUM X

> Lovely. Enjoy. Say hi to Mum. x

> OK WILL DO TAKE CARE DAD

Explode/implode

"What are you watching?" Luke asks, taking off his coat.

"It's amazing," I say. "You're just in time. Look." On the screen, a man in white coveralls makes careful incisions in the belly of a beached sperm-whale carcass. "Wait. It gets really good."

"Where is this?" Luke asks.

"Not important! Faroe Islands, I think. Okay, watch this—are you watching?"

"I'm watching!"

The whale explodes, guts and blood flying into the air, zipping many meters along the decking before slamming to a stop against a wall. The jumpsuit guy, nearly knocked off his feet by the force of the gush, scuttles quickly, comically out of shot.

"Did you hear the sound?" I say. "The way it pops! The gush! Let's watch it again." I hit "replay." The clip is prefaced by an advert for a honeymoon cruise package—an algorithmic joke?—and I recite with the voice-over in perfect sync, "Sail off into *your* happily ever after with Sunset Voyages—"

"How many times have you watched this?" interrupts Luke. He moves around the kitchen, opening cabinet doors.

"Not nearly enough. Here we go: are you ready?"

From the fridge he takes the milk and fills a glass by the sink.

I press "pause." "You don't want to watch it again?"

He lifts his eyebrows as he drinks, and the glass clinks quietly against his teeth. When he's finished, he ducks his head, slightly out of breath. "I've been dealing with blood all day. How has yours been? Did you not even get *dressed*?" A frill of milk runs along his top lip.

I return to the screen and click "play": pop, gush, scuttle.

"Imagine the pressure in there!"

"So what do you want to do tonight? DVD? If your appetite for quality film hasn't been sated already . . ." Luke tips his head toward the screen.

"Why are you making me feel bad?"

"How am I making you feel bad?"

"Never mind," I say quickly; but his hackles are up.

"No, go on—what did I do?"

"Don't be so defensive. God!" I say. He strides to the fridge and slings the milk back inside. "Maybe you should cool off while you're there. Long day, was it?" The door thunks shut and the fridge judders.

"You're going to have to help me out here."

I enumerate, pointing a thumb at him. "Try: you making snide, unhelpful remarks about me not 'even' getting dressed on a *Saturday*, when I've been working all week." Next comes a forefinger. "And hassling me for taking a two-minute break from my—really quite stressful—job hunt to watch a natural *spectacle*, which you seem bizarrely intent on pretending not to find interesting even though fourteen million"—I check the views count—"Okay, but still, one point four million hits would beg to differ."

"As *if* two minutes," he mutters.

"What was that? Another snide remark? Ten minutes, then. Fine, fifteen minutes. Happy?"

Luke steps behind me and massages my shoulders. "I'm really happy with you," he says in the joke-sappy voice we sometimes deploy when things are getting too heated; on this occasion, however, he couldn't have made a worse call.

"Ow!" I say, shucking him off.

For a long time neither of us says anything.

"You have no idea," I say finally. "You get to wake up every morning and go and do something you love, which also, conveniently, happens to be one of the most worthwhile things you could do in the world. How can I *possibly* compete?"

"You don't need to compete! This is a *relationship*." He pulls out the chair next to me, sits and takes my hand like the doctor he is. "We're a team."

"Right, and I'm the dead weight dragging you down."

"I don't like hearing you talk like this." He grazes my knuckles with his lips.

"Sorry," I say. "Sorry if you don't *like* it. Sorry if I *upset* you."

Luke drops my hand and palms his kneecaps. "Whatever. I'm going to take a shower. I don't know why you're being such a—" He stops.

"Such a what?" I say. "Say it. Such a what?"

"It's not worth it. I'll let you get back to your precious sperm whale." He stands up. At the door, he places his hands either side of the doorframe. "I've been nothing but supportive of whatever this thing you're going through even is."

"Yeah, and it's so *annoying*! Stop being so *nice* all the time! You can't bring yourself to call me a bitch when I'm being a horrible bitch to you! It's really so fucking boring!"

"I'm taking a shower."

"You already *said*." The door slams. "And you've got a milk mustache!" The shower powers on.

"What are you looking at?" I say to my unhappy face, glowering in the sleeping laptop screen.

Standardization

I take a walk to get some air and some perspective (and maybe, if I'm being totally honest, so Luke might worry, thus dissipating the storm of ill will I've gone and stirred up in the flat). But all I can think is, *Why* don't they make these concrete slabs stride-sized? Really, how hard can it be?

Empty

I skulk past our flat a few times, hoping to see Luke keeping an anxious lookout, but the front-room windows are empty and dark: blank as when we moved in five years ago. Buying the place had felt impulsive and exciting, the first truly proper grown-up thing we'd done together; but the process quickly declined into a bitter slog, with the seller growing increasingly belligerent for reasons that were never really made clear.

On the day we got the keys, it was pouring with rain, and after heaving all our boxes up two flights of stairs we finally closed the door behind us. I flicked on the light switch, only to discover that in a final act of malice, the seller had taken every last fixture and fitting not specifically itemized in the contract: doorknobs, cabinet and drawer handles, picture hooks, towel rings, toilet-paper holder and—crucially in that moment—lightbulbs. Worse still was the bleak detritus left behind: a ceramic teddy bear holding a heart emblazoned with "I LOVE YOU," filthy rags and twisted bedsheets, broken wind chimes and a single, fetid tennis shoe.

"Oh shit." Luke sank onto a box. "What have we done?"

"It isn't so bad," I said. "We just need to clean and unpack. Once our stuff's in, it'll begin to feel like ours."

"I thought it would look bigger with nothing in it. What were we thinking?" He went through to the kitchen. "We spent our life savings on this. I spent my *grandparents'* life savings on this." He walked out, shaking his head, and wandered up to the bathroom and the bedroom, taking a call from his parents.

"Yeah, we're in . . . No, it's . . . fine . . . It's great . . ." His voice echoed through the naked rooms, nothing at all to absorb his disappointment.

I wanted to cry: not because it was a shithole, but because he didn't seem to get that it was *our* shithole. Instead, I opened a box marked ESSENTIALS and—deciding against the bottle of warm, cheap-looking Chardonnay the real estate agent had shoved ungraciously into my hand along with the keys that morning—retrieved mugs, kettle, teabags, cookies and some non-dairy creamers I'd pocketed from the McDonald's a few doors down. When I went to find Luke, he was staring at the black street, where a succession of flashing police cars screamed past.

"I promise, promise, promise we'll make it nice," I said, handing him a hot mug and a chocolate cookie.

He held the tea with one hand and put the other arm around me, dunking the cookie so I was in a sort of headlock.

"I *guess*," he said, "you already are."

Confrontation

When it starts to get dark, I head for home.

"Hi," I say in a small voice at the door—so small I think Luke hasn't heard me. "Hi?" I try, a little louder.

"What do you want?" comes Luke's voice from the living-room gloom, where he sits in silhouette, channel-surfing on mute.

"To say I'm sorry." There's a long pause. On the screen, a cartoon's playing, one of the old Warner Bros. ones with Porky the Pig. Watching him trotting around, I feel the same sickly rise of boredom I used to get as a kid, in that impossibly wide, drab space between Saturday afternoon and Saturday night, when my parents would take to their bed for "a nap," which of course, it suddenly occurs to me now, with head-smacking clarity, was obviously a euphemism for *sex*, leaving me orphaned downstairs with these hectic critters for guardians.

Luke's silhouette breaks its silence. "You don't seem to realize there's a limit to how much a person can take. Sometimes it feels as if your sole aim in my life is to find the line and piss all over it."

I fight the overwhelming impulse to point out that I can't be both unaware of the limit *and* make finding it my sole aim.

"While I wouldn't necessarily endorse that assertion or . . . image," I say, choosing my words with tremendous care, "I will concede I was being pretty awful earlier." Luke's silhouette doesn't move. "For which, again, my most 'eartfelt apologies, sir."

"Titchy Pip isn't going to get you out of this," he says, and I know I'm in trouble: in happier times, Luke loves my Victorian street-urchin character, a plucky young shoeshine with nothing to 'is name but a tin o' boot polish and a pocketful o' dreams.

I drop the voice. "Seriously, I was horrible and I apologize. Though I would like to say, both for the record and in my own defense, that you were being quite mean."

"Well, *I* will concede it's a shame you felt that way, but I really, definitely wasn't."

"Okay, but . . . what I'm saying is that you *were*."

"I don't understand how you can say that when it's simply not true."

"Well," I explain in my most patient, helpful voice, "because it's possible to *be* mean without *meaning* to be."

"Are you actually sorry? It sounds to me like you might be trying to score points with twisted logic."

"I don't want to score any points. I just wanted to let you know my experience."

"Well, now you have."

"Luke. I really am sorry. I don't know what's wrong with me. It hasn't been a good day. I spent hours and hours staring at the computer, and it just felt like all these months in a microcosm, doing hundreds of aimless searches based on stupid, vague ideas I have about what might be a meaningful, or even just nice, way to spend my days. I wasted a full morning on an application to be a TV script editor: I've never seen a TV script! I just like watching TV! But I went through all the criteria, kidding myself that I could make my skills sound relevant, and then as soon as I read over what I'd written, I realized how deluded I sounded. *Then* I texted my parents to say, 'Hi. How are you guys?' and my dad basically replied saying, 'Please let us enjoy our muffin in peace.'"

"Muffin?" says Luke.

Encouraged, I take a step toward him. "They were in Starbucks. You know they go every Saturday afternoon as a treat for a latte and half a muffin each?"

"I didn't know. That's cute."

"It's weird hearing you talk without being able to see your face. You look like those protected witnesses on the news. One who's in hiding from his evil girlfriend." Luke's silhouette-head moves very slightly and I think (hope) he is smiling. "So what's the verdict: do you still hate me?" I say.

"No, I suppose I don't totally hate you," he says, and his silhouette-arm rises up, and his silhouette-fingers beckon me under.

We lie pressed together like sardines on the sofa, watching the still-muted TV and playing Guess What the Advert Is For.

"Car! Honda! Ford! Mazda! Nissan! Peugeot! Yes!" shouts Luke.

"That's not how it works!" I object. "You can't list every single brand of a thing to cover all the bases. I can't hear myself think!"

"Uh, the game is the first person to say the right answer. I didn't hear *you* saying the right answer, so I make it one-zero to me."

"It should be your *first* answer," I say, then shout at the screen, "Stella Artois! No, Nastro Azzurro! I meant Nastro Azzurro!"

"Nastro Azzurro," says Luke, quick as a flash just after me. "Oh, bad luck. Now it's two-zero to the Duuuuuuke!" His arms are up, victorious antlers.

"I said it first!"

"No, you said Stella Artois first. Don't come crying to me: it was your idea to do first answers."

"We hadn't started that new rule yet," I say. "I didn't think you even heard me. You didn't formally agree to the change. There have to be rules about rule changes. We need to have a vote. Otherwise this whole thing's a farce."

If I'm going down, I'm going down fighting.

Luke flicks the channel to a program where a man and a woman are watching TV, a wildlife program. A zebra is being busily savaged by a pride of lions.

"Did you know," I say, "that the reason so many people on TV watch wildlife shows on *their* TV is because it's stock footage and there's no copyright fee?"

"Oh. That's disappointing," says Luke. "I always assumed it was meant to be some commentary on what's going on with the characters. I thought I was quite clever for getting that."

I reach up and cup his chin with my palm. "You're too clever for all of them. Turns out they're just a bunch of cheapskates."

"Where do you *find* all this information?" he murmurs in wonder.

"I honestly think it finds me."

Piqued

First thing in the morning, I turn on the radio.

"And finally, there's no reason on earth," a chipper fellow is concluding, "why it can't play you a tune, for example, or give you directions, or tell you the weather. It is, I would hasten to add, egg-shaped and very approachable."

"What is?" I ask aloud, but it's too late, and now I'll never know.

Inconsistency

This American gent who only moments ago showed such concern that he accidentally cut in front of me waiting for coffee displays none of the same as he barges past now to swipe the last free table.

Luke

The way everything curls as he sleeps: fists, spine, eyelashes.

Last-chance saloon

In a wine bar, waiting for Rachel, whose lateness has just migrated from acceptable to rude, I tune in to a neighboring date for diversion. A furtive look puts the woman at mid-to-late thirties, while her companion's back, other than being impressively broad, gives away nothing, including his apparently monosyllabic replies.

"Do you like classical music?" she asks.

"..."

"Do you like *music*?"

"..."

"Fair enough. What . . . films are you into?"

"..."

"Really? Well, do you like to read?"

". . ."

She scours the ceiling for inspiration. "What *do* you like, then?"

". . ."

"Oh. Right . . . Who do you support?"

". . ."

She's shaking her head. "Never heard of them." Her lips have disappeared. They leave, exchanging grimace-like smiles of resignation, just as Rachel finally appears.

"I'm so sorry I'm late," says Rachel. There's a deep stress-line between her eyes.

"What's wrong?" I ask, and she bursts into tears. The human rights lawyer she's been sporadically texting (and even more sporadically sleeping with) has finally put an end to things.

"He said, 'I don't think this is right for me anymore. I need some time to myself.' As if seeing me once every three weeks was too demanding."

I teeter perilously on my bar stool to embrace her. "I know it feels really shitty at the moment, but I think this is ultimately a good thing. It's so much better to have a clean break than to be embroiled for another six months or a year. Now you can focus on meeting someone worth your time and emotional energy."

"I really thought he *was*, though."

Coming from such an intelligent person, this strikes me as beyond ridiculous, but I proceed with caution.

"You just said you saw him once every three weeks."

"I know I always complained about him, but he could be so sweet: he cooked me shepherd's pie after I told him it was my favorite. And the last time I saw him, he said he thought I'd get on really well with his sister."

I try to look impressed by this gallantry.

"I honestly thought it was going somewhere. What if he *was* the One and now I've pushed him away and I'll be alone forever?"

I tell her there's no such thing as the One. I tell her it's a conspiracy, a myth peddled by the Big Three: Hollywood, the government and the free market.

"How do you explain you and Luke, then?"

"Look, let me put it this way," I say, "that was nothing more than pure luck and good timing. Luke's great, obviously, but believe me he is *far* from perfect—and I don't have to tell you I'm no picnic. There are a million little compromises involved every *single day*. Doesn't it seem too unlikely that there's only one person out of seven billion who's right for you? And if that were even true, what are the chances that *I*, of all people, have found mine?"

"Okay," says Rachel, "but you know I could say the same to you about a job."

"Well, that's a bit different—"

"How? You're always talking about finding the right thing. But who's to say there aren't five or twenty or fifty jobs you could love if you were just a bit more open-minded? Doesn't it seem equally unlikely that there's only one thing that's right for you and all the rest of us have found ours?"

"But . . . No. It's not . . . Okay. Maybe. Fine. Why don't we agree we both have a point?"

She holds out a hand, and we shake on it, firmly.

"Deal."

We leave after last orders, and at the bus stop just a few feet away, who do I see but the very same couple from the unsuccessful date, kissing with the fervor of a departing soldier and his sweetheart, while the night buses sweep up and down the wet roads.

Obsession, compulsion

Where? my scrabbling fingers scream into the gritty depths of my bag.

Same place, my phone, cool and oblong, answers, *as the last twenty-five times you checked.*

How the mighty fall

One tiny little error in judgment (the number of tissues you think you'll need) is all it takes to become who you thought you never would (the person hawking back phlegm on the bus).

Co-op/priorities

Seven different varieties of hummus; zero varieties of apple, lemon, carrot.

Mixed messages

I'm woken by Luke, propped on an elbow, singing "Happy Birthday" in creepy falsetto.

"Come and get me when you're done," I say, burrowing under the duvet.

He lingers on the last note, feeling for my hand, and presses a small wrapped cube into it.

"Ooh." I rip off the paper. "Earrings?" I guess.

"Not *ear*rings but . . ." he says as I lift the lid of the box, "*a ring!*"

"Oh!" I look at him then at it until it blurs.

"What?" he says. "Is it okay?"

I nod.

"Are you sure?"

The rapid nodding continues as I extract it from its little velvet bed and lay it flat on my palm.

"This is from the same place as Sarah's—I remembered you really liked hers. But obviously it's a different ring. Try it on."

"Obviously. Because Sarah's was an engagement ring." I slide it on. There's a pretty gold rose where the stone would be, were it an engagement ring.

"Exactly. The woman called this one a 'cocktail' ring? But I think that just means 'normal ring.'" I try to smile, but my bottom lip will not play ball. "So, to confirm: you do like it," he says.

"I really do." My shoulders are bunched around my ears; when I try to drag them down, they ping back up.

Luke crawls around on top of the covers so that he's kneeling in front of me. "And you definitely . . . don't . . . *want* . . . it . . . to be an engagement ring?"

"No! No. No, no, no." I turn my head slowly left to right, left to right. "No way. Not yet. We talked about this. You know I don't."

"Do I?" Luke takes my head in his hands. "Claire, look at me." I open my eyes. "Are you crying?"

"I always cry on my birthday; it's a tradition. I was *born* crying: ask my mother."

Mixed messages II

The bell goes and I open the door to see the postman, already re-treating.

"Hey! Hello?" I call, and he turns, seeming astonished and ir-ritated that ringing the bell has resulted in someone opening the door. In his personal life, he might be a biker: his ears, eyebrows and abundant beard are spiked with piercings, and he's accessorized his uniform with a paisley bandana that no one could call regulation. He hands over a huge pink envelope, far too big to fit through the letter flap.

"You know, some people have mobility issues," I say. "You should wait a bit longer before assuming no one's in."

He sighs. "Sorry?"

"Some people can't get to the door that fast," I say slowly, enunciating carefully. "The elderly, for one. I *sprinted* downstairs and still nearly missed you."

"I heard you?" he says. "I was apologizing?" His manner could not be less apologetic.

"Oh. Right. Well. Good. Thank you. I appreciate that. And sorry if I overreacted, but . . . you know. I'm a bit . . . It's my birthday today."

He nods, hitching the mailbag more securely on his shoulder. "Happy birthday. Enjoy your massive card."

In the hall, I look at the envelope, which is addressed to Claire Flannery in the neat all-caps style my father has in common with psychopaths. It might be, excepting forwarded bank statements, the first thing he's ever posted to me.

I rip it jaggedly open and coax out a correspondingly huge card adorned with ribbon, glitter, glued-on satin rosebuds and the words FOR OUR SPECIAL LITTLE GIRL, featuring multiple fonts, scalloped edges and a poem spanning many pink pages—really, it's more of a booklet than a card—an epic in blandness, which leans rather too heavily on "day" as an end-rhyme (preceded by "to-," "birth-," "special," "ev'ry," "on this," "birth-" (again), "your big," "wonderful" and "lovely"); in other words, an all-frills job, which, through its scale and flamboyance, serves only to highlight the very lack of motherly love it was doubtless trying to disguise. I leaf through it in search of a personal message, and about to give up, turn over and see on the back, CLAIRE at the top, and FROM DAD AND MUM beneath the words "Time 2 Celebrate"; not a message, as my father apparently thought, but the manufacturer's logo.

It's always worth remembering

I didn't work hard at school and go to university so I could spend my life sending emails.

These people are not your friends

I find Geri semi-reclined on the sofa in her office. Her dog—a small, docile mongrel named Captain Popkin—lies on her lap, chin resting ruminatively on his front paws.

"Hmmm." Her eyes are closed as I enter, and when at last she heaves her attention my way, letting out a long, languorous sigh, I feel like I've trespassed on an intimate moment, though it was she who summoned me here in the first place.

"Claire, take a seat." She swings her feet to the floor and slaps the sofa cushion beside her. "How are things?"

"Things are great!" I say. "This could be a good time to catch up on where we're at—I think everything's in really good shape—"

"That's good," she interrupts, "but actually, I asked you in here because I wanted to say a big hip, hip, hooray and thank-you for doing such a terrific job. And to say how much fun it's been having you around."

"You're very kind," I say, wondering if she knows today is my birthday—perhaps this praise is her gift? "Well, it's fun for me too

It's really nice to feel useful again. I was worried it might be a bit strange—a step backward, you know? But it's really made me realize how much I missed everything: colleagues, the office, not to mention the work itself . . ."

Her eyes race between mine before she speaks again. "I'm glad you've *got* something out of it too." She leaves a beat. "It's great you've *had* a good time."

"You're . . . letting me go?" I say.

Geri lifts the impassive Captain Popkin so his head eclipses hers, and says in a pouty, poochy voice: "We're going to miss you so much." She wags one of his paws at me: *Bye-bye, Claire.*

Because I cannot get on board with this sort of behavior, I stare assiduously at the floor.

"Oh! Okay. Can . . . I ask why?"

Her voice drops as she lowers the dog. "Budget meeting this morning with Justin—won't bore you with the details, but what it comes down to is, we've way overspent. Hands up, it's my bad. Blame me."

"No, of course it's not your fault!" I say and catch my thumbnail between my teeth. "But if it's a cash issue, we can talk about that. There's only a couple of weeks' work left, I reckon, and I could try and finish sooner if that would help . . ."

She turns Captain Popkin over, cradles him in her arms like a baby, cooing into his raggedy belly. "I soooo wish there was something I could dooo! But it's out of my hands, I'm afwaid. Yes, it is!" She looks up, her face a pantomime of concern. "We *did* always say this was a short-term thing. Didn't we? I'm not leaving you high and dry, I hope?"

"Not at *all.* It's actually probably for the best anyway. I really should crack on with the old job hunt. Which was why I left here in the first place, if you think about it. You're actually doing me a favor in a funny way."

She gives me one of her "sincere" smiles, the least convincing in her repertoire. "You're such a great sport," she says.

I stand up to leave. "Is it still okay to put you down for a reference?"

Her attention has already drifted elsewhere, and when I say her name, she looks at me in surprise. "What? Oh yes. Get Bea to draft something and I'll sign it."

"Okay," I say, with my hand on the door handle. "So, my last day is when? Friday? Should I start wrapping things up?"

Geri puckers her mouth, shakes her head. "I was thinking sooner."

"Oh. As in today?"

She nods, thrusting Captain Popkin toward me. "Cuddles for Claire-Bear!" she says, and despite my various noises of refusal, the dog is now trembling in my arms, emitting a high-pitched whine and looking at me, wet-eyed and cock-eared, with what feels uncannily like pity.

Packing up

"Could you hold my bag open for me?" I ask Bea, who is barely visible amid the carnage of her workstation. The chaos is so deeply entrenched it has come full circle and evolved an intricate internal architecture: teetering towers of three-ring binders (which famously don't stack well) are buttressed by clumps of dirty tea mugs and various heavy-duty office supplies—stapler, hole punch, reams of photocopier paper.

"Hang . . . on . . . one . . . sec," says Bea, staring intently at her monitor. She has pushed her hair up into a pile and secured it with a pencil. Another pencil is tucked behind her ear. I have encountered her in a rare moment of industry: the touch-typing hunch she assumes when social networking has unfurled into a stately, straight-backed posture, hands poised rather high and fingers striking the keys in a slow, staccato rhythm, as though every character is of weighty importance.

"Forget it," I say, clattering my armload onto the filing-cabinet desk. I've gone in for one final stationery-cabinet sweep, and boy, have I made it count. My self-imposed criteria was medium-ticket items I wouldn't purchase myself, but which I'm confident will come in handy at home: highlighter pens, stapler, multi-pack of notebooks, gel pens, Scotch tape. One by one I hurl them into my bag.

"So. Guess what?" says Bea, hitting "return" with a flourish that ends above her head.

I put a finger on my lips. "Let's see. Is it 'I just got made redundant from the job I already quit'?"

"What? No way! Shit," says Bea. She tugs on an earlobe. "I hope it wasn't my fault."

"I very much doubt it has anything to do with you," I say, "but thank you for the concern."

"No, I really think it might be my fault. I asked Geri if I could take on some more creative stuff. And she said I could work on your project. I assumed that meant I'd be working *with* you— that's what I was about to tell you."

"Well," I say, "you assumed wrong." She looks a bit hurt and I feel a bit bad. "Don't worry about it. I don't even know why I care."

"I'm *sure* it's only because of my dad," suggests Bea, with uncharacteristic self-awareness. "I'm going to talk to Geri. I'll tell her to leave things as they were."

"Please, please, I *beg* you, don't bother. What's done is done—" I stop because we have been plunged into darkness. From the kitchen doorway the office manager's face flickers, deranged in the light of birthday-cake candles.

"*Wonderful*," I say as my almost-ex(-again)-co-workers unite in an atonal dirge.

You win some

I'm trying to decide exactly what this woman, dressed from suede-platform-booted toe to fedora-feather tip in a single, arresting shade of green, might have lost. Her inhibitions? Her mind? A bet?

Evaluation

It's the fifth day of now-involuntary unemployment. Every afternoon I've decked myself out in sports gear but failed to go for a run, leaving the house only to go to the Co-op. My usual cashier seems impressed today.

"You're training very hard for something," he says.

"Marathon," I say, lobbing a register-side chocolate bar in with my shopping by way of celebration. Never before has an assumption about me been so wide of the mark yet so generous.

Outsourcing

I'd happily split any money I earned, fifty-fifty, with someone who'd tell me what to do with my hair, what to eat, how to dress, when to bleed the radiators, get the windows cleaned, paint the walls, which articles in which publications to read, the salient points of this Syria thing and the best use of my skills and time on this earth.

Spam

Store your DNA for eternity!

Four a.m.

I worry that London will keep on expanding until it has swallowed up everywhere else.

I worry that legal deposit libraries will do likewise (though at a much slower rate).

I worry about everything else shrinking: bank balance, potential, fertility. Habitable land for the children I won't have because I'm definitely barren.

I worry about the integrity and future of the folksy organic smoothie manufacturer who sold out to a major multinational corporation.

I worry that waking up at four a.m. means I have clinical depression.

I worry that worry causes cancer.

Dream

A large pill, but no water to help it go down.

Meeting

I go to meet social-media whiz Andrea in a new cafe called Atelier. There's a "Mission Statement" printed on the back of the menus informing patrons that all furniture has been repurposed from authentic wood workshop fittings, and sure enough, the communal tables bear the scars of G-clamps, handsaws and drills, no doubt used to make the actual tables now shunned in favor of the tables they were made on. It's eerily quiet: every single customer is in silent thrall to a MacBook with white buds in their ears like stethoscopes, and Apple icons glowing like synthetic hearts.

"Hey," I say to Andrea, clambering gingerly over the bench to make as little noise as possible. Talking aloud here feels vaguely transgressive—akin to not saying, "Bless you," when someone has sneezed. Andrea closes her laptop with reluctant politeness, picks up her phone and starts scrolling.

"I can't be long. I have to chair a hub chat at three o'clock. Hope that's okay."

"Of course. Where's that happening?"

"The hub chat? Online?"

"Yeah, obviously," I say. "I meant where, as in which *site*?"

"What, do you want the URL? Actually, that could be great if you joined. We need numbers. Virtual . . . bodies . . . in the"—she flexes her thumbs at her phone a few times—"you know . . . thing. Okay, sent you the link. Starts at three." In my bag, my phone hums

"So what exactly do I need to do?"

"Come up with some questions? It's about how to harness momentum generated by bedroom campaigns."

"Could you give me an example?"

"Okay: not this. This is a really bad example, but say . . . say a woman dies while doing a triathlon. She overdid it, burnt out. On social media, someone coins a phrase like, I don't know, 'Pace yourself for Grace'—her name's Grace—"

"Convenient."

"Yeah, I *said* it's a bad example. Anyway, some initiative about planning your race in advance, seeking medical advice beforehand, blah, blah, and everyone's using this tagline 'Pace yourself for Grace.' So the question is, how do *we* become part of the conversation, in order to help drive traffic to our site?"

"Piggybacking on a tragedy, in other words."

She shakes her head, irritated. "I said that was a bad example! I'm talking about any campaign or movement—it could be political or topical, whatever's captured the consumer imagination."

"Consumer?"

"Fine: public, then." She tuts with impatience and rolls out a rehearsed-sounding tirade about the liberal media's "holistic Montessori bullshit"—i.e. their insistence on peddling the idea that we're all so "*pwecious* and unique." "I'm sorry," she says, wrapping up with a flourish, "but I'm not the public's *mum*."

"*That's* true," I concede, adding silently, *More like its scary maiden aunt.*

"Look, when you use most websites, you're a potential consumer: that's the deal you make when you log on. That's how the Internet functions. We don't do what we do for the good of our health." I refrain from asking what it *is* she does, having done so too many times before, but I'm firming up a feeling that she handles social media for social-media companies. She's still going, tapping her phone against the table while the poor MacBookers stare in bewilderment as they struggle to process the novelty of live human-to-human speech. "If *we* don't capitalize on this stuff, someone *else will*. It's simple economics."

"I don't know . . . It seems kind of cynical. A bit . . . leechy."

She looks me up and down. "Maybe you shouldn't come to the hub chat. We could do without the negative energy."

"Actually, can't anyway," I say, showing her my palms as though it's written there. "Just remembered I have a dentist's appointment. Can you believe I haven't been for five years?"

Andrea clenches her teeth in horror. I hadn't noticed before how white and perfect they are and decide I really *will* go today.

"Because you're scared?" she asks.

"Give me some credit. Being afraid of the dentist is like hating traffic cops—too easy. I like to think I'm a little more particular with my phobias: spontaneous shooting sprees on crowded trains, poisonous spiders laying eggs in my luggage on holiday—that sort of thing." I've lost it: Andrea—eyes askance—seems to think so too. "Sorry, this is what happens when I spend too much time alone. I'm not sure what avenues are worth going down."

"I'd better get moving and set up this thing."

"Okay," I say. "Good luck."

We sit looking at each other. She slowly lifts her laptop lid.

"Oh, you're staying here. You want *me* to go. And, obviously, I have to go to the dentist's." I clamber backward off the bench. "We should do this again soon."

"Sure," says Andrea, but she doesn't sound it.

Teeth

Coughing and sneezing at the doctor's is one thing; at the dentist's, it's a whole new level of disgusting. I'd walk straight out of this spluttering germ-pit if I hadn't already lost ten minutes (and counting) to the registration process.

"A glass of wine is two point four units," the receptionist says, watching my pen hover over the form as I try to work out an acceptable figure. "A *small* glass," she adds, with a pointedness I can't help but take to heart. I bite my lip to hide any telltale redwine stains, before remembering I had a night off.

"I'd be more worried about the ones who *don't* need to count, who know *exactly* how much they drink. That suggests obsession, addiction," I say, buoyed by yesterday's virtue.

"Or moderation, self-control. Sister Frances! First floor!" the receptionist calls, and a tiny nun scurries past

———

I flip through a magazine, two years out of date, then return it to the table by a dried-out plant. I'm hopeful the attention to detail lacking out here has been plowed instead into hygiene, staff training. Like Sister Frances before me, I've graduated to the first floor—another waiting area, where doors fly open and shut with the frequency of a boring silent farce. On the opposite wall is a safety poster: "If you discover a fire . . ." Step one is: "Stay calm."

Wisdom

My baby-faced dentist is a jovial sort. He seems much younger than me, not just in his looks but the way he speaks (he insists I call him Rohan, even though I am sure I'll have no need to) and the pair of Nikes peeping from beneath his scrubs. My childhood dentists were all distinguished older gentlemen who wore white coats, bow ties, and brogues. Rohan asks questions with laconic good-naturedness: Any problems? Do I floss? What is it I do? Because my mouth is wide open, full of fingers and metal, my responses (No; Sometimes; I'm not sure) come out like strangulated laughter.

"Insurance?" he asks, of my last answer, and I nod, because, well, why not?

"Oh yeah? What sort?"

"Ha, ha?" I say, just sounds now. I'm curious to see where this will lead.

"Healthcare?" he guesses.

I nod. Maybe it's a sign. Maybe I've discovered a new career service: it feels no less arbitrary than any other approach.

When my mouth is empty once more, I say, "Go on, then: what's the damage?"

He laughs. His own teeth are good, not perfect, which suggests both respect for nature and tolerance of imperfection: values I can get on board with. Were we protagonists in a romantic comedy, this would bode well for our future. "There's some thinning enamel we need to keep an eye on"—he gestures on a chart—"but generally things are looking pretty good in there."

"No sign of any wisdom teeth yet? I thought they were meant to have come up by now."

He grins. "But they *have*: full house."

"Oh! Oh. I didn't even notice."

"Some people go through a lot of trouble with those guys. You should count yourself lucky."

I nod, but truthfully I'm disappointed: the tiniest, stupidest part of me hoped they might live up to their name.

Desire

In bed, I recount my meeting with Andrea. She doesn't come out of it well.

"She's obviously not very nice. I don't understand why you're friends with her," says Luke.

"I'm not."

"So why do you waste your time with her? You only get one life."

"She asked to meet up and I feel bad saying no. She knows I don't have a job—I have no excuse."

"You don't have to explain yourself. Say you're busy next time."

"I don't think there'll be a next time. I don't think she likes me."

"So no problem, then."

"But I *want* her to like me."

"But you don't like her!"

"Because she isn't nice!"

"So what's the issue?"

"I *am* nice, so she should like me!"

"You do know it's okay if not everyone likes you," says Luke.

"If that was true, it would feel okay, but it doesn't, so it *can't* be."

"All right, you've lost me. Sleep time now."

"Don't you want to have sex? We said we would."

"Do *you* want to?" asks Luke.

I weigh my options. I don't, but I'm not ready to be left alone in the sickly orange streetlamp wash beyond good night. "I don't *not* want to."

"You make it so hard for me to resist."

"Don't you want to?"

"I do, but . . . tomorrow? *Definitely* tomorrow."

"We *always* say that."

"But this time we really, really mean it."

7

Ephemera

Things have been piling up over the last few months in the corners and at the edges of the rooms in our flat: stubborn, uncategorizable items that have no proper place but aren't rubbish either. In the wake of a spate of huffs and hints from Luke (who has somehow managed to absolve himself of any responsibility for the stuff) I gather everything together and sit down to go through it all in one go.

There's a cord from my e-reader (which my computer doesn't recognize); a lightbulb, which might be old but might be new; three keys, all incompatible with the locks in my life; a set of portable speakers rendered obsolete by our recent mobile phone upgrades; spare buttons in little polythene bags; a cardigan left after a dinner party; the order of service from my grandfather's funeral; a cigarette lighter left after a different dinner party; a red ribbon; two jokers from a pack of playing cards; the instruction booklet for a desk fan; and a used plastic disposable camera: contents unknown.

I leave the other stuff for later and take the camera to the first drugstore I find, one of the dusty village-style variety with a window display themed around evening primrose, incongruously quaint on this grimy London street between a tanning salon ("Spray It Like You Mean It!") and bookies. A bell tinkles when I open the door and I'm hit by the smell—a powdery, fudgy, floral nostalgia-blast, encoded in my brain at some long-ago point to signify "femininity," and I realize with a vague sense of disenchantment that this phenomenon—femininity—has not manifested itself at all as I expected, in the form of vanity table, crystal perfume atomizer, kimono suspended from silk-padded hanger, et cetera, but instead as a tangle of grayish underwear, old sports T-shirts for nighties and an unruly drugstore-special-offer-dictated assortment of half-finished moisturizers, packets of face wipes and bunches of tampons.

I select from the shelves a prettily packaged tube of cuticle cream—the first step toward the boudoir of my dreams!—and take it to the counter along with the camera, which I submit for one-week development.

Recurring dream

Last night, the wolves that used to feast on my flesh fed on a mountain of steaks instead. Am I meant to read this as some kind of progress?

Surprise

I turn on the TV to reports of a terrorist attack on the news— rolling footage of charred remains, grave shock in the voice of the presenter, and with a sinking heart, I think, How are we still surprised? Is it as simple as *we forget*? That planes crash; babies get bigger; cells mutate; volcanoes erupt; sometimes it rains; years go by; regimes grow strong; humans lie; economies fail; children die; bins get full; clean clothes get dirty; darkness always falls early in winter? Is this how we keep going, one day to the next?

"M" is for "Mother"

A text out of nowhere, like a small detonation. *can u meet. M.*

Olive branch

I take a table alfresco—i.e. outside the cafe's glass front, but inside the train station overlooking the main thoroughfare. I have an absurd fear I won't recognize her, that in the months since I saw her she'll have turned gray, aged aggressively. Then she emerges: fingers primping her hair, rearranging her scarf, her collar, her hair again, eyeing herself sidelong in every shop window—so self-absorbed that for a moment, even as I'm flooded with love and relief after these many months without her, I find myself also furious with her.

"Mum," I call, trying to rise, but things are tight between table, chair and window, and the result is a bowlegged squat. She's overshot by a few feet and is startled to see me when she turns.

"Oh! Claire. I missed you there." Instinctively she reaches out for me, then remembering, withdraws a little, and squeezes my hand the way a distant elderly relative might.

"I missed you too," I say.

"What? Oh right. Yes, I see," she says, still holding my hand.

———

Once she's settled with coffee, she gives me the customary once-over.

"*That's* a nice top," she says. "Is it new?"

Tugging the hem, I say, "This? No."

"Still. I've always loved blue on you." Her eyes continue to rove. "Hair back." (Meaning: *scraped up*.) She touches her own, voluminous as ever.

"You're looking great," I say, taking the cue. She tweaks her shoulders and sits up a little straighter.

"Well. At my age you have to make the effort." There's a pause. We smile at each other, look away, smile again, wider, a little more desperate.

"So. How's Luke?"

"He's fine. Work's busy, exams ongoing, but you know Luke: always has his eyes on the prize."

"And . . . things between you are good?" Her head is tilted to one side, casual fashion, though the tendons stand out in her neck, and I'm seized by the paranoid, squirming feeling I get whenever I'm asked a direct personal question.

"Things are brilliant! Better than ever!"

"Good! I thought . . . No, that's great."

"What?"

"I didn't say anything!" She throws her eyes upward, tutting. "That's always been your problem, Claire—you see everything, even things that aren't there." She stirs her coffee, takes a dainty slurp of foam. "I was only going to say, I thought you two had decided to take a step back."

"What does that mean? Where did you get that idea?"

"Oh," she says lightly, "I thought there was something about deciding not to get married, but perhaps I'm mistaken."

"Was this from *Grandma*?"

Her lips and brows gather in exaggerated thought. "I suppose . . . yes, it must have been. So *is* it true?"

"No! Not at all. Well, only in the sense that it's always been true: we're not married and have no current plans to be."

"No plans, or plan *not* to? I'm allowed to ask! I'm your mother— you can be honest with me."

"Apparently only when it suits you."

She jerks back in her seat, offended. "That's not nice. Don't I have a right to know whether to expect a wedding from my only child? Or if I'm ever going to get to be a grandmother?"

"Honestly? I'm not really sure you do." I stare at my hands. The nails I've spent months not biting are raggedy edges now.

"Are you taking folic acid? You should take folic acid if you're even thinking about *thinking about* having children. You're lucky to have the benefit of my experience. I didn't know I was having you until it was too late."

"Too late. Wow." I compress my lips and stare wide-eyed at the sugar pot.

"Oh, you know what I mean. Stop being difficult. Too late to take the folic *acid*."

"Mum, you haven't spoken to me for months! I could have almost *had* a baby in that time and you wouldn't even know."

She looks briefly, guiltily hopeful; tries to cover her tracks with a wounded frown. "Your father and grandmother have kept me up to date. I'm not inhuman: I've been thinking about you."

I study the wood grain; try a wobbly smile.

"It's been hard for me too," she continues. "I've been working through things, trying to come to terms with my own grief and . . ." She closes her eyes, tosses her head and begins again, placing her fingers carefully on the tabletop. "I wanted to see you today because I've been doing a lot of soul-searching and I feel I now might understand."

"Understand what?"

"All this . . . unpleasantness. I've been doing some reading around it." She reaches into her bag and takes out a sheaf of pages, rolls it tightly into a baton and hands it to me. "I found these articles on the computer. You don't need to read them now, but I think you'll find it all very interesting."

I loosen my grip and the pages spring open. The first is a printout from a psychology website in a questionable font. I read the headline aloud: "'False Memory Syndrome.'"

"It's a very well-documented phenomenon." She leans forward, prodding at a paragraph halfway down the page, flanked by handwritten black asterisks like spidery henchmen. "Read that and tell me that doesn't fit."

It begins, "Sufferers may fixate on the imagined memory in order to distarct from problems in real life." In the margin she's put *YES*, underlined three times.

I look up.

"Well? What do you think?" she asks.

"They've spelled 'distract' wrong."

She tuts. "You would pick up on that of all things. It makes *sense*, though, doesn't it, the timing, if you think about it? You'd just left your job, and would have been feeling a lot of uncertainty about the future, and then there's whatever might be going on with Luke." She holds up a hand, preempting objection. "That's your business, I know. I'm saying nothing. And of course, Daddy— Gum—had just passed away. Grief does funny things to a person." She puts her hand over mine. "I hadn't realized the pressure you'd been under, and"—she laughs—"oddly enough, *I* wanted to apologize to *you*, to say I'm sorry for not being there. Obviously this isn't the way I'd choose for it all to come out, but I want you to know: I *understand*. It's okay." She grips my hand harder, beaming with compassion, or at her own magnanimity.

I take a deep breath. "Mum. I'm so glad you're ready to talk to me again, and I really appreciate what you're trying to do, honestly, but this isn't . . ." I take my hand back and leaf through the pages. "Look, some of this stuff is completely bananas! There's a whole section here about alien abduction."

Her eyes widen. "That's actually a very interesting parallel—there's a book I got on Amazon. I'll lend it to you."

"*Mum.*"

"What! Don't tell me you *believe* in that UFO stuff, Claire. I thought you were a bit brighter than that."

"Of course I don't! That's the whole point! Do you really think *alien abduction* is an appropriate comparison?"

Her fingers seek out her necklace and worry at the pendant. "So what exactly are you saying? That Daddy—your grandfather—was some kind of—" She stops, looks over one shoulder, then the other, and slowly, distinctly mouths, "Pervert."

"No. No! We've been over this. I'm saying what I've said right from the beginning: I made a badly timed, lighthearted remark that has been blown out of all proportion."

"So it *was* a joke, then? He didn't actually"—she gestures downward—"you know, *show* himself to you."

"No, I mean, he did, but not . . . 'Show' isn't right; it was always more like a flash." The word choice is unfortunate; I quickly move on. "It wasn't that he necessarily intended to, or if he did, it was just . . ."

"Just what? I'm sorry, you're going to have to help me out here."

"I don't know!" I flick away sudden tears with my knuckles. Passersby peer at us, then avert their gazes. "You'd need to ask him!"

A bitter laugh escapes. "Well. I'm afraid it's a bit late for that."

"Maybe . . . maybe it was some kind of . . . weird impulse he didn't understand. Something from his own childhood. Maybe."

"You just said it was a lighthearted remark! Now it's some deep-seated trauma from his past. Which is it?" I open my mouth, but nothing comes. "What about this: wait, hear me out." She taps urgently on the pages. "Could you have walked in on him in the bathroom? Mightn't the shock of that have confused you at a young age, made you misinterpret what was happening?"

I swallow. "I understand why this isn't a comfortable conversation. I'm sorry if it's complicated your view of him. But I don't think me *pretending* it didn't happen is helpful or . . . right, and maybe part of me feels a little let down that as your daughter—"

"*Why* won't you at least consider this? I thought you wanted to work things out. You're the one who's been calling me and begging my—Thank you *so much*. That was *lovely*." She turns on the charm with bewildering speed for the waitress who's appeared to clear her coffee cup. "Begging my forgiveness. And now here I am, making an effort to understand what possessed you to make these frankly bizarre accusations out of *nowhere* at the poor man's *funeral*! All I'm asking is for you to take and read this. *Then* tell me if you don't agree, but please don't dismiss it out of hand . . ." She presses a fist to her lips. Her entire irises are visible: blue, bright and hard against the whites. I feel so exhausted, trapped by her desperation, and by the relentless stream of travelers, churning back and forth, that all I can muster is a single deep shrug. She gathers up the printouts, shunts the edges flush, hands the sheaf to me.

"You know, Claire," she says with tenderness, reaching across the table to pluck a stray hair from my shoulder, then gracefully releasing it into the air, "there's no shame in being wrong."

I nod because I have to agree with her there. In this instance, there's only shame in being right.

Going dark

Luke greets me at the door like a faithful pet.

"How was it? Are you okay? Did you sort things out?"

I go straight to our room, crash facedown on the bed.

"Guessing that's a no."

I give him muffled directions to my bag and the printouts.

"Yikes," he says, once he's taken a look. "So this is the new party line?"

"So it seems."

"Shall I make a cup of tea? Something stronger? Glass of wine?"

"Is there a drug I could take that would knock me out for a while?" I ask.

"What, you mean a sleeping pill?" The mattress dips as he hops on beside me.

"I was thinking a bit longer term. More like a few months?" I turn to face him. He looks concerned, as though I'm exhibiting signs of something serious, so I slightly change tack. "I thought you could set me up in the living room with a drip. Actually, could you rig it so I lose a few pounds? Kill two birds with one stone. It'll be great: you'll come home, watch some soccer and your beloved foreign films, and I'll be right beside you but you won't hear a peep. Just like now, but without any talking. Could be really good for our relationship."

Luke nods and frowns. "But what about sex stuff?"

"What about it? I said it would be like now—i.e. not a factor."

"But what will I do about food? And washing."

"Yeah, you'd have to take care of that yourself," I admit.

"I *knew* there'd be a catch."

"You're right. God, what was I *thinking*?"

"It's off! Coma's canceled." He puts his forehead to mine. "Claire. Are you really okay?"

I pull my knees to my chest, roll away from him. "Oh, you know. I feel as if . . . I could just do with a bit of time off."

"Time off from time off? Wait, I'm pretty sure there's a cure for that. It's what we in the medical profession call 'getting a job.'"

"Why are you still here? Fetch me some wine!" I say.

Since the voluntary coma's not a goer, I'm going to need to resort to plan B.

Dream

Can't speak because my hair's all tangled up in my teeth.

Snapshot

The disposable camera I left at the drugstore turns out to be from a trip my parents went on at some point in the last ten years or so. The results are nearly identical to every other set of their holiday photographs I've seen over the years: alternating between solo portraits of my mother in poses of staged relaxation (reclining in sunglasses and straw hat on a sun lounger, arm spread dramatically toward a building or view) and my father dutifully taking his turn against identical backdrops, but squinting, teeth clenched, arms stiff and fists balled with the effort of appearing natural.

I can't stop looking at the last in the set, the only one of them together, late in the holiday judging by their tans. Relegated to the bottom left of the shot, Dad has his arm around Mum's shoulders and both are smiling with sweet uncertainty—spared, only just, by the vast blurry thumb of some anonymous stranger eclipsing all else.

Apathy

Not the first time I've jumped at that dust ball in the corner mistaking it for a spider or worse; pretty confident it won't be the last.

Domestic

"Should we get a cleaner?" Luke asks, rooting through the sink for something.

"We don't need a cleaner. We can't afford a cleaner. Why do you think we need a cleaner?"

"Things are getting a bit . . . wild," says Luke. "The black stuff on the tiles in the bathroom, and cobwebs everywhere, and in here there's, like, general grime. Look at the stove top."

I look at the stove top. It's dull, flecked with various bits, some identifiable (bean sprout), some less so (sludgy beige splodge).

"If we're dishing out orders, here's one: *clean* the stove top," I say.

"I'd prefer to pay someone."

"I'd prefer not to."

"You wouldn't be paying them. *Where* are all the knives?"

"What's it for?"

"Claire, no. I just need a knife."

"If it's for buttering that bread, you can use a spoon," I suggest, wielding one. "It's better than a knife for spreading—you use the back."

He pulls it from my grasp and clatters it on the counter. "I don't want to use a spoon."

"Honestly, try it—you'll never look back," I say. I bump him aside with my hip to get to the cleaning supplies and hunker down at the cabinet. "What do you mean, I wouldn't be paying?"

"What do you think I mean?"

I put my knuckles on the ground to steady myself. "You said you wouldn't do that."

"Do what?"

"Hold me to ransom with your income. We agreed."

"I'm doing exactly the opposite. Freeing you up so you can spend *more* time getting a job."

I straighten up. "This isn't about 'getting a job.' I can 'get a job' anytime. I'm sorry if that isn't straightforward, but I always told you that was the plan." I spritz too much Mr. Clean around the stove top.

"How are we on this? I just wanted a knife!"

"You're undermining all the work I do around the house. You never say thank you, you never ask if you can help, and you never hear me complaining that you basically don't do anything." I move the dirt around in soapy swirls.

"Oh my God! You're right! I'm *not* finishing my medical degree to secure our future while also paying the mortgage and bills."

"Hang on, that's not fair. That's only been the case since Geri fired me: I was paying my way until then. And whatever happened to what's yours is mine? You said you were happy with this arrangement!"

"I am!"

"As long as I keep everything spotless and don't complain?"

"I don't think there was ever any danger of that happening."

"Fuck *off*!" I say. We're both a little stunned. "I'm sorry, but I don't know how it's turned out like this. I just wanted to try and take control of my life and somehow it's turned into me doing everything around here."

"Which is why! I'm suggesting! A cleaner! For God's sake, Claire, I just want things to be a bit nicer!"

"But I don't want you to want that! I want you to think this is enough!"

He leaves, sighing, with no breakfast, abandoned packed lunch (two unbuttered slices of bread) on the counter and me staring into the sink at a wooden spoon drifting facedown in the greasy debris.

Great expectations

I've only ever really asked two things of Luke: one, don't have sex with anyone else, and two, don't leave clean bowls faceup to dry. Yet in the drying rack here I find three faceup bowls, with murky, chalky water pooling in the bottom, and now I have to wonder where we stand on number one.

Three new messages

I grit my teeth and listen, all in one go, to my mother's latest voice missives:

1. *Monday, 3:35 p.m.*
   "Oh! Claire, it's me, just calling to catch up, see how you are . . . Did you *have* a chance to look at those things I printed out for you? No, I'm not pressuring, there's no rush, I'm just curious I suppose, to know what you thought and . . . There was something else . . . Oh yes, that was it, I got chatting to a girl who was at school with you: Becky? Reddish hair, very striking, pharmacist. Anyway, she was so interested to hear how you're getting on career-wise—were you married? Any children? She's a *pharmacist*. Did I say that already? Two boys, three and one, she told me their names but I didn't quite catch them, a bit unusual, but no, still, nice, something different . . . and Becky's mother looks after the little ones when Becky's working—I'll give you a laugh: they call the granny Moo Moo! Isn't that lovely? I thought that was lovely, and of course Moo Moo's completely besotted and Becky's delighted to have both, the career *and* children—it suits her, anyway . . . So . . .

and . . . yes, she said to say hello, *full* of praise for you and how clever she thought you were at school, she'd always predicted great things for you, expected you'd be in *journalism*—not a bad idea, actually. I said to her that you were thinking about a new direction, not that you were [whispered] *unemployed*, but just working things out—just some food for thought, what do you think? Oh yes, you're not there, of course. So okay, I'd better get moving, but we'll speak soon, if you have a moment, give me a ring. So okay, bye now, bye now, bye . . ."

2. *Wednesday, 4:23 p.m.*
"Hi, Claire, yes, no, just a quickie to say I saw Dr. Patterson and he was wondering had you found a job yet, and I said you hadn't—I hope you don't mind . . . No, not that you *should* mind, well, you know what I mean—but anyway, his nephew, Brian is his name, I think, works in recruitment in London, very high up in, see if I can remember what it's called—no, it's gone, but it's a big firm, you'll probably have heard of it, I hadn't—but anyway, Dr. Patterson thought he might be able to put in a good word, so I've given him your email to pass on to the nephew—I do think it's worth following up, Claire, because you never know the doors it might open, and it would help, you know, if you wanted to go for the Dee Oh Ell Ee, it's your business, but you'd need to show you're being proactive about looking for a job—I was thinking you might as well do that, you know [whispered] *sign on*, you wouldn't need to *tell* anyone you were, but when you think there are plenty *without* your education and experience taking full advantage—but anyway, that's your business, and I'll let you get on with it, but give me a ring if you get this, just to touch base. I know you're busy, so no rush. Okay, bye now, bye . . ."

3. *Thursday, 12:18 p.m.*

"I've seen a dress in Marks & Spencer that is *absolutely you* and I'm wondering will I get it? I thought if you were going to a wedding or summer party, it would be just the thing. I'm looking at it now, lovely shape, flattering, flares out at the waist and has little sleeves and a collar, not right for me at all, but for you it's perfect, more your age, really, trendy, in a sort of abstract pattern with circles, orange, roses, are they? But I'm not really doing it justice a *pinky* sort of orange, very pretty print. I'm wondering if I should chance it anyway . . . I think I will, I'll treat you to it—you can look it up, the girl I spoke to said they'd have it on the website, type in 'orange dress' and it should come up, or try 'pink' if not or *'cerise'* . . . Do I mean cerise? . . . Sorry? Oh, *would* you? Yes! I'm on to my daughter . . . Yes, oh, Claire, the lady next to me just said salmon . . . Thank you, yes, it is *exactly* salmon with flecks of green . . . Anyway, you'll find it, I'm sure. Get back to me, I'll wait until—what are we now? Twenty past—I'll wait until half past, but I can always bring it back, I suppose, and I really think it's *so perfect* for you, so: yes, I've decided, I will, I'm going to do that, I'd *like* to do this for you. No need to call back. Okay, speak soon. Bye for now. Bye."

Invitation

At six p.m., my friend Polly calls to ask Luke and me to a "spontaneous supper" at the new house in Wimbledon she's bought with her fiancé, Will, a hedge-fund manager boasting aristocratic roots (hence "supper"). I'm standing in the bath wearing old boxers of Luke's and a sleep T-shirt I've had since I was eight—it's a big T-shirt: I was a big eight—scrubbing the blackened grouting with a toothbrush and bleach. I tell her Luke's working late, but I'd love to come.

"I won't be drinking, though, just to warn you—I'm not pregnant, just giving the old liver a rest. Who else will be there?"

"Mainly Will's friends."

"Oh." I hesitate, almost retract the not-drinking pledge but decide this is exactly the sort of challenge I need to face up to. "Fun! If it looks as if I'm about to cave on the booze front, please, please will you stop me?"

"I'll do my best. See you seven thirty for eight?"

Guest

I turn up at eight fifteen to avoid awkward sober mingling and make voluble but vague apologies about buses as I take the only remaining seat at the table—a corner spot on a flimsy folding chair.

I can't help but feel that the delicious-smelling food—billed as "eight-hour Moroccan lamb"—exposes Polly's claims of spontaneity to be somewhat bogus, and more relevant to my invite than the "supper" itself. Certainly, it seems unlikely that so many apparently important, successful people would have been free at such short notice.

"Hi. I'm Claire," I say to the girls—women, really—on my right, both vaguely familiar and wearing dark, sleeveless clothing that seems designed to showcase their slim, toned arms.

"Okay, hi," says the brunette.

"Sorry, what are your names?"

"Clem, Totty," says the blonde, pointing first at herself, then her friend.

"Lottie?" I say, thinking I must have misheard.

"Totty? As in Antonia?" says Clem, and with a condescending

smile leans away on an elbow to thwart further interaction. I take a moment to recover, then turn, beaming, to my left.

"Matthew," says my gingery, freckly, toothy neighbor, offering his hand. I've definitely met him before.

"Claire. You don't remember me, do you?" His brow crimps in confusion and I wish I'd just played along with his ignorance. "Don't worry, happens all the time. I don't tend to make a first impression."

"I think you make a very *good* impression," he says with the bullish politeness of the extremely well bred.

"No, no, I don't make *any* impression—you've just proven my point. We met at Polly and Will's engagement drinks. You're a radio producer for the BBC . . . specialist factual, recently bought a flat in Battersea?"

He shakes his head. "Amazing. You should be a spy."

"We prefer 'intelligence officer.'" He looks a tiny bit alarmed. "Obviously I'm kidding—when you're as prodigiously bland as I am, even MI6 fail to take any notice." I shrug. "Occupational hazard."

"Their loss," says Matthew. "So what do you actually *do*?"

"Um. Well. I guess at the moment I'm a housewife."

"That's terrific!" He laughs, delighted at the novelty. "I've always said there are too many people and not enough jobs—good for you for opting out of the rat race and directing your efforts where I'm sure they're most appreciated."

I hold up a hand. "Whoa, hang on there. Sorry, Matthew, before we go any further, I should say I was sort of joking."

"Ah. So you're not a housewife at all?"

"Well, it wasn't a deliberate career move. I'm in a sort of flux period." I tell him about my plans to take some time out to discover my purpose, and how I've somehow ended up being made redundant by the company I originally quit. "Which has set progress back even further, sadly. I feel pretty useless most of the time, if I'm honest. It's scary how steep and quick the descent has been from productive human to waste of space. So that's my story: any suggestions gratefully received."

"How about some Shiraz?" He must have noticed me gazing at it like a lovelorn adolescent, and hovers the bottle temptingly over my glass. "Or why don't we start there, anyway?"

"Thank you, but I'm on the"—I consult one of the two organic soft drinks I bought on the way over, which together cost more than I'd normally spend on a single bottle of wine—"wild raspberry and elderflower water, gently sparkling. Cheers!" I take a sip, and wince at its perfumed sweetness.

Resolve, dissolving

"Claire's boyfriend Luke's a brain surgeon!" Polly calls down the table, apropos of someone else's conversation.

All startled faces turn my way.

"Well, *trainee*," I say. "He's not fully qualified yet."

"Oh, wait," says Totty, "you're Claire as in *Luke* and Claire?"

"Luke and Claire, Claire and Luke. Both work. You know Luke?"

Totty is eyeing me with sudden snake-ish interest and instantly I decide this is much, much worse than being ignored. "A great friend of ours, Fi, works with him . . . at UCH?"

Fiona. Ugh. She *would* have awful friends: I should have recognized them from her Facebook photos. "What a small world," I say.

"So. *You're. Claire*. Huh," says Totty.

Clem, the blonde, grins darkly.

"I've never met Fiona, but I know Luke thinks she's wahn-derfuuul." I seem to be unintentionally mimicking Totty's plummy vowels, and pray no one's noticed.

"Isn't it so exciting about Johns Hopkins?" says Clem.

"Sorry—John who's that again?" I say, flustered, and Totty bucks back in her chair with an unconcealed snigger.

"*Johns* Hopkins? The hospital? In America? Where they're doing the six-month exchange."

Everything dims, sort of fizzes at the edges.

"Six months?" I say stupidly, then get it together. "Of course. Sorry, I'm with you now. Yes. Amazing news. Really exciting!"

"Will you go out and visit, do you think?" asks Clem. "No, wait—you don't work, do you? Are you planning to tag along for the whole residency?" Speechless, I guzzle my soft drink, throwing my eyes around in a goofy *who knows?* sort of way.

"Well, anyway, tell Luke that Tots and Clem say hi," says Clem, who, having had her fun, turns her fabulous blow-dry on me again.

At my shoulder, Matthew is brandishing the wine. "*Sure* I can't tempt you?"

"Oh, go on—why not?" I say with huge relief, waving away Polly's frantic signals of discouragement.

Next level

When Polly emerges from the kitchen with a tray of bowls, her fiancé, Will, taps his glass with a fork.

"I'd like to raise a toast, if I may, to Polls's salted-caramel ice cream, topped with crushed amaretto biscotti." We raise our glasses and he adds, "The biscotti are shop-bought, I'm afraid, *but* authentic at least—I brought them back from Bologna."

"Is that why you didn't have time to make them yourself, Will? Because you were in Bologna?" I'm as surprised as anyone else to hear my voice cutting through the convivial buzz.

Will looks confused. "Sorry?"

"You apologized that they weren't homemade. I just wondered why you didn't have time to make them. Maybe you could have done that while Polly made everything else we've eaten tonight."

"What?" says Polly with a nervous laugh. "Claire, shut up."

"Uh, I was *working?*" says Will.

"Oh right, so does Polly not have a job anymore, then? Or did she make this entire meal *as well as* holding down a job?" I shrug. "I'm just curious."

Everyone has gone quiet, save for the scraping of silverware against bowls.

"Is there . . . a *problem*, Claire?" asks Will. He glances around the now silent table, seeking allies.

"No, none at all. *I* don't have a problem." I pick up my spoon and load it with ice cream.

Tentative micro-conversations resume: hesitant platitudes— "Anyway . . . ," "Er, so, yeah . . . ," "What were you saying?"— anything to fill the scorching silence. But it would seem I'm not done yet.

"It's just I wondered why you'd apologize about things not being homemade when you didn't actually make anything yourself. Not really your place, in my opinion." I shrug again and wedge the spoon in my mouth.

"*Claire!* For fuck's sake!" says Polly.

"Hey, shh, Polly, it's cool. I've got your back. I'm just having a discussion with Will."

Will clears his throat. "I don't really think it's *your* place to criticize *me* in *my* house, in front of *my* friends."

"Well, you're entitled to your opinion."

"Sorry, have I missed something here? Polls doesn't seem to have an issue. Polls, did I offend you?" Will asks, though he's looking dead at me.

My head drops onto my folded arms. "She hates being called

that! *Everyone* knows she doesn't like being called that. It's Poll-*y*! Her name! Is Polly!"

Toothy, freckly Matthew pipes up, "Ah—I think this might be partly my fault? I made her have some wine when she didn't want to, and I think she's had rather a lot. Quite quickly. Perhaps a bit more than she's used to."

Will snorts. "Oh, she's used to plenty, don't you worry, mate."

I shoot upright. "*Mate!* I am *here!* I! Am! Right! Here!" Then back down to the forearms and blessed darkness I go.

Swirling

"Sorry, she's not normally like this. I don't know what's wrong with her," says Polly's voice, far away.

What's *wrong* is, I would tell them, if I could be bothered, were anyone even interested, but they wouldn't understand, so what's the point? But . . . what? Oh yeah, what is *wrong* with "her"—i.e. *me*—is, I'm the spare human in the world. If you counted everyone up, I'm the one who'd be left over, the one who *does nothing,* only takes, always *takes* things, a drain on everyone, completely pathetic like the poor old—poor old thing, the poor old wooden spoon, floating in the dirty sink . . .

8

Morning

Not awake exactly, more emerging from blackness, I open my eyes and try to piece it all together. The stiff T-shirt smelling of unfamiliar washing powder, the towels I'm lying on in the strange bed, the silent house, head utterly numb, throat dry and sticky, mouth a foul and fuzzy cave. A persistent buzzing detaches itself from the general assault of light and thirst and pain and queasiness, and I muster everything to locate the sound, which turns out to be coming from my phone, inside my shoe, under the bed. Three missed calls from Luke. I ring him back.

"Hi," I croak.

"You're awake." His tone is brisk.

"Um." I try to sit up again, decide against it for now. "Yeah, not feeling great. I'm still at . . . I guess I must still be at Polly's? Sorry I didn't come home. Things got a bit . . . much."

"Evidently."

"Did Polly call you?"

"She did. As did you, five times. So, not a good night for either of us, it would seem."

I close my eyes. "I'm so sorry. Was she angry with me?"

"I'd say more worried. Are you coming home?"

The clock by the bed says 8:47 a.m.

"I will be. Might need a little bit of time to turn myself around here, though."

"Well, I'm leaving for work now, so I won't be in."

"Oh," I say pathetically. Then, "I cleaned the house," as if this somehow explains or mitigates last night's behavior, and the state I'm in now.

"You said already. Quite a few times."

"So I'll see you later?"

"I'm staying at the hospital tonight. I guess I'll see you when I see you." He hangs up. *Hospital.* The word triggers a new sick feeling, unrelated to the alcohol. I'd forgotten all about it: Johns Hopkins, six months.

Tube

The journey home is hell, testing all my basic faculties: movement, sight, balance, breathing, temperature control. Everything seems completely absurd and utterly pointless, not least the ad for a new chocolate bar repeated all the way down the escalator wall.

As I'm waiting on the platform, a recorded message advises passengers to heed the safety advice printed on signs around the station.

On the train, I watch a lonely corn puff roll on the floor, before it's crushed to cheesy powder by an indifferent desert boot. My car fills up with a crocodile of children holding hands, all wearing red school caps. One of them, a small girl with stringy brown hair, stares at me, her mouth a tiny "o," and shrinks away when I attempt a smile.

Paradox

Nausea equaled only by snarling hunger; but there's nothing on this earth I want to eat.

Fighting talk

On my road, a woman strides by in an uncomfortable-looking suit, screaming into her phone, "*What* are the side effects? *What's* the life expectancy?"

Dad

At home, I send flowers to Polly and Will with a note reading, *Sorry for everything.* I mooch around the house in leggings and one of Luke's jumpers ("boyfriend fit" being more snug than magazines and the fashion industry would have me believe). Waking from a short, deep nap on the sofa, I see I have a voicemail from my dad. I listen—the phrase "nothing urgent" crops up four times. I phone back immediately.

"What's wrong?"

"Ah! It's Claire! My favorite child! I'm just at home, sitting down to some lunch!" He sounds exactly how someone being told to "act normal" by a gun-toting madman would sound.

"At home? Do you have the day off? Eleven thirty's early for lunch." On his end, the landline starts to ring. "I can wait while you get that."

"No, no, don't worry—it's no one. A nonsense caller."

"Huh? Oh, nuisance, you mean. How do you know?"

"If it's important, they'll call again. So, what can I do for you?"

"You left me a message. I was phoning you back."

The ringing stops.

"It was nothing urgent. Just, ah, checking in to see how things were with you."

The ringing starts again, somehow more insistent the second time around.

"Honestly, it's fine to get that. I'll call back in—"

"One moment." There's a crunching noise and it ceases, mid-ring. "There! It's stopped! Everyone happy?"

"Dad, you're being weird. Is everything all right?" In the silence, a new sound like a sort of *panting* in the background. "Is that . . . ? Can I hear a *dog*?"

"Possibly."

"In the house? You hate dogs. Mum hates dogs."

"She doesn't mind Walnut."

"Walnut . . ." My addled brain tries to make sense of this. "Do you mean . . . Hazelnut?" Hazelnut belongs to their neighbors a few doors down.

"Whatever. I hope it's him, anyway. Otherwise I don't know who I have here."

"Pretty sure Hazelnut's a she."

"Listen, do you think I should give it a tomato?"

"Dad, what's going on?"

"Nothing. Doesn't matter. Completely normal. Anyway, how are you? Did I already ask?"

"I'm good. No news really." I shut my eyes tight to ride out a splitting headache, and try a different angle. "How's work?"

After a few seconds of silence, he says, "The thing I want you to remember, Claire, is that the person in charge on a day-to-day basis is a small, shortsighted, arrogant arsehole."

Now we're getting somewhere. I have a thousand questions, but decide to let him continue, in the hope that any logic will emerge in the telling. His narration, though spirited, is typically roundabout: amid the twists and turns I identify a clear villain (the shortsighted, arrogant arsehole—I honestly can't tell if "shortsighted" means this person wears glasses, lacks judiciousness or both), a victim (Dad) and an ongoing campaign of persecution. Dad makes more references to Hitler and the Jews than I'd let him get away with were anyone else listening, but he's clearly in a bad way, so I park my objections and make a mental note to return to them later. At last, he gets to the crux: a frank exchange of words this morning (the Hitler–Jew analogy among them, alas), resulting in my father being asked to leave.

"Asked to leave the premises or to leave the firm?"

"Claire, I don't know."

"Is Mum with you?"

"She is not."

"Have you told her?"

"Not yet."

"I think . . ." I take a stab, "I might come over if you don't mind? I have no plans today anyway, and it sounds as if maybe you could do with some company."

"Well. I have Walnut."

"Hazelnut, of course." I'd forgotten all about the dog.

"It's been answering to Walnut," he muses. "Do they answer to anything if you use the right tone of voice? Peanut!" There's a pause. "Marmalade!" Another pause. "Andrew! No, that didn't work."

"Shall I come over, then?"

"If you wish," he says.

I pull on my shoes.

Home

From the train station, I take a taxi to my parents' house. Dad greets me at the door with the dog by his side. Over suit trousers and shirt he has on a frilly pink apron—an ironic gift someone gave years ago to my mother, who hates cooking. His hands are enormous in oven mitts, feet surprisingly small in socks. He reminds me of one of those dancing bears trussed up in a tutu.

"Hi, Dad," I say. His embrace is tight; the mitts up around my ears muffle his greeting. "Is this your special dog-handling outfit?"

"Guess again." He pulls away, making for the kitchen, with Hazelnut sashaying slowly at his heels.

The oven is open and a delicious, comforting aroma has diffused throughout the room.

"I was just checking on it when you arrived," he says, tilting the cake pan, teeth clamped appraisingly over bottom lip. "Needs a bit longer." He shoves it back in and slams the oven shut. The kitchen is in total chaos: utensils and ingredients have taken over every surface. By the bin, a whole tomato sits in a saucer.

"She might prefer a bit of meat," I say. "Don't you have some chicken breast or something in the fridge?"

"If she's really hungry, she'll eat it," Dad says, a horribly familiar refrain from my youth.

"Shall I at least slice it up?"

He looks at me. "And tuck a napkin in her collar too?"

Gag

I sit cross-legged beside Hazelnut, who is sprawled in front of the oven, and ruffle her fur.

"So, the dog."

"What about it?"

"Come on, Dad."

He nods in defeat, swallows the end of a mug of tea. "It was in the garden. I went out to investigate and it got into the house."

I look at Hazelnut lying on her side. She doesn't look capable of swift action.

"Have you told the thingies yet—the Thompsons?"

He tuts, lowers his voice. "Odd people. What's the one worse than vegetarian?"

"Vegan?"

"Precisely. *She's* all right, but he's a bit . . . odd. Calls himself a poet. Came round selling copies of a book he published, wrote our names in the cover without asking. Mum thinks it's so we can't take it to the thrift shop."

"Are they any good, the poems?" I ask.

He wrinkles his nose. "I looked at one or two, but couldn't make them out at all."

"I think you should phone and let them know you have their dog."

Dad slides a hand into the apron pocket, frowns, pulls out a tiny strip of paper, squints at it, feels in his shirt pocket for his glasses, which aren't there, so holds it at arm's length. "'It looks like . . .'" he reads. His frown deepens. "'Rain dear'?" He stares at me. "What does that mean?"

"Turn it over? I think it must be from a Christmas cracker."

Presumably the last Christmas we celebrated together, pre-rift, pre-cruise, just the three of us and a turkey we called, for reasons

I can't remember now, Roy: so enormous he made our little gath-
ering seem even smaller by contrast. Roy was still cropping up in
soups and stir-fries when I visited well into April, thanks to Dad's
thrifty freezing.

He turns the paper over and reads, "'What does Mrs. Claus say
to Santa when she looks up at the sky?'" He shakes his head. "'It
looks like rain, dear.' I've heard that one before."

"She's old, Dad," I persist.

"Mrs. Claus?" He roots around again in the apron pocket, and
produces a folded square of gold tissue paper.

"You know who I mean. Hazelnut. They might think she's
been run over. They'll be worried."

He opens the paper out into a crown, dandles it over me, as
though distracting a cranky infant. I grab it.

"Well, she hasn't," he says. "So they needn't be. Your grandma
told me a good one." He chuckles. "Did you hear it?"

I hold up a hand. "I don't really share Grandma's sense of
humor."

"You haven't heard it yet."

"I speak from experience."

"Why don't you let me tell you and then you can judge?"

"I will if you tell me en route to the Thompsons' with the
dog."

"Claire, it's under control." His palms press the air for empha-
sis. "Please. Let me handle this. I'm waiting until your mother
gets home." At the mention of my mother, everything falls into
place: the dog, the cake, the mess. In the midst of all this orches-
trated chaos, he's hoping the job thing might seem like just another crazy detail. It makes a kind of desperate sense.

"I'm sorry," I say. "I'll let it go."

"Well. I think I'll have a beer! Will you join me?"

My hangover has receded to the point where a drink seems to
be not just the best but the only course of action.

"I wouldn't say no to some wine," I say, sliding on the paper crown.

Overdone

"Buggeration," says Dad, waving an oven-mitted arm through the smoke and slamming the cake pan on the counter. We stand over it. The top is very dark brown, the raisins blistered and burst.

"Oh no!"

"Don't worry! It's fine. We'll just"—he puts his mitts on his hips—"isolate and eradicate the locally affected areas."

"Cut off the burnt bits."

"It isn't burnt."

Delayed reaction

While Dad removes the top layer, I mix up some water icing. I keep getting the consistency wrong—too thick, too thin, too thick, too thin—and end up with way too much.

"Did you wash your hands?"

"I've been cooking for myself for over a decade. You don't need to ask that sort of question anymore."

"We don't know where that animal's been." He sets a bowl of burnt cake pieces down next to the tomato.

"Hey, remember when we used to frost cookies on Sundays?" It was our weekend "baking" tradition: cookies coated with messy white goo and decorated with sprinkles and colored icing. I'd present them proudly on a tray with a cup of tea to my mum when she returned from wherever the short reprieve from mothering took her.

"Did we?" Dad says.

"Yes! Every Sunday."

"I don't think every Sunday. Maybe once or twice."

"No, it was every Sunday!" I don't know why this is so important. "Mum would go out and you and I would put icing on the
cookies."

"Oh yes, Sunday cookies; now I remember," he says in the robotic tone he uses when my mother corrects him about something.

I drain my glass; fill it back up again.

"Looks . . . nice?" The surface is lumpy owing to Dad's limited
carving skills. Because I was too impatient to wait for it to cool,
the icing has melted and run into ghoulish drips. "Considering."

"I've had an idea," Dad proclaims, grabbing a tub of glacé
cherries from the baking Tupperware. He places one in the middle. It looks a bit lonely.

"What about a face?" I suggest. We add two eyes and a smiling
mouth.

"That's better," says Dad.

"Much," I say. Hazelnut pads over to Dad's side. There are
charred bits caught in her fur. "Wow, she really went for that
crust."

"Told you it wasn't burnt." The smoke alarm starts to shriek.
"GOOD TO KNOW IT WORKS," Dad booms.

"If you'd call that working," I say.

Body language

"Do you think you should talk to an employment lawyer, find out
what your rights are?"

"I don't know." Dad clasps his hands behind his head. I once read in a magazine that soccer players do this when they miss a goal because it mimics the support of their mothers' hands cradling them as babies.

"Maybe I'll get someone to recommend one. I have a few friends who are lawyers."

"I always said *you'd* make a good lawyer." Hazelnut stirs at his feet, places her chin on his knees and looks up at him.

"Never once heard you say that."

"To your mother I have. Very fond of a loophole," says Dad, scruffling under the dog's ears.

I think about it. "It involves too much information for me. I'd probably get distracted by all the incidental stuff."

He nods. "Maybe." Takes another swig of beer. "You made a good decision, Claire."

"*I* did?"

"Getting out of that job if you weren't happy. Took guts."

"I thought you thought I was a bit of a dropout."

"Well." He jiggles his head, seeing my point. "In my day, if you went into a job, that's where you stayed for forty years. If you didn't like it? Too bad."

"But you did like your job. Do like it, I mean."

"I might have preferred to be an architect." He says this so frankly it breaks my heart a little.

"Oh. I never knew that."

"Ah, yes, but you see, Claire, you never asked."

It's true. I'd always assumed he was happy where he was, that he didn't have the imagination to question it—when in fact, all these years, *I* was the one who lacked the imagination to find out. I draw a "C" in the sugar dusting the table, then scrub it out.

"You're right: I never did. I'm sorry." He waves my apology away. I prop my chin on my palm. "I wish I wanted to be an architect."

"Ach. It's not the most secure profession nowadays."

"I mean, I wish I knew *what* I wanted."

"Maybe . . ." Dad lifts his can, puts the opening to one eye and peers in, as though seeing the future inside, "there isn't going to be a magic job that will solve all your problems. There's a whole world between *any old* thing and *the* thing. What does Luke think? About your situation."

My mouth droops and the fog of self-pity closes in. "I think Luke's had enough of me."

Dad's mobile thrums in his pocket; he lowers the beer, takes the phone out and freezes. "It's your mother," he whispers. His eyes dart to the window in a move I recognize at a near-genetic level: wild paranoia that she's out there watching him. "What'll I do? Will I answer? What shall I say?"

"Take it," I say, "but I'm not here."

"Well, hello!" he warbles in the same too-bright voice he used when he answered me earlier. "I'm terrific!" He snaps his fingers at me in this urgent, dictatorial way, then at the dog. Though it would be easier for him to leave the room, I take Hazelnut by the collar and guide her into the hallway. When I get back into the kitchen, he's saying, "Everything's fine. No-no, nothing, no-no, nothing, nothing urgent. See you soon, then. Cheerio!" He drops his phone on the table and massages his forehead. I hand him another beer from the fridge.

"When is she coming back? Let me help you clean up some of this before I go."

"Aren't you going to stay?" he says.

"I'm not sure that's such a good idea."

"I thought you two had sorted things out."

"She's talking to me again, which is something, I suppose, but . . ." I sigh. "She's cooked up this theory, and even though I know going along with it's the path of least resistance, I just . . . I can't. It feels like a betrayal to myself. To child-me. I don't know." I run a finger around the mixing bowl, decide I'm drunk enough to ask: "What do *you* make of it all? This stuff with Mum about . . . whatever. Gum and the war wounds and his, you know, with me in the bathroom and everything." The batter is delicious: sweet, silky and rich.

Dad twists his wedding band, mouth in a line.

I say, "You know what? You don't have to answer. You're in a difficult position. You've probably only heard her version anyway." I scoop up another round of batter.

"If I'd—" He stops, starts again. "Claire, if I had known at the time what was going on, I would have found it very difficult—"

"Which is why I never said anything! I didn't want to cause trouble."

He clears his throat, still twisting the ring. "I hadn't finished. I would have found it very difficult not to give the old bastard a war wound he'd have been in no hurry to show off."

I laugh, looking up at the ceiling so that the pooling tears won't spill. Dad slaps his hands on the table.

"Now! If you'll excuse me, I'd better go and check that our hairy colleague hasn't defecated in the hall."

Dog

Before Mum comes home, we clean up the kitchen: I wash; Dad dries, in accordance with age-old tradition. Afterward, we have some bread and soup to soak up some of the alcohol. Hearing pounding at the door, we look at each other, and get up to open it together. Sue Thompson is standing with an empty lead in her hand, craning her neck to look down the street.

"Sue! We were just about to call," Dad improvises. I look at him admiringly: who knew he had it in him? "We've had a visit from your little furry fellow. Claire, why don't you go and—" but Sue's already marched in past us.

———

"Where did you find her?" she demands in the kitchen, crouched by the dog but fixing us each in turn with a blunt, unrelenting gaze from behind her glasses.

"Out the back," says Dad. "We were going to call, but then you showed up."

I nod, obediently, corroboratively, sidestepping to block the beer cans from Sue's view.

"I've been out in the car, searching all over, and was about to give up but thought I'd knock on doors just in case . . ." She draws her eyebrows together. "Did you say you only found her just now?"

"Is Hazelnut a *Labrador*?" I ask, before Sue can get too intimate with the timeline.

She allows a smile. "Labrador retriever."

Hazelnut wanders over to Dad, sitting alert but very still at his feet.

"She's lovely," I say. "I'm not really a dog person"—Sue's smile falters a tiny bit—"but she's . . . really great."

"You might have heard she's getting an award next Monday," says Sue, pronouncing it "Mundy."

"Really? A dog-show sort of thing?"

She looks affronted. "A Community Spirit Award. From the mayor?"

"Wow," I say, not daring to look at Dad. "That's wonderful. I didn't know there was such a thing."

"Ceremony at the town hall. Everyone welcome. Mundy at four." Her head periscopes from me to Dad and back again. "Evan's giving a reading of a poem he's written specially."

"What a talented family," I say.

"That . . . sounds like a very . . . unique . . . occasion," Dad manages.

"Well, she is very unique." Sue explains that in her dotage,

Hazelnut has become a locally renowned and much-loved assistance dog, who divides her time (and Sue's) between old people's homes, primary schools and libraries, spreading cheer among the immobile, shy and lonely folk in the local community.

"I hope I'm never up against Hazelnut for a job. Her resume blows mine out of the water," I say.

"Well," Sue says, not contradicting me, "it's a gift she has, really, an extraordinary way of seeking out the people most in need. You either have it or you don't." She gives a helpless shrug. I glance across at Dad, who is frowning down at his feet, absently stroking Hazelnut's glossy head. In the heel of one of his socks, a tiny perfect circle of flesh glows white through the worn gray fabric.

Mum

At the sound of Mum's key in the door, Dad and I lift our drinks in solidarity.

"Did you have any luck with the missing bin lid—Oh." She stops, seeing me, the drinks, the cake. "A party."

"Surprise!" I hug her.

"What are you doing here?" She pulls away, taking in my leggings, Luke's jumper and (eyes lingering at head level) the Christmas-cracker crown I'd forgotten all about. Sue Thompson must have thought *we* were the crazy ones. "Interesting outfit. Did you have an accident?" she says.

"We've been baking!"

"And drinking, I see," she says, stepping toward the cake.

"Well, Dad baked. I did the icing."

"Okay. Is it supposed to be a . . . snowman?"

"It's supposed to be a fruitcake. But it got burnt."

"*Excuse* me," says Dad. "All that happened was, the top browned at an exponential rate vis-à-vis the remainder."

"You're home early," Mum says to Dad, in an uncharacteristically non-accusatory way that makes me suspect she's already assumed the worst.

"Yes," he says.

She sits down still wearing her coat: I always hated this when I was a child, fearful she might take off again at any moment and never come back.

"What happened?" She closes her eyes. "Don't tell me: McKinnon. You let him have it."

"In a nutshell."

"How bad?" she says, opening her eyes. "Wait, I think I need a drink first. 'It looks like rain, dear.' What's this?" She's picked up the small strip of paper from the kitchen table. Somehow it's survived the clear-up.

"Christmas-cracker joke," says Dad, mixing her a very potent-looking gin and tonic. "Not a good one, but there you are."

"I have one," I say, "I think. Hang on." I straighten my crown while I settle on the wording. "Okay. 'What . . . ' No, 'How does an Inuit fix his broken roof?'"

"Don't know," says Dad.

"What's an Inuit?" says Mum.

"Eskimo," I say impatiently.

"Oh, an *Eskimo*," echoes Mum, nodding. The ice cubes in her drink ring against the glass.

"But you know that's not really PC? The right term is *Eskimo*." I simply can't resist the gift-wrapped opportunity for a little lesson in cultural sensitivity.

"You just said Eskimo was offensive."

"It is. What? You're confusing me. *Inuit's* the correct term." I'm drunk. "Do you want to hear the punch line?"

"I can't remember the beginning now," says Mum. "Remind me?" She closes her eyes and leans forward, cupping her ear.

"'How does an Inuit fix his broken roof?'"

"Don't know," says Dad.

"Well, no, hang on," says Mum, "we can work this out. It'll be an igloo, won't it, so it's got to be something to do with ice . . . or snow . . ." Her eyes pop. "I bet I know!" She points at me. "He covers it snow-ver."

"Nope," I say, "that's not it."

Mum looks at Dad in disbelief. "Well, I can't imagine what it is, then."

I grin at one then the other in anticipation. "Shall I tell you?"

"Yes," says Dad.

"No!" says Mum. She ponders for a few more seconds, moving her lips, though I think she's just reciting 'covers it snow-ver.' "Okay, go on, then."

"'*Igloos* it back together!'"

"Huh," says Dad, after a few seconds.

"Igloos. It back. Together." Mum turns the words over stiltedly, completely destroying the cadence. "No"—she shakes her head—"I'm sorry, that doesn't make sense."

"Dad gets it."

"*Do* you?" she says, turning to him, astonished.

Dad nods. "It's fine. No worse than that other one. Oh, *there's* a job for you, Claire: cracker-pack jokes. Someone must have to write them."

"Igloos," I say urgently to Mum, "like 'he glues.' Igloos it back together."

"Oh," says Mum. She pulls her coat tighter. "No. Preferred my one. He covers it snow-ver." She laughs. "That's much better. You should use my one next time you tell it."

"Thanks," I say, "but I'm going to stick with mine."

Lost it

"Where's the pepper?" I ask, fanning all the cabinet doors open and shut in turn. I'm helping to set the table for dinner, but my parents have reorganized the kitchen and nothing is where it should be. "And the napkins. Hang on, don't you even keep place-mats here anymore?"

"Did you want to borrow some proper pants or a skirt or some-thing before we eat?" Mum asks, clearly still disturbed by my slouchy leisurewear. "I've got a nice blouse you could put on too. And you can try on that dress I told you about. Did you get my message? Come up and I'll show you. Wait—first, let me lend you a brush. What way is your hair under that paper thing? Not at its best." She starts to dig, elbow-deep, in her handbag.

"Well, Mum," I say, thumping down a jug of water, "*I'm* not at my best. So thanks for pointing that out."

"There's no need to fly off at me. I just thought, you know—"

"*A little bit of effort makes all the difference.*" She flinches at the imitation, which isn't even an imitation, really, more a sneery whine engineered to make her feel as small and ridiculous as pos-sible. "I don't *care* how I look right now, okay? I know I don't al-ways wear makeup and earrings and have my hair the way you think I should, and I'm sorry if that embarrasses you or upsets you to have to look at me *not at my best*"—that voice again—"even inside the privacy of your own home. I get it. Okay? I get that I'm not the daughter you wanted!"

"Now, Claire," says Dad from the stove, red plastic spatula raised like a warning. "There's no need for that. Why don't you go sit down in the other room while we finish up here? Take a breather. Go on, I'll call you in when things are ready."

I turn back to Mum. Her hands are still inside her bag, but they have ceased moving. Her mouth is in a troubled pinch.

"Please! Can you stop! *Looking* at me!"

She lowers her eyelids with such swift sorrow I'm instantly overcome by shame, and slide down against the cabinet to the floor, my face heavy in my hands. "Oh God. Of course I didn't mean that." My head goes back, smashes against the cabinet door, but I've had too much alcohol for it to hurt, and in any case I've just been stricken, really, properly for the very first time, by the idea of *me with them as a baby*, completely revelatory through the exhausted red-wine fog. "You're my mother! You *made* me! Of course you want to look at me. I can't believe I've never once said thank you!"

"For what?" says Mum.

"Everything! You—you both did, *everything* for me. Fed me, clothed me, changed my shitty diapers and nursed me through, like, *chicken pox*. You didn't even have the Internet to check you were doing it right! And I've never said thank you. How fucking disgraceful is that?" I swipe away hot tears with the cuffs of Luke's jumper, livid and astonished at my thoughtlessness.

"Claire, please, it's all right, shh. Just . . . try to calm down, love, shh," says Mum, clutching her elbows and leaning down toward me, wanting to help, but perhaps a little afraid to come close. I can only imagine how dreadful things look in the face department—pink eyes, nose red and glistening, mouth a downward gash like a tragedy mask—but it feels *good* to give in to this sorrow, so bleak and fathomless it's almost funny.

"It isn't all right! I know you didn't really plan to have children, and I just came along and gate-crashed your lives, and I was such a ni-hight-mare that you didn't want to have more! And now I'm . . . I don't even *know* what I am, and I don't know what to *do* with myself, I'm such, such, such a fuh-failure, and I'm pushing *Luke* away to Amer-hic-a, he didn't even tell me, he's running away, I've ruined everything, by being such, such, such a complete disa-ha-ster!" The tears take over completely, a descending scale of high-pitched sobs, *uh-huh, huh, huh,* so pitiful and child-like they sound put on. Mum—impelled maybe by some Nean-derthal impulse—rushes to hold me and I cry into her coat, soaking the scratchy-soft fabric; then a moment later I feel the embrace intensify, as Dad, who might have just lost the job he's had for forty years, moves in to complete our little tableau.

Recovery

Once I've removed the froth of used tissues from the floor where I wept, downed a glass of water, washed my face and brushed my hair (Mum and I even managed to laugh at the latter), the three of us sit down to have dinner together. I'm ravenous, and devour two huge servings of spaghetti bolognese made with turkey mince—my parents haven't allowed beef in the house since the Mad Cow hysteria of the mid-nineties.

"And now, some lovely fruitcake for dessert!" Dad announces, bearing it ceremoniously to the table. In what I take to be an effort to lighten the mood, he's donned my paper crown.

"Hey—turkey and fruitcake, like Christmas," I say.

"To make up for the one we missed with you," says Mum, cov-ering my hot, rough hand with her cool and moisturized one.

9

Symbolism

Back at the flat the next day, I bathe my face multiple times in warm water, hideous still from the crying jag. As I'm blotting them with the towel, my swollen eyes fall to the cup on the shelf above the sink, where my toothbrush and Luke's stand at opposite sides, bristling stiffly away from each other.

"Too much," I say to the universe.

Reality

"So. Johns Hopkins."

Framed by the kitchen doorway, gaze downcast, Luke says, "What about it?"

"When were you going to tell me?"

He repositions himself so that he's standing sideways, feet straddling the door. I watch him wind the doorknob tight, let go and recoil slightly as it shoots back.

"There wasn't really any point."

"If you want to break up, it might be worth just letting me know," I say. "I mean, I'm getting the message pretty clearly as it is, but it'll be over much quicker if you come out and say it."

"Are you kidding?" he says with apparently authentic surprise. He actually sounds quite angry. "I don't want to break up. Why? Do you?"

"No, I don't." I sit on my hands, so as not to bite my nails. "I assumed you wanted to. Why else would you keep something so big from me?"

"Because there's nothing to tell."

"What? They said you'd be there for six months—that doesn't sound like nothing."

"Who said that?"

"These terrible girls. Friends of Fiona's who were at Polly's dinner."

"Yeah: Fiona's going; I'm not."

"Really?"

"You must have a pretty low opinion of me to think I'd just up and leave without telling you. And an even lower one of yourself."

"Well . . . *why* aren't you going?"

"Honestly? I didn't think you were in the best place. To be left on your own."

Puff-chested, I leap to protest. "That's not really for you to—"

"Imagine if I'd been over in the States instead of here, getting those calls the other night. You throwing your guts up, sobbing down the phone, making absolutely no sense. Then *Polly* phoning in floods of tears, asking if she should get an ambulance, and how to put you in the recovery position. It was fucking scary, Claire."

I quell the urge to defend myself. "Okay. Yeah. When you put it like that. I'm sorry: that was not how things were meant to go." I straighten out my legs, line my feet up side by side. "I promise I'll never . . . I promise I'll try to never do that again. But you still should have told me." He shrugs. "What even is this Johns Hopkins thing, anyway?"

He sighs and rubs his head briskly so his hair stands on end. "It was a six-month residency for junior doctors to work in the neurosurgery department there."

"Luke! That sounds amazing!" A tense smile. "So what—you applied and they picked you?"

"It's irrelevant. I'm not going."

"Luke."

"Yes, I applied, but didn't think I'd ever get it—"

"But you did. You were offered a place."

"Yeah, but—"

"You turned it down because you were worried about me?"

"Yes."

"Without even thinking to tell me. Well," I say, "we need to fix this."

"What do you mean?"

"This isn't how we work. You don't get to make big decisions for both of us on your own. If you thought I was in such a bad way, you should have told me and we could have talked about it."

"You've had enough to worry about. I didn't want you to feel like you were holding me back."

I laugh grimly. "*How* am I not? You've been so patient all this time while I've been stumbling around trying to sort out my life and career. Then an unmissable opportunity for *yours* comes along and you don't take it because of me!"

"Yeah, well. I guess I love you."

"I can't believe you would do that for me. I can't believe you care about me so much." I thought I was all cried out, but feel perilously close to a fresh deluge.

"Claire, you'd do the same for me." This pure, simple faith—in me, and my love—is like a steadying hand and somehow I regain control.

"You're amazing. I know how much you must have wanted to take it, and how worried you must have been about me that you didn't, and honestly I can't really find the words to say how touched I am that you would make that sacrifice. But, Luke," I continue, as gently as I can, "please tell me: how exactly does turning down an opportunity like this really help anyone?"

"Well, look, it's done now. I'm sorry if you think I made a mistake, but I've already told them I'm not going, so we don't need to have this conversation anymore."

"No."

He flinches: I know I'm speaking too loudly.

My voice is creaking with resolve. "You're going to call them and tell them you are."

"Claire." Now he's getting really annoyed: his hands have petrified into claws. "I can't. I already . . . It's unprofessional. They'll think . . . It's too late now to just turn around and say I've changed my mind."

"I bet it isn't."

"Claire! *Seriously.*"

"Okay! Okay." Sensing his limit, I relent for the moment, palms out in surrender, sitting back in my chair.

He continues, calmer now that he thinks he's won the battle. "It's fine. Which is more than I can say for you. Don't take this the wrong way, but, God, you look absolutely *awful.*"

I nod fervently. "Thank you for not thinking this is how I look normally." I touch my cheek. "I cried so much yesterday I think I cured myself."

"Of . . . your hangover?"

"No: cured like pork, from all the salt tears."

"Ooh, I'm *hungry*," says Luke, clutching his stomach. "Is it dinnertime yet?"

Old habits

In the Co-op, we discuss what to eat, huddled in the chill of the refrigerator aisle.

"It's your special night," I say. "Anything you want."

Luke says, "I can't decide. You choose."

I reach for a pack of salmon fillets.

"Or pizza?" he says.

We each head off to gather various things and arrange to reconvene by Oils & Vinegars. When I get there, he's stooping, hands on knees as he surveys the bottom shelf: scruffy sneakers, the soft cardigan that used to be his dad's hanging slightly too big on his frame. Little boy, old man, Luke through the ages. I set down the basket, and thread my arms around his waist.

"Which one should I get?" he asks, pointing to the olive-oil selection. "Look, there are five, no, six different kinds."

"It doesn't matter. Just pick one," I say, cheek pressed to his back. He does, and I steer us, still holding tight, toward the checkout line.

Reality

After we've eaten, we watch *Don't Tell the Bride*. The groom has allocated half the wedding budget to a Dolly Parton tribute act and bucking-bronco hire.

"Uh-oh," says Luke when the bride states to her bridesmaid in no uncertain terms that the one thing she categorically doesn't want is for the wedding to have a Wild West theme.

"Where exactly is Baltimore," I ask, "in relation to, say, New York?"

"Claire."

"Yes or no."

"It wasn't a yes-or-no question," says Luke.

"Is it close?"

"Ish. A three-hour drive."

"So if, in theory, I knew someone who was doing a junior-doctor residency at Johns Hopkins in Baltimore, and if, in theory, I were to visit, would it be possible to spend the weekend with them in New York?"

"Claire . . ."

"I said in theory."

"Stop it."

I give him a little respite, then, feeling generous, a little more. The bride is trying on the wedding dress her fiancé's chosen: a white lace and satin saloon-girl outfit, complete with feathered headpiece.

"I can't believe it. I actually really love it!" she gushes. "Oh my God, it's stunning!" It's unclear whether the Wild West implication has properly sunk in. I mute the TV.

"Hey!" says Luke. "I want to hear what she says about the cowboy boots!"

I throw the remote across the room onto the armchair, out of reach. "You have to listen to me for a minute." He stares mutinously at the screen. "Luke. I honestly, truly, completely, unequivocally, passionately think you should go. It has one of the best neurosurgery units in the whole world. It's *crazy* of you to pass this up."

"I already told you: it's too late."

"I bet it isn't. I'm sure it isn't. There's always a way—you have to at least ask," I say. "They already accepted you. The hard part is done. Just explain you had some personal matters, which have now been resolved. Is any of this getting through? Luke? Will you do that? Will you ask?"

He finally peels his gaze away from the TV and studies me: wary, but a little hopeful too.

"You *really* would be okay with me going?"

"One hundred percent. Do you promise you'll ask?"

"I'll ask."

"Do you promise?"

"I do."

At the wedding reception, the bride's astride the bucking bronco, whirling an air lasso above her head and having the time of her life.

"Will you lie on me?" I ask.

Luke obliges, pressing the full weight and warmth of his body on mine.

"Don't die, okay?"

"On the mean streets of Baltimore?"

"I meant ever, but now you say it, the crime rate over there isn't ideal, is it? Don't get mixed up with any drug lords." I squeeze him so hard his bones crackle.

He raises head and shoulders up to look into my face, as though deliberating whether to speak. "You're *sure* you wouldn't mind that Fiona's going too? I know you have a weird thing about her. Completely unfounded, obviously."

"Please," I say. "I've met her friends: I'm not worried. I really don't think you'd last five minutes with someone who consorts with *Totty* and *Clem*."

"Oh, *them*! I've met them! They're not *so* bad."

"Totty. A person who calls herself Totty." I sigh. "Have I really got you so very wrong all these years?"

He puts his head on my chest and we lie there in silence for a while.

"Ow," I say. "Knobbly knee. Ow, shoulder. No, *your* shoulder in my arm. Collarbone—your chin's digging in mine!"

We wriggle and shift, realigning our edges. "Better?" asks Luke.

"Yes." There's a brief pause. "I'd *miss* you if you died, is what I was getting at."

Symbolism II

"Why don't you come?" Luke says. We're brushing our teeth, and what really comes out is, "I oh oo uhm?"

"No, thanks." ("O anx.") I spit. "I have things of my own to get on with."

"Such as?" he says. ("Uh ah?")

"Making plans. Still need to work on the finer details, but I think I've decided I'm going to temp for a bit to save up for a proper trip somewhere."

"Oh." He thinks about it. "That's a good idea. Cuba? Or Peru. I can't believe we've never been to South America." He resumes brushing.

"I was thinking more like Iceland. Or Canada. As I say, need to work out the specifics."

"Those don't really appeal so much," he says through gritted teeth, white flecks flying everywhere.

"That's fine," I say. "You're not coming. You'll be in Baltimore."

He spits. "But . . . how will that work?"

"Well, instead of me being *here* while you're at Johns Hopkins, I'll be somewhere else."

"I thought you said you wanted to meet me in New York."

"I could still do that on my way to wherever."

"Why don't you just come out and stay with me? Free accommodation. New city. We can go on weekend trips on my days off."

"Because you'll be there to do *your* thing. I'd just be hanging around like a spare part. I want to do something for me. Aside from these last few months, I've been in full-time work or education for over twenty years."

"Okay . . . so then what happens after your trip?"

I sit on the edge of the bath. "I'll come home and get a job."

"Yeah, obviously, but what? Isn't this just putting off the same old problem?"

"I think I'm coming round to the idea that there's a whole world between *any old* thing and *the* thing." Luke looks quite impressed, so I decide not to credit my father with this wisdom for now. "I know what I'm like. Being somewhere different will make me nostalgic for a routine. I'll find something, give it a go. If I don't like it, I'll try something else."

"I'll hire you," he says. "A new role's just opened up, actually, in the Department for Hugs and Kisses." He looms toward me, clumsy like Marshmallow Man, toothpaste froth spewing from his lips.

"Maybe six months apart isn't nearly long *enough*," I say, leaning back into the bath.

He grins, rinses his toothbrush and drops it in the cup, where—as random good fortune would have it—it swings round to nestle next to mine.

Parental guidance

I phone Dad to hear how things panned out at work.

"What's the verdict?"

"It's over. I'm out."

"I'm so sorry. Can't you appeal?"

"No, Claire: I resigned! I told them I'd had enough of being treated like a second-class citizen."

This, I really did not expect. "Oh wow. Are you okay?"

"I think so," he says, but after the spirited announcement, he sounds a little shaken and tired.

"Congratulations, Dad. That was very brave."

"I took your advice. If something isn't making you happy, change it: isn't that what you said?"

"Did I?"

"Maybe not in those words. But that's what you did, leaving your job. The first time, anyway."

Alone in my kitchen, I allow myself a small, unconcealed smile of pride.

"Does this mean early retirement, then?"

"No."

"Yes!" my mother, hitherto latent, calls from the background: speakerphone strikes again. "We can access the pension in a few months' time. We'll be fine."

"Hi, Mum!"

"We need to sit down and work out the budget," says Dad. "I think I'll need to do some consulting part-time. A colleague said he has some good contacts."

"Still, you'll have more time for yourself. Any big plans?"

"I might try and get the garden sorted."

"No!" says Mum. "House first, then garden. We agreed! Claire, don't mind him—he's pulling your leg."

"I think he's pulling your leg, Mum," I say. "Dad, you could take a course in something—architecture maybe? I'll send you some links."

"I'd be too old for that," he says. "I'll be dribbling onto my drawing board by the time I qualify."

"Not to retrain," I say, trying to banish the dribbling image. "Just for fun. Maybe I'll sign up too: we can go together."

"What about me?" says Mum. "Could we find something all three of us might enjoy? Ooh—flower arranging?"

"Um," I say.

"Salsa? Bernadette's big into her salsa and says it's great fun." There's a stomp-clack noise, which I take to be her heels tapping out some moves on the kitchen floor.

"Cha-cha-cha," says Dad.

Mum laughs, stomp-clacking again.

"I think that's something different," I say. "I think that's the cha-cha."

"Cha-cha-cha! Oh, hello, Mr. Snakey-hips! You should see him, Claire!" Mum hoots, and I give brief wordless thanks that I can't. Then there's a rustling noise on the line, and Mum starts to shriek, "Oh *no! Stop that!* Put me *down!*"

"I think you guys should go for it. Salsa's more of a two-person thing anyway," I say, over their breathless laughter.

Party time

Aunt Dee is hosting a birthday party for Grandma: the cousins are in our usual spot—crammed round a couple of folding tables in the hallway, with seats scavenged from throughout the house, while the adults live it up on coordinated furniture in the adjoining dining room. Sophia, one of the twins (perched on a linen chest), thanks me for organizing Grandma's present from the family—an iPad, plus broadband installed in her home.

"No problem," I say, waving a hand and propelling myself back and forth as much as limited space will allow. I've got the rocking chair, and feel every bit the wise elder at the table. "I thought it would help with the loneliness. Imagine having never been online—it's a form of exile, when you think about it." I'm conscientiously watching my wine intake, but I've had just enough to bring fire to my cheeks, and grand hypotheses to my tongue. My cousins nod, willing to grant me that one.

"Not it for teaching her how to use it," Stuart says quickly.

"But you work in computers!" This is from Faye, who has had unfortunate wispy bangs cut, and who I still haven't fully forgiven for blabbing about the Gum business way back in the first place.

"Last time I went over there, I tried showing her how to use Google on my phone." Stuart rolls his eyes, segueing into a spot-on impression of Grandma. "'Ask it my name . . . How old am I, then? . . . Should I have soup or sausages for dinner? . . . Well, I don't understand how you can say it has the answers . . . No, I'm sorry, I really don't understand how you can say that.'"

A cork pops in the dining room. "Children! Cake!" calls Dee, glugging champagne into flutes. We troop in obediently round the grown-ups' table and I stand behind Mum, my hands light on her shoulders. Dad reaches back and puts an arm around my waist. We launch into a stirringly tuneful round of "Happy Birthday" to Grandma, who, clapping along—decked out in party sparkle and fake fur, thin white hair teased to soft peaks like whipped cream—looks all set to lift off from the table, powered by delight at the attention, plus the enormous helium balloons tied to the back of her chair.

Epilogue

Monday morning

I wake early to go for a run before work, kissing Luke on the shoulder when I leave; in sleep, he puckers reciprocally.

Outside, the air is cool, but the clear sky promises a scorcher. The streets are in shadow as I set out, overtaking street sweepers and dodging early commuters. I head east toward the canal, and on every street exploding from buildings and gardens and railings—bright purple buddleia sprays bop in the breeze: clusters of supporters lining my route to cheer me on my way.

ACKNOWLEDGMENTS

I would like to thank:

Thomas Morris, Jessie Price, Kiare Ladner and Thomas Eccleshare, for early readings and astute feedback.

Jane Finigan, for instant and enduring faith. Also, David Forrer at Inkwell Management and Juliet Mahoney at Lutyens & Rubinstein.

Francesca Main for boundless passion, eagle eyes and invaluable guidance. Also, her brilliant colleagues at Picador.

Kara Cesare at Random House, and Martha Kanya Forstner at Doubleday Canada, for editorial savvy and vital encouragement.

My family, for a lifetime of love.

Simon, for everything.

ABOUT THE AUTHOR

LISA OWENS was born in 1985 and grew up in Glasgow and Hertfordshire. *Not Working* is her first novel. She lives in London.